THE BEFORE TIMES

THE BEFORE TIMES

Sam Mills

The Before Times

Copyright © 2019 Sam Mills

Content Editor: Mallory Miller
Copy Editor: Catherine Lynch
Editor-in-Chief: Kristi King-Morgan
Formatting: Kristi King-Morgan

ISBN: 978-1-947381-19-3

Dreaming Big Publications
www.dreamingbigpublications.com

I wish to give a shout out to the following friends and colleagues who have been instrumental in the success of my novel. My wife, Adele, is always the first person to hear each and every chapter as I complete them, and her suggestions and support are always appreciated. Once I have completed the original draft, my daughter, Katie, serves as my in-house copy editor, editor-in-chief and agent. It was through her efforts that my work was able to attract the interest of a publishing house. I also wish to send my thanks to the people at Dreaming Big Publications including Mallory, my editor, who required me to add and subtract many passages to make it a better read. And finally, I wish to express my whole-hearted gratitude to Penny Kelly, who allowed me to loosely base my futuristic setting and global circumstances upon her prophetic, published work, *Robes, a Book of Coming Changes*, which describes the future history of mankind and planet Earth.

PART ONE

When I see an old neon sign flashing "Excelsior Hotel" in bright red letters, I know I have discovered my final resting place. I park my crimson BMW convertible in a nearby lot and bid it farewell. I grab my suitcase and walk along First Avenue for a block and a half. The air is muggy, and the sky means to rain. A wall of clouds turns it dark gray and hangs pregnant overhead like a swollen sack waiting to burst open. Just as I push the revolving door and enter the lobby of the hotel, I feel the inaugural drop splatter on my hand.

It is even darker inside. Weak florescent lights give off a dull glow overhead, and an old iron chandelier hangs below in abject despair. None of its incandescent light bulbs seem to work anymore, and probably haven't for a long time. Their snap-on floral shades haven't been dusted in years. Underneath, a couple of well-worn couches face each other across a heavy wooden coffee table. It is littered with outdated magazines, dinosaurs such as *Life* and *Look* that went out of circulation with the advent of the digital age. I feel as though I have entered some kind of time warp where the past has refused to budge and make way for the normal flow of events.

An elderly, balding man with gold-rimmed spectacles sits in a high-backed reading chair adjacent to one of the couches. He holds a faded copy of *Life* in his lap. It is open, but upside down. His watery eyes rest on me without interest, as if I am a familiar object he has seen a thousand times before. His mottled skin is blotchy with age, and his few remaining teeth are more yellow than white. His indifference gives me the creeps.

An open doorway to my right leads to a gloomy hallway directly behind the old man while a steep staircase rises to the upper regions on my left. An elevator with an "Out of Order" sign taped to its closed doors is stationed next to the check-in counter along the back wall. A half-moon dial numbered one through ten hangs over the elevator door, its arrow-like hand permanently frozen on the number one. I wonder how long it's been since that dial circled around to the other nine numbers.

Another graying gentleman stands behind the well-worn counter and stares at me with mild curiosity. Behind him, a wall of hollow cubbyholes, void of letters but not of keys, suggests that the Excelsior has seen better days. The whole place feels vacant, bereft of vitality. A fossil of its former self.

The weary attendant watches as I approach his counter. He manages to arrange his lips into something of a smile, as if my intent to rent a room is some cause for mild celebration. I start to speculate how long it has been since the last guest checked in. Was it yesterday, last week, or last year?

A sudden thunderclap erupts overhead, shaking the windows facing out on First Avenue. The lobby lights blink off and on as the sound of a heavy, monsoon-like downpour pounds the sidewalk.

"Your timing's perfect, sonny," the clerk notes. "Had you taken another minute to get here, you would have been soaked through." His voice sounds rusty as the pipes that vein this decaying structure.

"This must be my lucky day," I respond, feeling anything but lucky. "I'm looking for a room for one night." I don't bother asking if there are any vacancies. It seems unnecessary.

"Well now, one room for one night. Just passing through, are ya?" His eyes match his slate gray hair and bore into me like drill bits. I resent the intrusion.

"I am definitely passing through," I reply, refusing to divulge any more information than I have to. He nods like he understands exactly what I mean. He turns an old register around and pushes it toward me.

"Please fill in your name and address on the first empty line. I'll give you Suite #13, right down at the end of that hallway over there. I think it will suit you just fine."

I enter the information as requested. Much to my surprise, I notice a previous entry was made this very day. For some reason, I feel more reassured that at least one other person is staying at the Excelsior tonight.

"How much do I owe you for the suite?" I ask.

"The usual price. Fifty bucks, cash or credit. The suite will cost you ten bucks more than a regular room, but it's worth it. You get a little parlor to spread out in." He pauses and reconsiders. "If it's too much, I can put you in the room next door?"

"No, no," I hastily respond. "A suite sounds perfect, and fairly priced at that. Suite #13 will do fine."

Given the circumstance of my visit, I feel like splurging.

The clerk smiles back and nods his head with evident satisfaction—maybe too much satisfaction. He is tall lanky, and reminds me of an old baseball player, rangy looking and probably agile in his day. He could be well into his seventies or early eighties. His hair is still pretty thick, but his face is all creased and weathered like he's been out to sea for a long time. He wears a green tweed jacket over a white shirt. His light blue silk tie has a few stains on it, and his brown woolen slacks are as wrinkled as his face and hands. But it's his eyes that define him the most. They are too clever. I feel like he is playing me somehow. His shrewd disposition suggests that he holds all the cards and that I am in way over my head.

For Christ's Sake, he's just a fucking hotel clerk, I scold myself. *Pay him and get on with it*. I do so, procuring my room key—a real key at that—and head for my room. When I pass the man in the reading chair, he stares into nothingness and ignores my passage completely. I feel invisible. I could be a ghost. He remains so still I can't tell if he is dead or alive. *He* could be a ghost, for all I know. I gratefully enter the dimly lit hallway and proceed to Suite #13.

The key works, and I enter what I know is my final accommodation. I close the door and survey my surroundings. The suite does indeed suit me just fine. A sagging couch snuggles a papered wall featuring various floral patterns that repeat themselves every fourth time. The edges of the paper are fading golden with age. Two worn padded chairs keep the couch company, and a stained wooden coffee table with fold-up sides squeezes in between them. A couple of shaded lamps provide light for the homey, if not slightly dingy setting. The room reminds me of my mother's parlor, where she spent most of her time recuperating from life. This room smells old and stale like hers did. The adjoining bedroom boasts a king-sized bed with a pink cotton blanket draped over it. A closet door is halfway ajar, and a plain white bureau stands nearby. Another door leads to the bathroom. I am delighted to see a rust-stained bathtub with an old-fashioned showerhead and a dull gray, plastic shower curtain that boasts more than several years of use. It will suit my needs perfectly. An ornate, gold-framed mirror hangs over the sink next to the tub. The mirror outclasses the rest of the bathroom and feels out of place.

I set my suitcase on the bed and take in the little parlor. I notice a painting to the right of the door hanging over a small writing table, where a plain black phone without any call-buttons squats next to a mud-brown leatherette blotter. From across the room, the subject in the painting looks like a walking skeleton. I approach to study it more carefully. Up close, I face the Grim Reaper. The skeletal figure carries a large scythe as if he is in the process of harvesting a crop of newly deceased souls. His face grins out into the room and reminds me of the hotel clerk in the lobby. His smile suggests that the joke is on me; that no matter how long or short my tenure or how large or small my contribution, he will be waiting.

"Sooner than you think, buddy," I wisecrack back at his grinning countenance. But there is something weird about the painting, something that doesn't sit right. I scrutinize it carefully and discover what is wrong: the skeleton's pelvis is reversed with the back facing forward. No wonder he is grinning at me. He wants to see if I will notice his little joke. Well, I do. Now, I wonder if the gray-eyed clerk with the weathered complexion knew what I was planning to do. Why else would he direct me to this Grim Reaper Suite? But no, it must be a coincidence. I don't believe in God, or miracles, or in the "other side". What I see directly in front of my nose is plenty real enough for me. Plus, my recent experience has taught me that destiny is a crapshoot and dreams of happiness are fruitless. Then the Reaper winks at me, but when I focus on his eyes they are just as immobile as always. My imagination must be playing tricks with me, which I don't appreciate. There is nothing amusing about my current situation.

***

Why just the day before yesterday I was in my fancy office down on Second Avenue making more than enough money to live comfortably. Most importantly of all, I was happily married to Janice, the love of my life. My world could not have been more on track. I had advanced myself the hard way to vice president of an investment house of considerable repute in charge of private accounts, with my best friend working alongside me as a top analyst in the firm. Together, we'd hoisted our way up the big ladder, one step at a time, building on Ted's acumen with charts and my ready smile and glad hand. He was great with the numbers, a real whiz kid, and I was good with people. By coupling our respective gifts, we rose steadily among our peers and gained real status. Then I go out of town on a two-day business trip, return home a few hours early, and now I'm standing in front of the Grim Reaper, emotionally devastated and completely alone.

***

"Go ahead and smirk at me, you fucker," I say to the Reaper. "The joke is on me, after all." I head to the couch and sit down. An old RCA television set faces me from across the room. I wonder if it even works, but don't bother to find out. There's nothing that I want to see. Any kind of news seems inconsequential and seeking entertainment would be like trying to drink from an empty well. The notion of comedy makes me want to puke, and the need for drama or tragedy would be like telling a coma patient to get more sleep. Janice, my love, my wife of ten years, has left me for Ted, my best friend and closest colleague. I am abandoned and betrayed by the two nearest and dearest people that I know. And I didn't even see it coming.

I rise from the couch and walk into the bedroom. I open my suitcase and pull out the kitchen knife I grabbed hastily on my way out of the house. I carry it back to the parlor and place it on the writing table directly under the painting of my new roommate.

"That's my ticket out of here, buddy," I tell him. "A couple of quick cuts and I'm history." I leave it beneath him to pay homage to his coming harvest. Soon, I will be chaff on the edges of his ever-relentless blade. I bow to him in mock reverence and return to my couch. I'm not quite ready to perform my final ceremony yet. I want more time to ruminate on my woeful lot in life. I also need to work myself up for the task at hand.

***

The three of us met in college. Ted and I were fraternity brothers at Phi Kappa Delta. We both majored in business and shared a lot of the same classes. We also shared a passion for baseball and played on a club team together. It was during our junior year that he and Betty, his girlfriend at the time, introduced me to Janice. All it took was one look and I knew I was meeting the girl of my dreams. Up until then I had played around some but had never really been all that interested in members of the fairer sex. After meeting Janice, she was all I could think about. I fell in love for the first and only time. She still looks a lot like she did when I first met her, a strawberry blonde with blue-green eyes, and she smiled like she meant it. Her hands were so delicate I could hold them forever. She was 5'4" and a little on the skinny side, but she was so spirited, she felt larger than life. Her features were delicate, like her hands, and perfectly proportioned. She beamed intelligence and radiated sweetness, and she was funny too. She'd tease me a lot about how serious I was. And she was right. I was serious back then.

I grew up in a household where I got to learn all about envy. My mother was always tired, she had a poor heart, and my dad toiled drearily as a science teacher at the local high school. During summer break he worked as a driving instructor and somehow managed to survive, though he had a few close calls with kids who panicked and almost drove him straight into oncoming trucks or roadside trees. These tales only caused my mother to worry more about him and his overall welfare, though neither parent seemed to worry too much about me. We never had much in the way of spending money, especially since mom was constantly in and out of therapy because of her depression. She lost her will to live and withered away when I was only twelve years old. She simply refused to eat and asked my father to let her go. She died in her sleep. It was like she willed herself to die. To be totally honest, I didn't grieve her passing all that deeply because she wasn't all that present when she was around. She was too busy suffering from her condition to care about me, but my dad took her death really hard. I think he felt guilty because he followed her instructions and didn't let the doctors keep her alive intravenously. After she was gone, he just kind of went through the motions as a single parent, like he inherited her depression.

When it came to getting what I wanted as a teenager, like cool clothes or a car of my own, I had to hustle after school at a series of different jobs. In the springtime when I played high school baseball, I had to work day and night on the weekends. I worked at the local diner, busing table after table all day long. Meanwhile, my father took up drinking to cope with his emptiness and, as a result, never had much money left over for anything as extravagant as allowance. I learned to fend for myself. He did manage to put a little something aside for my higher education because he maintained that schooling was an important step if one wanted to excel in life. He squirreled away enough to cover my first year at State, where I studied hard and did indeed excel. After that first year, I earned my own way through grants, scholarships, and loans. I was so driven because I didn't want to end up like my folks, depressed and alone. That's why Janice would sometimes tease me in order to get me to lighten up. She was good for me, in that regard.

My dad died from liver cancer three years after I graduated. His passing left me alone. My few remaining relatives lived on the East Coast, and I hardly ever saw them, except at my parents' funerals. I had nothing in the way of extended family and didn't really care. I had Janice, and she was all I needed. Janice and my career.

***

I hoist myself off the couch and go to the bathroom to take a leak. After I finish my business, I glance at my reflection in the mirror and experience a slight tugging sensation in my chest, like something is pulling at me. I think of Janice and decide it is my broken heart acting up again. I still can't believe that she left. I return to the couch and sit down. My new roommate is still grinning at his little joke. As far as I'm concerned, it's already getting old.

***

Janice said she felt drawn to me too. We started going together right after we were introduced. She was a year behind me in school and still deciding on her major. She loved to write and was thinking about a career in public relations. We both wanted professional lives and yearned to rise above our upbringings. She came from a decent middle-class family. She had a sister and a brother, and everyone seemed pretty normal to me. I grew to love and respect her folks as much—if not even a little more—than my own father, whose spirit was drowning in the alcohol he was consuming in increasing dosages. I was especially close to Janice's mother, who was so attentive and caring compared to the depressive, indifferent behavior my own mother showed me. Now, as I sit alone in my suite at the Excelsior Hotel, I realize I have lost them too. My pride would never let me stay involved, even though I know I would be welcomed to do so. Ted can have them. Fucker.

I sigh, pushing down an innate feeling of guilt. I never thought I'd call him that. He is my only real brother in arms. After we graduated from State, I went right into the firm we'd both end up working at while he went on to get his MBA. Because my GPA was near the top of my class and because I was so ambitious and determined, I interviewed with the most prestigious investment house in town, Williams & Howe Capital Investments. They snapped me up like I was popcorn at the movies. Morton Williams, the older founding partner in the company, took me under his wing and steered me toward client relations. My street smarts and work habits taught me to know how to read people and anticipate their needs. It didn't take long for me to develop a secure client base and a reputation as a reliable producer.

Two years later, Ted finished graduate school and followed my lead. I introduced him to Bob Johnson, our chief analyst, and the two hit it off. Ted joined the firm and soon established his own credentials. He began feeding me his best picks, and before long my clients' portfolios were prospering from his astute recommendations. As the years piled on top of each other, which they did with ever-increasing speed, Ted and I rose to considerable prominence in the firm.

Meanwhile, Janice also thrived in her profession. She worked for a pharmaceutical company that specialized in veterinary medications. She organized several annual public relation campaigns, including a program that encouraged people to adopt homeless dogs and cats. She also spearheaded a movement to neuter all prospective pets at regional animal shelters. Janice always loved animals, so naturally, we adopted a dog. Scampers became our surrogate child, since neither of us was in any hurry to have kids of our own. One of our favorite routines was to play rigorous games of fetch every evening over at Harrington Park, which happened to be in easy walking distance from our cozy home on the south side of town.

We finally agreed to marry six years after we started going out together. It was a modest ceremony. Ted served as my best man. He was in between girlfriends at the time. Janice and I went to Puerto Vallarta for a very romantic honeymoon. Everything was perfect. Our careers were on track, and our relationship was sweet as fresh honey in a hive. We purchased a small three-bedroom home in Collins Wood, a desirable neighborhood that was trending upward, and our futures were secure. The only real question mark in our relationship was whether we would produce any children. Janice wasn't in any hurry, and I was content waiting for her to take the lead. She never did.

The years flew by. Most of our friendships were work-related. Slowly, many of the couples that we associated with had children. Janice and I soon became godparents or honorary aunt and uncle to a few kids whose parents were particularly close to us. We gradually settled into an easy and comfortable relationship with each other and were quite content to remain a married but childless couple. We joined a health club together, went to the movies, and ventured out for brunch with the Sunday paper. Life was ideal.

Ted remained my best friend through it all. We double-dated with him occasionally, depending on whom he was with at the time. He went through girlfriends like a kid goes through Halloween candy. He sampled a variety of flavors, sometimes simultaneously, and never did settle down with anyone for more than a few months before his wandering eye led him in a new direction. Janice and I came to accept that marriage and monogamy were as foreign to him as everlasting peace on earth. How was I to know that Ted had wanted Janice ever since he introduced her to me fourteen long years ago?

His betrayal suddenly hits me where it hurts. An intense anger burns in my chest, and I jump up and pace around the room. How could Ted betray our friendship so suddenly and so completely? I trusted him like he was my only brother. Tall, lean, and as blond as I am dark; we're opposites in so many ways, yet we still fit together perfectly. His blue eyes and ruddy complexion reflect his Irish blood, and his devil-may-care disposition balanced out my steady, driven manner. I think he enjoys analyzing charts and trends, numbers and percentages, because it brings some order into his naturally chaotic character. We complemented each other so effortlessly that I felt like I already knew him when we first met.

In retrospect, I think I was too close to both of them to notice that they were attracted to each other. My familiarity and affection for both Ted and Janice blinded me from detecting the growing intimacy and desire that must have crept into their relationship over the years. The three of us hung out together so often, especially when Ted was in between women, that I just grew comfortable with him always being around Janice and me. I should have seen it coming at some level, but my unconscious denial secured the door to that perception and locked it out of my awareness.

Maybe I was too determined to be happy. I grew up resenting the imperfections of my parents, my mother's lifelong melancholy, and my father's sullen tendency to settle for less. I was going to do life right, and I felt confident that I was achieving all my goals with the unerring determination of a man fully in command of his own destiny. Well, my destiny train went off the tracks earlier today when I walked in on Ted and Janice fucking on my living room couch.

***

I head over to the writing table, pluck up the knife, and hold it before my eyes. I scrutinize its sharp serrated edge. I consider how close love and hate are when circumstances intervene in a way that changes one quality into the other. My own heartfelt love for Janice and Ted has morphed into a wretched, vengeful hatred so complete that I am tempted to open an artery right here and now, just to show them.

But I don't. I return the knife to its appointed place beneath the portrait of the grinning Reaper. He will have to wait a little while longer. I'm not ready yet.

I lie down on the bed and stare at the ceiling. Flakes of dull white paint are curling away from the plaster and threaten to fall to the floor. A spider crawls along the top of the molding, looking for something to devour. My own appetite has ceased to function. Any hunger I had abandoned me when I stopped caring about everything that once mattered. This betrayal has sucked the will to live right out of me and left me empty inside. I am nothing but a hollow husk of my former self.

***

"What the fuck is going on here?!" I shouted when I discovered them entangled together. I was so shocked, I didn't know what else to say. The business trip had taken me to clients on the West Coast, but I caught an earlier flight back when my last client canceled unexpectedly. I decided not to call Janice from the airport so I could surprise my wife, just for the hell of it. Obviously, I wasn't expected home yet.

They disentangled from each other and stood up. Both of their faces reddened with shame as they struggled with their confused emotions. They said nothing.

"How long has this been going on?" I asked accusingly. I could feel panic seize my chest and squeeze tightly as some deep intuitive part of my psyche sensed that my life as I had known it had come to a sudden and screeching halt.

Ted stared at the floor, too ashamed to face my rising rage. But Janice looked directly at me and came to grips with our destinies with an iron will that chilled me to the bone.

"Jason, Ted and I have fallen in love. I'm sorry, but it's true. I know it's not fair, and I deeply regret that I have betrayed our marriage, but it's something that we both have no control over. It just happened, and it's very real."

"How long has this been going on?" I repeated less forcefully. I could feel the steam draining out of my righteous indignation. The steely certainty of her words had unmanned me completely.

"It started two years ago. We both tried to deny our feelings for each other, but we couldn't. I'm so sorry dear, I really am." Her tone had softened a little but remained steadfast, nonetheless. Ted raised his eyes and looked at me sheepishly, like a kid who had just been caught stealing. He shrugged his shoulders as if to say he couldn't help himself either.

I turned and left the room. If I owned a pistol, I might have gone and fetched it. But I don't, and I didn't. I abhor the use of firearms as a general rule, and I've always maintained that society is way too gun crazy and violent as a whole. But at that moment, I wished I had one in my possession. Instead, I went to the bedroom that was no longer ours, dumped out my suitcase, and threw in some clean garments and my unzipped toilet kit. Then I swept into the kitchen, grabbed the sharpest knife I could find, and slipped it into my bag, and left the house. Ted and Janice had hardly moved when I passed them on my way out the front door.

I drove back downtown and scouted for a place to die. Twenty minutes later, I checked into the Excelsior Hotel. I am now where I want to be.

***

I look over at the Grim Reaper and see him thrashing away as always. He is lucky. He is already dead. He has nothing to lose and everything to gain. If I could have bought an equity position in his operation, I'd be richer than Bill Gates; the Reaper never runs out of paying customers, all dying to give him their business. And now, at long last, my time has finally come. I can feel it in my gut. I am finished. I don't want to have to think about Janice and Ted ever again. Fuck them. I am ready to move on. Money and success no longer tempt me to excel. All of my motivation had to do with providing for the security of my happy little home. She can have it, she and Ted. The house, the dog, all theirs. I have nothing to live for. My tank is dry.

I suddenly feel exhausted, like I'm completely drained of life and energy. I could fall asleep easily, but instead, I force myself to get off the bed and go into the bathroom. I head to the sink and turn on the hot water. I wait for it to show up. When it finally arrives, I fill the sink bowl and wash my face. Then I lather up and shave. After that, I comb my hair and brush my teeth. When I am done prettying up for my final act, I take one last look in the mirror. I look okay, considering what I am going through emotionally. I'm in great shape for my age and could have gone on living for a long time, given my disposition and habits. I was dedicated to my job and devoted to my wife. And now she is gone, and my moment of truth has arrived. I turn to fill the bathtub, but before I can leave off looking at my depressed self, something happens.

A strange force reaches out of the mirror and grabs me with invisible hands. Someone or something is pulling me into my own reflection. I feel myself spinning like a cyclone, even though I sense that my body is still standing in front of the sink. My mind and emotions swirl around like I'm in a blender, spinning in circles so fast that all I can see is one constant blur of motion. I become aware of an endless void surrounding me.

And then, just as suddenly, I am standing still, looking at my reflection in a bowl of water. I have a dark, smooth complexion, deep brown eyes, a long curly black beard beneath a shiny shaved head, and I am grinning at myself because I'm so full of happiness and joy.

PART TWO

And why would I not feel such joy? The High Priestess, Enheduanna, has just promoted me to a new position of considerable importance. I am chief priest-elect in charge of matrimony at the Temple of Ur, and I am to perform my first duty today. Oh, how my heart throbs with anticipation and thankfulness! I am only twenty winters old and already I have reached such lofty heights within the Temple's hierarchy. Mighty Inanna, the goddess of love and war, skill and deceit, daughter of the moon god, must surely be smiling down and bestowing her blessings upon me.

Given my auspicious origins as the firstborn son of a successful foundry owner, I was well positioned to succeed in life. My mother and father provided me with the best education available to those who could afford such privileges. I was instructed in the art of the scribe and showed considerable ability from an early age. I was clever with sounds, and my hands were nimble with the pressing tools used for inscribing the cuneiform letters onto clay tablets. My talent allowed me to be considered as a candidate for the priesthood, a profession that was normally reserved for those of the noble class. I could have been a man of commerce like my father before me, but my heart and my destiny have led me to a life where I may dedicate myself in service to the gods and goddesses who dwell in our holy Temple and watch over our destiny.

I entered my apprenticeship as initiate-elect two years ago and in that time have gained the confidence of the High Priestess. From my arrival, I have served as an assistant to Kitushdug, her chief scribe, and when called upon, I carve tablets of verse as she dictates with her soft, melodious voice the many inspirations that flow through her like the refreshing currents of air circulating the various passageways of our vast Temple. Often Kitushdug allows me to substitute for him, as he has a family of four children and a demanding wife in his apartment in the *gipar*, the section of the Temple compound reserved for the High Priestess and her entourage. Luckily for me, his family demands much of his time and energy.

Her Holiness quickly came to appreciate my agile mind and determined disposition, and sequestered my services, even over the protestations of Uri, her chief priest in charge of Temple affairs. The old goat would have preferred that I had trained under his more severe tutelage, especially as I am not of noble birth. Uri had actually preceded Enheduanna in authority and reigned as en-priest himself until her father, the great and powerful Sargon, King of Mesopotamia and beyond, placed her in ascendance as the en-priestess of Nanna, the moon god. Uri was required to relinquish his own authority and bow before her and her good fortune. So, as my star rose in the High Priestess's firmament, my standing with her second-in-command plummeted in equal measure. Two years later, I remain ever vigilant and wary in his presence, for I know full well that he would do me harm, but he is restrained from doing so as long as I hover in the good graces of the en-priestess herself.

It has been decided that I am to replace Uri as the priest in charge of matrimonial affairs, and he has been training me in my new duties. It is very apparent to me that this is a responsibility he detests, but I eagerly follow his directions and tend to the details of mastering my new position while ignoring the undercurrent of hostility that festers beneath the surface of his solicitous manner. I am mature for my years and an astute judge of other peoples' inherent dispositions. Uri can smile all he wants; I still sense the disguised disdain and envy he fails to hide within his jealous heart. Happily, my training period is at an end, and today I begin my new service in the Temple of Union.

I am thankful for the High Priestess's sponsorship just as she herself benefits from the ongoing support of her father. His accomplishments began in his youth and continue to this day. From Akkad, where Sargon established his throne, he managed to conquer all the lands that embrace the twin river valleys of the Tigris and Euphrates and that stretch between the two large seas in the northwest and the south. The young usurper has essentially created the largest kingdom known to man, thereby proving he is truly destined to be a unifier of power. He is a brilliant strategist and a man of tremendous vision, and I am fortunate enough to be a favorite of Enheduanna, his only daughter.

Having gained control over of a vast area of warring states, Sargon moved to create a centralized form of government that reported back to him in Akkad. As a result, a time of prosperity has enveloped the region. A multitude of trade goods swell the King's coffers: lapis lazuli, cedars, silver, jade, silks, linens, slaves, precious gems, and many other commodities pour into his kingdom from distant ports all over the known world. Lying as it does along the banks of the Euphrates, Ur shares in this prosperity. Traders from all over the empire pass through the city, fostering and expanding commerce and new wealth. My father's foundry prospers as Sargon's armies are in constant need of new swords and sharp spearheads, which is why I grew up the son of a very wealthy man.

Ur was conquered twenty winters before my advent into this world. I know nothing of the old days when Sumerians ruled in Sumer. I speak and scribe in Akkadian as fluently as my native tongue and am accustomed to Sargon's kingship. It is modern to recognize the importance of Akkad in our culture, and to speak and think Akkadian is both practical and wise.

And so, under the roof of our Temple, the Sumerian gods still holds sway, but with the appointment of our Akkadian High Priestess over two decades ago, subtle changes are afoot. Nanna is the chief deity of our Temple. Many ceremonies revolve around the cycles of the moon, and many sacrifices and offerings are made to the moon god to help ensure that herds of cows will be productive and yield much milk and cheese. He is considered to be the shepherd of the stars along the great celestial way. However, gradually under the High Priestess's tenure, a change in emphasis is slowly occurring. Nanna and Ningal are losing regard in the High Priestess's own esteem as her passions are directed toward Inanna, their daughter, the goddess of love and war. She is also called Ishtar in the Akkadian tongue and is much beloved by Sargon, who believes she has bestowed upon him many blessings and much good fortune. Over the years, Enheduanna defers to Inanna more and more in her supplications. I feel the status of the fierce warrior goddess rising in importance in the eyes of the other priests, priestesses, musicians, singers, castrates, and scribes; all except for her predecessor Uri, who stubbornly remains loyal to Nanna. He and some of the more traditional elderly priests have had difficulty letting go of the old ways. They remember when the last great Sumerian king, Lugal-Zage-Si, held the reins of power and are far less comfortable bowing down before the dictates of the Akkadian usurpers from the north.

Perhaps Uri thinks I am a traitor to the traditions that preceded the rise of Sargon. If so, he is correct. I am quick to follow the dictates of the High Priestess, whom I admire greatly. After all, I know her mind better than most, for have I not been privy to some of her deepest and most sacred thoughts which I scribe for her in the cuneiform text of old Sumer? I always find her dialogue with the gods and goddesses quite profound and bold in both openness and honesty. Her inspirations seem to come directly from them, almost as if she hears them speaking directly to her. Clearly, my mentor believes that the gods and goddesses are every bit as real as we lowly humans who bow down before them. As a prospective priest, I too must learn to submit to their celestial authority.

A breeze enters my chamber and stirs the water in my reflection bowl. I hear steps approaching and turn to see Ada, the High Priestess's handmaiden, enter my room.

"Please forgive my intrusion, Ishme, but Her Holiness wishes to speak to you immediately in the Temple of Union."

"I will join her there at once," I reply, nodding to Ada who bows in acknowledgment and withdraws from my private chambers. My bedroom is a modest space with a simple wooden bed and a straw mattress covered by hand-woven blankets of soft Egyptian linen, a gift from my mother. I also have a small writing table upon which lays a bundle of freshly cut reeds that I use to impress the soft clay. My water bowl sits on a stone pillar and serves as a mirror and a sink for my daily ablutions. It stands in the corner of my room, next to a chamber pot cast from bronze, which is stationed near the door. The pot is emptied and washed by the Temple servants every morning and evening.

I glance at my reflection one more time and note that my thick curly beard is ready for another trim by the Temple barber. I will endeavor to hunt him down later today and arrange for a time that will suit both our schedules. My dark, heavy beard and my serious, ambitious nature belie the fact that I am so young. Many people suppose that I am older than I am, a deception I secretly take pride in. I also notice that my head once again needs to be shaved and oiled, something that requires attention every few days. Needless to say, the Temple barber is a very busy man.

I exit the room and proceed down a long corridor. Several bedrooms open out onto the same hallway. The corridor runs along the outer wall of the central nave of the Temple. Its multiple arches create a domed ceiling that is wide across and even longer in length. It is truly a majestic space. This is where the large ceremonies and sacrifices are conducted on a daily basis. Nanna demands many offerings as he is constantly rising and falling and expanding and shrinking himself in relation to us mortals.

On the other side of the central nave is the *gipar*, where the High Priestess and her staff live very comfortably in a maze of rooms that rival the Governor's Palace in luxury and scope. Enheduanna manages the land around the Temple and the growing of many crops and foodstuffs. She rules over a vast empire of farmers, shepherds, fishermen, and gardeners. Since her primary concern is the fecundity of the land, she oversees the selection of crops to be planted and manages the distribution of produce at harvest time. A large kitchen that provides meals for the entire complex is also located in the *gipar*. It is constantly swarming with cooks and other house servants responsible for the many meals that need to be served on a daily basis.

I turn right at the end of the long corridor and pass through the forecourt of the Temple, where a beautiful pond glistens in the early morning sunlight. I enter a midsized room on the far side of the courtyard that serves as the Temple of Union. Here, the legal work is assessed, contracts are inspected, and approval is sanctioned by the priest in charge of matrimony—who, as of today, happens to be me. A sacrificial ritual will be performed to bear witness before the gods and gain their approval of the union at hand. The wedding ceremony will then be performed in the days thereafter, usually in the home of the bride.

When I enter the Temple of Union, I see Enheduanna standing next to an altar at the far end of the room. A large wooden table with several chairs squats stolidly in the middle of the chamber and separates me from the High Priestess. It is where the official business of the day will be conducted. Should both parties be satisfied with the contractual agreements, a sacrifice and blessing will be performed in front of the altar.

Enheduanna is still very beautiful given her mature age. She is surprisingly tall for a woman, partly enhanced by her erect posture and her long and elegant face. Her snow-white complexion is flawless, but a few age lines crease the corners of her deep brown, oval-shaped eyes and edge around her wide and firmly formed lips. She is old enough to be my mother, but too sensual and alive to appear at all matronly. Her long black hair, which is usually tossed up and covered by her conical ceremonial cap, flows unadorned across her shoulders and down her back. Occasional streaks of gray reveal that she is no longer young or innocent but is instead middle-aged and much experienced in the ways of the world; though at a distance one might be fooled, for her figure remains surprisingly trim for one so seasoned on the vine of life.

She is arranging fresh-cut flowers on the altar. She has placed them in two tall earthenware jars and is busy cutting and sorting them into a beautiful relationship with each other. Colorful red poppies, white lilies, and purple irises are equally distributed between the two jars. She glances at me when I enter.

"Oh good, you're here. I'm delighted you will conduct your first ceremony today, especially for this couple, who are blessed to come together in holy matrimony." Her voice echoes slightly in the confines of the enclosed room but still sounds as clear as the spring water that feeds the sacred ponds embellishing the fountains of our great Temple. The quality of her voice serves to calm those who communicate directly with her. I am surprised to see her arranging the flowers herself; normally, Ada would have been delegated to handle such a task.

"I am honored to be selected to perform such a scared ritual, Your Holiness, and am grateful that you have entrusted me with such a precious responsibility."

She smiles, and a sense of joy beams from her with such radiance I think I might surely go blind. "You have earned my trust and faith in you, and I am pleased to have a hand in your advancement. But even so, I will continue to call upon you to record some of my musings, for I will need you to substitute for Kitushdug on occasion. At the same time, I want to increase your authority, for you are adept and diligent in all you do."

The chambers of my heart puff up like an adder as I accept her kind words, but I keep my face from flushing and instead bow humbly in thanks. She cuts and places the final stem—a lily—into the jar, steps back to appraise her work, and turns to join me a few paces back from the altar.

"I enjoy working with flowers. I miss gardening so much. Did you know that my father was a gardener before all else and that his adopted father was a water bearer?"

"Yes, Your Holiness. It is said that the King was rescued from the Great River as an infant and raised by a family of gardeners. That is part of the legend that precedes him wherever he goes."

"Yes, I suppose it is common knowledge—and he went to great pains to make it so. My father is adept at creating drama around him. He enjoys fostering his own legend, for he appreciates the power of myth and the importance of having a respectful relationship with the gods and goddesses. He maintains that Inanna herself led him to that water bearer, the *aqui,* who plucked him from the reeds and gave him a home. From this humble beginning, he claims Inanna guided him to his many accomplishments as a great ruler." She pauses to make an adjustment to one of the poppies in the jar on the right side of the altar, then she steps back to reassess her handiwork before continuing.

"As his daughter, and a very spoiled princess in Akkad, I could have chosen any suitor I wanted, for there was a long line of prospective husbands waiting to catch my eye." She smiles at me, and I quickly nod in agreement. I have no doubt that she would have been a much sought-after prize for any prince in the surrounding lands ruled by Sargon. "Alas, my father decided that I would be far more useful to him as an en-priestess in Sumer. Surprisingly, I was not at all disappointed with his decision. I quickly recognized the breadth of opportunity he was presenting and accepted his request." She smiles again. "Not that I had any great choice in the matter. My father is a man accustomed to having his will obeyed, but I was bored with the niceties of court life and felt restless and unproductive. I was as educated as my brothers and also inherited my father's ambition. The thought of settling into the future as a pretty and powerless queen in some backwater kingdom hardly matched my own aspirations. Ultimately, my father's vision of my future has proved to be far more satisfactory. As I trained to be a priestess, I developed a deep-seated devotion to the gods and goddesses who direct our destinies for good or ill. It was in my nature to do so."

She gazes at me, then confesses what may well be her deepest truth. "You see, Ishme, I can go inside myself and merge with the divine energies of our great unseen patrons and be inspired directly by their wisdom. Some of my teachings that you yourself have recorded have in fact come through me directly from the gods. It is my duty to have these transmissions transcribed so they may be shared with the priests and devoted followers of our many temples, and I find it very stimulating and exciting to channel these creative energies through me. I have truly been blessed by the gods and goddesses who inspire me."

"And I have been honored to act as your scribe, Your Holiness," I reply as I bow to her with my deepest respect. The High Priestess approaches the altar one last time to adjust the distance between two stems and then turns to face me.

"Well, now you must prepare yourself for your new responsibility. Today you will join my cousin Naram to his young and beautiful bride-to-be. He is a valuable officer in my father's army and in charge of the local garrison. He has fallen in love with a young Sumerian maiden whose family lives here in Ur. Perhaps you know her? Her name is Nagula, the youngest daughter to Ninband, who heads a noble family of long-standing influence in this community."

"I know of the family," I reply, "but have not met her, though I have heard tell of her beauty. She shall make your cousin a happy man if she is even half as sweet as she is reported to be."

Ur is a well-established city that nestles along the banks of the Euphrates. It has already existed for several hundred years and has consequently spread like a rolled-out carpet on both sides of the river. Several small ferryboats line the banks of the river and serve to connect both halves of the community together. Canals and ditches branch out and carry water to the city and out to the neighboring fields for irrigation. The Temple is located on the western shore, along with the major markets and more established, aristocratic residential neighborhoods. Needless to say, the family whose daughter is to be married to the military commander lives but a short stroll from the Temple.

I socialized with many families in that part of town before I became sequestered as a Temple scribe. Even though I was not born into the nobility, my father's wealth allowed me access to certain noble precincts. My father's private stores of foodstuffs are considerable, for he is a clever trader and has prospered greatly from his foundry's production of weapons for the King's army. Many of the noble families depend on his generosity in times of drought, for even the Temple stores can be drained if the gods are displeased with our people and withhold the rains that would nurture our crops. Before I joined the priesthood, I mingled socially with my betters simply because I could afford to do so. Nonetheless, the maiden in question, Nagula, is younger than me, and I have not crossed her path other than to hear whispers of a young girl whose beauty is blessed by Inanna herself.

"Well, my cousin is quite smitten and has courted her successfully," Enheduanna continues. "They shall both arrive shortly for their preliminary meeting. As you know, her father will also attend this meeting to represent the bride's side of this union. Should these proceedings arrive at a mutually acceptable arrangement, we will perform the actual ceremony at the girl's home down the street in a few days' time. I must assume that it will be a large affair, for her family is well known, and my cousin's status speaks for itself. I will represent the family in the absence of my father, who is busy administering justice in Akkad. You will take the lead in performing the ceremonial rites, and I will have Ada assist you. I trust that Uri has adequately prepared you for this duty?" She looks at me with a raised eyebrow that indicates that she might be concerned about my capability in this matter.

I feel a tinge of dread trickle down my spine, but I quickly respond with as much assurance as I can muster.

"He has trained me well, Your Holiness, and I am eager to apply my new skills." She smiles and nods her head in acknowledgment of my display of surety.

"Good, Ishme. I'm delighted to hear that you are so confident. This is an important event. My cousin's marriage into this family should help to further Sargon's peaceful control over the city, which couldn't come soon enough. There are rumors from the north that other sections of my father's empire are growing restless of late."

Although many years have passed with peace prevailing throughout the empire, as the King grows older, certain regions have begun to test the limits of the all-powerful ruler. More and more of Sargon's resources are being committed to putting out the fires of rebellion along the edges of his seemingly endless realm of influence. His daughter knows the importance of securing the peace closer to his seat of power.

"We shall meet them here shortly," she adds, "and review the contract to ensure that both sides of this marital equation are satisfied with the exchange and distribution of goods. She is from a very wealthy family, and her father will undoubtedly demand a high value for the hand of his daughter." Enheduanna smiles amusingly. "If my cousin were to depend solely on the pay his commission as an officer provides, he would be hard pressed to raise a sufficient payment to secure his bride-to-be. Fortunately for Naram, my father has amply rewarded his loyal service with both property and slaves, making him a wealthy man. His estate in Akkad is very comfortable, I can assure you. It is high time that he obtains a wife to help him manage his domestic affairs and produce an heir. I can only assume that my father will order him back home soon, especially since he has finally found a wife to share his seed with. My father desires as many blood relatives as possible to populate his court. I hope Nagula will mature into this role quickly, given the tenderness of her age in comparison to Naram's many winters of life."

The High Priestess notices a lily leaning too far back in the arrangement and adjusts its position to more adequately suit her highly developed sense of proportion. Stepping back to appraise her work, she turns to address me again.

"Since this is your first assignment, and an important one at that, I will closely observe how you handle these decisions. I have asked Uri to remain here to watch over the Temple's affairs, and he has graciously agreed to do so."

I bow before her. "I am grateful that you will shepherd me through my first official preliminary proceeding," I humbly reply.

I am pleased Enheduanna will oversee my duties in Uri's stead, for I know I will feel more support and approval from her. I also sense that Uri is probably displeased with this decision, for attending the joining of a highborn Sumerian maiden to a relative of the ruling family promises to be a greatly coveted invitation. Only the most powerful families will be lucky enough to attend. For me to perform the marriage rites instead of the former priest is both a great challenge and an unanticipated honor that I will hold dear for the rest of my life. It will also be a bitter disappointment to Uri—one that he may be slow to forget. At any rate, I am glad the High Priestess will be there. To practice a mock ritual is but a hollow attempt at the real thing. Soon I will execute the rites I have been practicing, and I know how difficult it could prove to be, especially given the importance of this particular union.

Ada appears at the entrance to the small temple. "Excuse me, Your Holiness, but the wedding party has arrived and is waiting in the outer courtyard."

"Thank you, Ada. You may show them in." Ada bows and leaves to attend to her mistress's request. As the sound of her footsteps vanish into the background, Enheduanna faces me.

"After I have greeted my cousin and the young girl, I will step to the side, and you will initiate the contractual review. You must determine that the terms are clear and that the price for this bride is agreed upon. If there is any disagreement, this is their last opportunity to come to terms. You may have to assist them in arriving at a suitable amount that satisfies both the groom and the father of the bride."

A jolt of nerves clenches my gut as I prepare to assume a responsibility that may well carry more weight than my young shoulders can bear. Enheduanna intuits my insecurity and reaches out with her hand, placing it gently on my shoulder.

"Fear not, Ishme. I will be standing right behind you in this negotiation, and if you falter, I will help to lighten your burden in any way I can. You must help them settle on a price that is acceptable to the father who is to give his child into the safe keeping of the man who is to assume her care. If you are lucky, they will have already reached an agreement before coming here."

I hear several sets of footsteps approaching the Temple entrance. The High Priestess and I turn in unison to face the expected wedding party. Ada ushers three people into the chamber. It is immediately obvious to me who they are. The eldest of the two men is Ninband, the bride's father. He wears rich vestments of the finest of linens, no doubt imported from Egypt whose styles and symbols are considered exotic and therefore very much in demand. His long gray beard and deeply lined face indicate that he has waited many seasons before he chose to engender the creation of his young and very beautiful daughter, Nagula, who enters at his side.

To simply call her beautiful would be as inadequate as describing the sun as a warm disc of light. Rather, her beauty radiates out from her like the fiery heat from one of my father's heavily stoked furnaces, enough heat to melt raw chunks of iron ore into molten metal. Likewise, I can feel my own heart liquefying inside my chest. Outwardly I wear the garb of a priest, but inwardly I am still a youthful male whose secret urges are as healthy and untamed as any man my age. Her raven black hair, unblemished complexion, dark amber eyes, and sweet inviting lips are perfect enough to tempt even the holiest of men. Fortunately, I am more ambitious than holy. I exert all my willpower to pull my focus off of her face and appraise the man who will have her as his own.

Naram is the same height as his intended, who is unusually tall and lean for a maiden. If his eyes are an indicator of his true nature, he is an intensely driven man, both willful and predatory. His presence and surety extend far beyond the boundary of his physical stature, which is average at best. He is dressed in civilian robes, plain and comfortable; if he has worn his sword, it was removed and left in the care of the Temple servants. A necklace of fine gemstones, rubies, emeralds, and sapphires encircles his neck like a collar and gives notice that he is a man of considerable wealth. While his thin wispy beard is starting to gray around the edges, his lean and erect posture suggests that he is still in fighting shape and well-disciplined in his ways. He is not a man I would care to confront or betray in any way.

Since the wedding party has arrived, it is time to settle down to the business at hand. The people of Mesopotamia approach most everything in terms of business. The movement of goods is an integral element of commerce, so my not-so-distant ancestors invented the wheel. The cuneiform alphabet was devised to facilitate the recording of financial accounts; only after did it occur to the priests that the alphabet could also be used to praise the gods and goddesses who watch over our prosperity. In keeping with this emphasis on accountability, the bringing of two hearts together in holy matrimony is first and foremost a business transaction. A contract must be written that clearly details the exact amounts and contents of the groom's purchase of the bride's hand in marriage. Only when the purchase agreement is acceptable to both parties and sanctioned by the matrimonial priest can the nuptial ceremony occur. Hence my purpose in this meeting.

Enheduanna steps forward. "Welcome Ninband, sage nobleman and elder in our city, father to Nagula, whose hand is now proffered to another. And welcome Naram, protector of our city and respected general in the grand army of Akkad. Please be seated at the table of council." She turns and bows her head slightly in my direction. "Ishme, the priest-elect in charge of matrimonial affairs, will serve as witness and counsel to these proceedings."

Naram looks me over as he might a new horse, sizing me up quickly to determine my strength and character. "You are young for such a responsible position, priest. Do you have the necessary experience to facilitate a matter of this magnitude?" His tone sounds skeptical, and his assessment of my capability is clearly lower than a drought-depleted streambed. He is trying to intimidate me with his scathing opinion, perhaps to gain some advantage in this negotiation. I steadfastly refuse to wilt before him and his beautiful bride-to-be.

"I have been trained by Uri, the previous priest in this position, and I am confident that I can see this proceeding through to its conclusion, Your Excellency." I bow slightly to him, in deference to his position of authority. I have used a title reserved for those of the highest stature. If he is flattered, he doesn't show it.

"We shall discover how effective you are, I am sure. I am well acquainted with your father and have had many business dealings with him. He is hard-nosed, but fair. Why do you dwell in the Temple when you have such an established legacy outside these walls?"

I am surprised he knows so much about me and answer him as respectfully as I can. "I have been drawn to a life of devotion and service to our gods, my lord, and have left the dealings of mankind to the capable hands of my younger brother who is better suited to the family business." Naram turns to face his cousin and raises his eyebrow to seek her own estimation of my qualifications.

"Ishme is young, but he is very astute," Enheduanna reassures him. "I shall watch over him and assist him when necessary. This is his very first assignment, and we shall be patient as he establishes his credibility. Won't we, cousin?" She smiles at Naram in such a way that all he can do is smile back and bow to her in agreement. The High Priestess glances at me and nods her head, signaling that I should begin the business at hand.

For the rest of the morning, I lead the negotiations on the value of Nagula's hand in marriage. It proves to be costly indeed. Ninband is extremely stubborn and unrelenting from the very beginning. He believes that the combination of his daughter's beauty and her vaulted status as a member of a high noble family should dictate a price commensurate with both of these factors. Naram is agreeable, but only up to a point. He concurs that his betrothed's beauty is beyond compare, an observation I can easily agree with, however he argues that the value of her family's status should be subject to negotiation. He goes on to say that the Sumerian city of Ur is, in reality, no more than a conquered Akkadian city and that his blood flows from the same veins as its mighty conqueror Sargon the Great. Needless to say, this proves to be a delicate issue and one that sorely tests the limits of my as-of-yet untested ability.

"While your point is an excellent one, Your Excellency," I cautiously observe, "and the quality of your ancestry beyond dispute, Sumer itself is an ancient city with a long and noble history of its own. Yes, it is true that it was assimilated into greater Akkad, yet it still remains a special jewel in the crown of your uncle's vast and glorious empire. The noble bloodlines of Sumer remain untainted and highly respected by the various and sundry peoples that prosper under Akkadian unification. Therefore, I would argue that Ninband's claim that his ancestry demands a high valuation is both reasonable and just." I glance at Enheduanna to determine if my intervention has met with her approval. After all, the same Akkadian blood travels through her veins, and perhaps she sides with her cousin's point of view. But the faintest trace of a smile that passes across her full and balanced lips suggests that I have managed the situation astutely in her eyes.

Nagula also glances in my direction. Her respectful expression stirs the hidden coals of my dormant heart into a wakefulness that is entirely out of accord with my current mantle of responsibility. I quickly look away and focus on Naram, whose sharp and penetrating gaze bores into me with the impact of a violently hurled spear. He turns to address his future father-in-law.

"I respectfully agree with the priest's august appraisal of Sumerian ancestry," he counters, "but I must still insist that Akkadian blood be valued at a premium, given the political reality of our situation." Here, Naram pointedly bows to Ninband. "But I will concede that Ur is an important city in my uncle's empire and will value the hand of your daughter accordingly. Therefore, I will offer fifty sheep, forty goats, twenty head of cattle, and a one half-share of a season's supply of grain as my final offer. My estate up north can ill afford any more drain upon its annual output and continue to sustain itself. This must be my final offer."

Ninband inclines his head in acceptance, and the deal is done. Over a hundred head of livestock in addition to half a season's supply of feed is a generous offer indeed. The old man smiles with satisfaction and nods to me in thanks for my part in the negotiation. His estate will be greatly increased as a result of the bargain, and his status in the community will benefit in equal measure. That his daughter's marriage to Naram will also connect him to the all-powerful ruler's bloodline is another feather in his cap. He smiles at Naram and grasps his hand to show his accord and seal the bargain. I set down the details of the agreement in writing and have both men stamp the document as the final seal. The time has come to bless this union.

I pour purified water into a copper urn that is specifically designed for the nuptial blessing. It has two separate spouts opposing each other; one for the groom and the other for the bride. I direct Naram and Nagula to stand before the altar. I place her father to her left, and Enheduanna immediately assumes the position to the right of the prospective husband. I stand before the group and raise my arms in salutation to the gods.

"I call forth the blessings from on high. May Enlil, great King of Heaven, bless this union and cherish it as any father would his newborn babe. I pray to Ninlil, mother of Nanna, the moon god. I pray to Inanna, her granddaughter. May they smile upon this marriage so that it may prosper and be fruitful. May this household be harmonious, and may they bear many heirs. I offer these prayers in humble acknowledgment that the gods are mighty in their ways and favor us with their blessings when we favor them with our respectful offerings." I grasp a hare from a basket set beneath the altar. The hare has been drugged and is docile to my touch. I hold its body upside down by the legs and slit its throat with a sharpened knife reserved solely for this purpose. It has a special handle, embedded with many colorful gems, and its silver blade is well honed. I deftly capture the blood as it pours from the rabbit's neck into a silver bowl that I have already positioned beneath the now inert animal. When I catch enough blood to satisfy the watching gods, I place the bowl on the altar in offering and give the animal to an attendant standing nearby. He places the carcass back in the basket and removes it from the room. I lift the copper urn and pivot to face the bride and the groom. I instruct the two principals to kneel so I may anoint them with the purified water, which I pour generously from each respective spout onto their bowed heads. At my bidding, Ada steps forward and dries their dripping heads with a woolen towel.

"You are now properly prepared through sacred ritual to join one another in holy matrimony," I state clearly for all to hear. "The gods have blessed this marriage in our presence and approve of your union. As priest in charge of matrimony, I declare that you may hold service for this accord as soon as you desire, and I will dutifully perform your marriage ceremony with great respect and devotion."

I bow to both of them and gesture for them to rise. They do so and smile gratefully at me before nodding respectfully to the High Priestess and to Ninband. Ada then leads the wedding party out of the chamber and guides them to the Temple's exit. As the sounds of their footsteps recede into the background, my mentor assesses my performance.

"I am proud of you, Ishme, for you handled yourself well with this proceeding. One word to the wise, my young friend: a priest—or in your case a priest-elect, for you still must declare yourself by sacred oath to this way of life—must seem to be in the background, especially when performing the sacred rituals. You must remember this, for the gods are watching and can become jealous and spiteful if they feel up-staged and disrespected." She stares deeply into my eyes, plumbing my capability to comprehend what she is saying. I suddenly feel very naked. Luckily, she is satisfied with what she sees, for she quickly moves on with her critique. "But your sense of management is well developed for one so young. My cousin is not an easy man to deal with, being accustomed to obedience and respect and yet you handled him adroitly, I must say. I will commend Uri for his excellent job of preparing you for your new position." She smiles wryly, for we both know that Uri will be anything but pleased by my success.

The High Priestess graciously nods to me and then exits the chamber to address other pressing demands. Now that I am alone, I must confess that I too feel proud and relieved to have passed my first real trial as the newly appointed matrimonial priest-elect for the Temple of Ur.

***

The following day flies by in a blur as I settle into my place among the Temple elite. Uri, my reluctant mentor, sends for me to join him in his private office. He is a thin man, slightly stooped at the shoulders, with almond-shaped eyes that are larger than normal and as black as a moonless night. His bald head is shaved and buffed; his beard is thin, white, and waxed to a sharp point below his chin. His pasty skin is colorless, as if he has avoided sunlight for all his waking days. His office is filled with clay tablets stored on wooden shelves, which cover three of his four walls. An ancient and musty smell seeps from the tablets, but thankfully it is boldly challenged by curly wisps of sandalwood incense, many scented candles, and the torch smoke that burns from several locations around the room. A hollow airshaft draws the excess smoke up and away from his underground domain. The elderly priest sits behind a wooden table carved with symbols that look to be esoteric in nature. Many of them are new to me, proving I still have much to learn about the secret teachings of the priesthood. The desktop is piled high with reports and accounts relating to the day-to-day operations of the various Temple programs and services.

He congratulates me on my "adept" handling of the negotiation process and my evident "mastery" of the sacrifice and blessing ritual, actually using some of the same words spoken by Enheduanna herself, then commences to counsel me, one final time, with the details of the marriage ceremony that I am to manage in a few days. As he reiterates the proper sequencing of the rituals I will be performing, I can feel his displeasure and ill will simmering beneath the dutiful facade of his seemingly benign instruction. I always find his unexpressed hostility very disquieting. I consequently feel obliged to conduct myself with the guarded deliberation I might exercise were I handling a poisonous serpent. I treat him with the respect his elevated station deserves and avoid any attempts to humor or personally confide in him as I might with someone I trust. All of our interactions are strictly formal and very cool. Despite the lack of harmony that surrounds my relationship with Uri, I experience a blossoming confidence in my abilities and a corresponding excitement building in me regarding the approaching ceremony.

When the wedding day arrives a week later, I dress myself in the ceremonial garb of my new office. It is planting season, and the sun is rising ever higher in the sky. I, therefore, select a white linen skirt as my undergarment, forsaking its woolen predecessor. I secure it with a thick pleated belt that has royal blue tassels attached to it. I find it very formal and elegant to have a splash of color to offset the white cloak I wrap myself with, leaving my right shoulder bare as is customary for most male attire.

I obtained the services of my new assistant, Grudea, a competent devotee a few years older than myself. He is tall and lean, as if the gods put him together from a bundle of cattail stalks, and he towers over me. His features are smooth and plain, impossible to read, although his long nose lends a sneaky suspiciousness to his countenance. We are both adjusting to our new relationship, and I am quickly learning how to issue commands and expect an appropriate response. I incline naturally to taking control and am beginning to get comfortable with the responsibility of leadership. Because it is Uri who appointed Grudea to serve me, I keep a careful eye on him, for I am uncertain where his true loyalty lies. I bid him fetch the jar of perfume that will be used in the ceremony. When he does, we leave the Temple.

Ninband's estate is only a short walk away. It is a large home surrounded by high mud-brick walls. Judging from the various thatched rooftops that poke into view, the compound has several out-buildings, probably for guests and servants. Traditionally, most residences in Ur are modest one- to two-room structures packed tightly together along narrow winding lanes. But in the area nearer to the Temple, many of the town's nobility congregate in significantly larger houses. The Temple itself is built upon a raised *ziggurat*, or terrace, so that no other buildings can approach its height and majesty. It has risen and crumbled many times over the centuries and literally lies upon the dust of its ancient past. Although Ninband's house is considerably smaller, it is still grand in scale. He is a very wealthy noble with large holdings in livestock and food supplies. My father, like Ninband, also built a fine home to raise his family in, not much smaller than the estate I now approach. But the neighborhood we lived in is farther away from the Temple, and many smaller houses surround our house. Some other wealthy merchants also live in that area with estates much like my father's, but overall most other homes are modest by comparison. In this part of the world, bloodlines count far more than gold or silver, and even though my father could afford to live near the Temple, his application would probably be denied given his merchant class upbringing. He's been wise enough to avoid the situation, knowing his place and respecting the mores of the land.

We stroll up the pathway to the front steps and climb to the gate where Grudea pulls a rope tassel that rings a warning bell. He then quietly steps behind me in deference to my superior station. Before long, the wooded gate pulls back and a short male servant ushers us into the grounds. We follow him down a lengthy corridor that has several doors leading off it. It opens onto a central courtyard where a beautiful garden forms the beating heart of the complex. Palms and date trees surround neat little pathways, leading hither and yon between fountains and ponds. The corridor encircles the garden on all four sides, embracing a generous paradise that is secreted away from the intruding eyes of those outside the walls. A larger fishpond is situated in the center with lily pads and cattails surrounding its perimeter. A spacious stone patio borders the pond, and I decide it will host the altar that I will construct for the day's ceremony. A gentle breeze graces the courtyard and cools the air to a comfortable temperature. *A good omen*, I think. *Surely, the gods are smiling upon the coming union of two such noble beings.*

Ninband appears before us dressed in another colorful robe, this time decorated with many Sumerian symbols of prosperity; cattle, sheep, goats, fish, and bundles of grain are all cleverly embroidered onto the linen cloak. Clearly, he is a man who likes to be seen. I am delighted when he selects the exact location I imagined for the ceremonial altar. Next, I set about transforming the patio into a makeshift Temple worthy of the upcoming nuptials. After inspecting several rooms, I secure a large wooden table, polished to a dark ebony hue, to serve as the proper altar. Ninband agrees with my selection and has his servants haul it from the dining room to the garden. I direct where they should lower it down, for I have the strongest vision of how the ceremony will proceed. I position vases overflowing with blossoms on each end. The flowers, all of which currently bloom along the riverbed and in private gardens, were provided by Enheduanna, who had Ada deliver them just minutes before I arrived. The middle-aged handmaiden remains available to help Grudea and me establish the proper environment for a wedding of this magnitude.

I respect Ada a great deal. She came to Sumer with the High Priestess from up north. She is Akkadian, sparingly built, and well-mannered and efficient in all she does. She keeps her hair short, which is unusual for the time. Her features gather themselves in a proper accord, giving her a pretty but somewhat serious appearance. She arranges the flowers on the altar, adjusting them in much the same way the High Priestess did in the Temple of Union. It is easy to imagine who's instructed her. The table is freshly polished and shines with a fine luster. Grudea hands me a silver jar of perfume that I position in the middle of the altar. Ada places a white veil next to the jar.

Meanwhile, Naram is waiting in a separate room, idling away the time with his male witnesses and attendants. Nagula is sequestered with her mother and bridesmaids in another part of the compound. No doubt they are preening and adjusting her garments and hair so that she will seem as fresh and welcoming as the gentle breeze that blesses this occasion. Just after we finish embellishing the altar, the first guests begin to arrive. Enheduanna parades into the garden, dressed not as High Priestess, but as a member of the groom's family. Her cobalt blue gown wraps around her and almost touches the tiled floor. She wears her hair braided and tied up with a matching ribbon. A few white lilies are tucked into the arrangement, adding elegance and natural beauty to her overall presentation. She is magnificent to behold.

Several officers of the King's army accompany her, along with a few noble lords with political connections and even the Governor himself. He is an Akkadian and has served his king for many years. They are the leaders of our community. The head servant of Ninband's family ushers them to a preferred location directly behind where the immediate family will eventually take their places. The High Priestess smiles at me, and I nod politely to her before I turn and inspect the altar for the last time. I leave the garden and join Ninband in his private office to wait for the marriage proceedings to begin. I can feel my anxiety steadily building the closer we get to the commencement of the ceremony.

Meanwhile other guests file in and find places on both sides of the pathway that divides the garden. A few servants are stationed along the way and guide the guests to one side or the other to ensure that the pathway will remain unimpeded for the bridal procession. When Ada informs me that the guests have mostly entered the complex, I accept that the appointed hour has finally arrived.

I leave Ninband and proceed to the garden. I approach the altar in a dignified way, not too fast and not too slow. I signal to Ada to notify the bridal party that they should initiate the precession. Quick as a wink, Nagula's mother is escorted to her place near the altar. Next comes Naram, along with his cadre of male witnesses who all appear to be Akkadian officers, very martial and burly looking. After them, the bride's female attendants proceed down the central pathway. They are young Sumerian girls, unveiled maidens who are obviously of noble birth. They dutifully parade in front of the guests, trying to maintain an air of solemnity since this is a scared ceremony and requires their respectful devotion, but it is clear to me that all of the girls are brimming with happiness and mirth as discreet smiles creep onto their serious countenances like shafts of sunlight breaking through an overcast sky.

Once the bridesmaids arrive at their respective places on the opposite side of the altar from Naram and his men, a silence seizes the courtyard and holds it captive. All eyes turn to the back of the garden in anticipation of the bride's arrival. Although only a few moments pass by, it feels closer to forever, so high are the expectations of the crowd. When Ninband finally appears with his daughter at his side gently holding on to his arm, no one is disappointed. Nagula is stunning to behold. Her raven-black hair, usually braided and twined into coils around her head, now cascades freely down upon her slender shoulders, indicating that she is a virtuous and unspoiled maiden. Her dark eyes eagerly seek out the details of her audience, drinking in the adoration that washes about her. Her long ivory gown fits her like her birthright. Her olive skin glows like honey, washed and oiled with sweet essences. Her smile, more coy than brazen, warms the hearts of everyone who beholds her in this, her moment of glory, a shining star in the center of her firmament, the bride on her wedding day.

I am speechless, drugged by her radiance and beauty. Thankfully, she and her father proceed slowly through the center of the assemblage, offering me time to try to regain my wits. Unfortunately, I am not altogether successful. I wade through the motions of the ceremony like the dazed novice that I am. Luckily, I regain my senses soon enough to finish strong with my benediction, sounding very much like the presiding priest I am learning to be. But it is the final ritual that really awakens me. I bid Grudea to present me with the silken veil that I may in turn hand over to Naram. My assistant sprinkles a few drops of perfume onto the dainty, almost transparent veil and hands it to me.

"May the groom approach the altar," I speak with enough authority to have him comply with my request. He strides the few steps that separate us with the inherent command of one of the King's most trusted generals—which, of course, he is. I face the congregation of guests. "The groom must now claim his bride in the presence of kin and peers and in witness to the gods who have willingly blessed this union." I turn to my right and offer him the snow-white veil. He slowly and gingerly takes hold and removes it from my grasp. He faces Nagula and smiles warmly at the young and dazzling maiden. It is obvious that he is very attracted to his beaming bride. He speaks clearly.

"I now, in the presence of my kin and peers and before the eyes of the gods who surround us, claim you, Nagula, as my wife and property, and as such I would veil you from the gaze of all but myself." Naram articulates the words so precisely that no one fails to hear him. He holds the veil before her and stares directly into her eyes, as though he and she are alone together in the privacy of their very own ceremony. I almost feel uncomfortable watching them, like I am trespassing in their private quarters. Dutiful Ada accepts the veil on behalf of the bride and attaches it to Nagula's hair with her clever and efficient fingers, gracefully stepping aside when her task is done.

The bride bows before her new master, the future father to her children should the gods decree it so. He offers his hand and raises her up, face to face, as man and woman, and then fervently places his lips upon both her hands, which he now grasps with both of his. I step forward.

"From this day forth, these two citizens of Ur are recognized by all who have witnessed this ceremony as lawfully united in matrimony. Please welcome them as man and wife." Friends and family quickly swarm Nagula and Naram. At the same time, the servants begin to transform the spacious garden from a wedding temple into a celebration hall, soon to be filled with music, food, and wine. My job is done and done well, and I happily join the others in offering my congratulations.

Sometime later, Enheduanna draws me aside. "Ishme, you did a masterful job for your first attempt. You seemed to gain strength and confidence as you went along. Isn't she beautiful?" The High Priestess points in the direction of the joyful bride, who is clearly in command of her performance. Everyone wants to be near her as she gaily converses with the lucky ones who can reach her side. Naram stands away from her, content to share her for the while. Later on, I suppose, she will be all his beneath the comfort of their silken sheets. I blush with shame as I imagine them lying together and quickly redirect my attention back to the High Priestess who stands in front of me. "Don't you agree?" Enheduanna presses on, not content with my silent response to her question.

"She is radiant, Your Holiness, and will make Naram a happy man and a proud father someday soon, if the gods be willing."

"If the gods be willing," she concurs. "They must spend as much time together as they can, for I fear that the winds of conflict begin to blow in the north. My father grows restless and stirs uneasily upon his throne. Naram may soon be called back to Akkad to serve his King and master."

The thought of having to leave such a beauty must surely vex him dearly, I think to myself as I admire her charm and grace from across the garden.

"He will probably leave her in the care of her family rather than cast her adrift at his estate back in Akkad," Enheduanna continues. "I doubt that he feels she has ripened enough to manage his vast holdings without his guidance. If Naram returns to Akkad, it will be to march off to tame the unruly tribes up north. Besides, Ninband has provided them with a private apartment on his compound, which I'm sure is more suitable than the groom's barrack apartment on the other side of the river." She looks around before she whispers, "I suspect he may plow her well and often, in the hopes of seeding an heir. I know my cousin well, and he is a practical and shrewd individual. I doubt he will waste any time, especially if he has to ride off to war. Time will tell."

At first, I am astonished that Her Holiness could be so frank and direct about such matters, but then I realize that she is a wise and experienced woman who has seen much in the ways of the world. She may be an en-priestess, but she is no figurehead. Instead, she manages a vast agricultural empire that surrounds the city and Temple of Ur. She emanates the qualities of a capable and grounded manager who has dealings with many different kinds of people, both rich and poor. She is comfortable in her own skin and with the power that lies firmly in her gentle grasp.

"I expect that you are correct, Your Holiness, for such a task would be no great hardship for any man who has eyes to see with." She smiles in agreement before moving on to mingle with the bride's family and other notables in attendance.

I am soon surrounded by a few of the bridesmaids, some of whom recognize me socially from my days as the young and restless son of a wealthy industrialist. The girls are very impressed with the sudden and rapid rise in my station. I receive their compliments for my adept handling of such an important ceremony. To be honest, to stand in the midst of such beauty is no real hardship for me. I happily converse with them and feel myself slipping back into my youthful ways.

Eventually, I gather together Grudea and our belongings and retire from the celebration. I have imbibed enough wine and praise, and sense that I best depart before I say or do something that is not in keeping with my priestly station. I take notice that the newlyweds have already retired to their private chamber, and I pray for a joyful and fertile consummation of their marriage. I experience a tinge of envy for Naram, which I immediately suppress. It is inappropriate. I can no longer harbor such emotions and desires for I am now a holy man, and my attention is reserved for the immortal gods, not for the base mortal urges that must be sacrificed on the altar of my devotion. Grudea and I return to the Temple, and after I have tucked the sacred vessel safely back into its proper container, I busy myself with other matters.

***

Time flows by as rapidly as the small fishing vessels that ply the currents of the Euphrates. Crops are planted, grow to maturity, and are harvested. Days grow shorter, and the winter rains arrive with their customary chill. The Temple corridors fill with smoke as the servants tend many small fires that burn in the rounded bowls placed in and around the compound. Since wood is scarce in Ur, they are forced to burn dried cow dung. The resulting stench is thick and musty, but the smell is easily tolerated in exchange for the welcoming heat the flames offer in return.

With the passage of each season, I have settled comfortably into my new role and have gradually mastered the various demands that come with the position. Occasionally, Enheduanna requests my services as her back-up scribe, and I am only too happy to oblige her. She is currently working on a collection of songs dedicated to the many different Sumerian temples that line the banks of the twin rivers that embrace and give abundant life to all of Sumer and beyond.

After the completion of four full seasons in my elevated role, I have determined that working as a priest-elect fulfills my highest expectations. I am happy with myself and with the level of respect I receive from my peers and the community that benefits from my services. Even Uri has become accustomed to my presence and treats me with less hostility. He is never really friendly, but his chilly demeanor has thawed into some modicum of civility. I continue to maintain my distance, but even so, I have many dealings with him since he is my superior and I am subject to his authority. Soon I will have to take the sacred oath and complete my probationary period as priest-elect. After I do that, there will be no turning back. I will be a priest until the day I die.

Winter retreats before advancing spring, and farmers flood the surrounding fields in preparation for the planting of crops that will eventually be harvested and collected in the underground storage bins adjacent to the Temple's kitchen. The winter rains have been ample, for the gods are pleased with the people of Ur and with the devotion and daily sacrifices that we priests demonstrate on their behalf. Unfortunately, the same gods are less pleased with the border regions to the north, and as such they have withheld the nurturing rains over the last two winters. This creates hardships for the northern tribes, whose food supplies have become seriously compromised. Uprisings are the inevitable consequence of this scarcity, and a rebel army has formed amongst these communities. It now threatens the city of Akkad itself.

Sargon has quickly responded to this crisis by raising an army he, himself, will lead against the rebel forces. His empire has been at peace for a long time, but even in times of peace, there are always regional disputes that the great King must contain and settle. His empire is vast, and the peoples he rules have many differences among them. But this current crisis constitutes a far more serious threat, for it is quickly growing like an unchecked grass fire into a full-scale rebellion. Therefore, the great King has summoned all his generals to marshal their commands and march immediately to Akkad.

Naram received his dispatch from Sargon and was forced to leave his lovely wife in the safe keeping of her family and march a majority of his soldiers north to Akkad. He left a skeletal force behind to man the local garrison. The lean and severe general rode in a war wagon at the head of a contingent of other charioteers and foot soldiers. I watched him ride by in his chariot drawn by four draft animals and studied his erect bearing. Dressed in his leather breastplate and wearing his copper helmet with a white plume sticking out of its summit, he looked every bit the hardened leader that he is. He held his gaze steady, looking ahead at all times while his driver managed the animals and impassively ignored the crowd that gathered to send him and his 250 troops off to defend the King's empire. He appeared completely focused and so purposeful that I had little doubt he would make a deadly opponent for any foe who should cross his path in battle. He is not the kind of general who will hold back in the rear of his fighting men. No, he will be at the fore, leading them on to victory or death. As I watched him lead his troops out of town, I wondered if he managed to leave behind more than just his beautiful wife. After all, a year has passed since he consummated his marriage to Nagula.

Since the army departed for the north, Nanna, the moon god, has completed his monthly sojourn, rising and growing to fullness and returning to the underworld to leave the night dark and lonely. Late one morning, I receive a request from Uri to go and visit with the general's young wife at her father's house. Apparently, she is pining for her departed husband and is in need of spiritual counseling. She has specifically requested my services.

It is common practice for the head priests to provide special counseling to the citizens of our community. Obviously, we restrict our visits to members of the nobility, though we include some wealthy merchant families who are charitable in providing support and resources to help to build and maintain our Temple complex. The mud bricks that constitute our various structures are in constant need of repair. In exchange for their generosity, the High Priestess doles out foodstuffs during times of drought, assuring that the more elevated members of our city receive their shares first and foremost. We have plenty of lesser priests and initiates who can attend to the needs of the less privileged. I have already paid several visits to other families on both sides of the river, conducting sacred fertility rites, removing curses, or performing sacrifices to the different gods and goddesses, depending on the nature of the request put before me. Sometimes, I simply counsel family members, mothers and fathers, husbands and wives, providing insights and blessings as needed.

The prospect of visiting Nagula as her private counselor sparks an excitement within me that should forewarn me to tread lightly and cautiously in her presence. Unfortunately, I am too young and emboldened to heed such sage inner counsel.

I grab a satchel containing certain objects of worship, exit the Temple, and walk along the lane that leads to her father's home. Off in the distance, I see several farmers leading oxen around their fields. Tilling the soil is hard work, and I am thankful to have been born into a wealthy family that allows me to pursue a less physically demanding occupation. I am slight of build and more refined in nature. Serving the gods requires less brawn and more acumen, which I have in sufficient quantity, unlike the rough, sunbaked laborers I see toiling in their lots. Once, the local farmers owned their land, but over time the priests have acquired much of it as an institutional holding for the public good. Enheduanna now exercises executive power and manages a great deal of the agriculture that surrounds the city. Many of the farmers that I now watch guide their oxen to stamp out the weeds labor on her behalf as sharecroppers. I notice that some meadows are still flooded and have yet to be drained. Soon the multitude of fields stretching between the dikes and reservoirs that channel the river water and provide sustenance will sprout several varieties of crops, including barley, millet, grain, and lentils.

Moments later, I ring the bell at the gate that opens into Ninband's expansive compound. A servant answers my ring and politely leads me into the garden where Nagula awaits my arrival. She reclines without a chaperone near the pond where I married her a cycle of seasons ago. She seems changed to me, less maiden-like, more grown up and mature. No doubt her marriage to Naram, a seasoned veteran, has contributed to her transformation. But I do not sense that she is with child, for her figure remains unchanged. Her countenance reveals immediate pleasure at seeing me approach, warming my heart in an instant. She speaks directly upon seeing me enter her space.

"Ishme, I thank you for coming to my father's home. I am in need of your counsel, for I am abandoned by my husband's call to duty, and I feel so terribly alone."

Her honesty and directness convince me that Nagula is no longer a girl of just seventeen winters but is in fact a woman with enough confidence to speak straight to the heart of her concern.

"Your sense of loss is understandable, my lady, for you have been sacrificed on the altar of service to our King and supreme ruler. Naram is a powerful man and has close ties to his uncle, who now calls him in this time of civil unrest. It is his duty to answer." Her beauty has increased like a flower whose petals slowly unfold and blossom over time. Last year she was still young, and while beautiful, she only hinted at the elegance and stature that her loveliness could attain. After a full year of wedded bliss, she has shed the fuzziness of youth and sharpened not only the features of her character but also the full focus of her depth and grace. Despite her age, I feel as though I am in the presence of a lady.

"Yes, my husband's rightful place is at the side of Sargon, but even so, I had grown accustomed to his presence in my life and am now bereft by his absence. The days have lengthened since he went away, and I grow more depressed with each passing moment." Nagula sighs deeply and lowers her head in despair. My heart weeps silently on her behalf, for it is hard to witness such exquisite vitality wilting under the weight of so much melancholy.

"It is normal for you to feel lonely and abandoned. Such emotions are commonplace when husbands march off to war. Perhaps you fear for his welfare, my lady, for he rides headlong into the gathering storm. We must pray to Naram's protector for his safe and speedy return."

She looks at me and inclines her head in agreement. "Naram always prays to Inanna. He believes she watches over him like she does his uncle. He even confided to me that she led him to my doorstep as a way of rewarding him for his virtue. Naram believes that I am second only to the goddess herself in beauty and form." She turns to me and smiles. "What do you think, Ishme?"

I feel the blood rising in my face and can only hope that the young lady will fail to notice my blushing complexion. "I am a humble priest who would never attempt to disagree with so powerful a man as your husband, my lady. Surely, your beauty rivals that of Inanna herself, but let us give her the victory, as she is our protector and we must defer to her in all things."

She smiles at my careful choice of words. "You are a wise man for one so young in years, Ishme, and are right to place Inanna before all others, including myself." She leans forward, as if to share something between us alone. "You, yourself, are young and handsome for a priest of the Temple. I know of many maidens in Ur who grieve that you have chosen to wed the gods and forsaken mortal companionship."

Now I am certain that my face must be turning red, for my youthful vanity is flattered by her words. "I am too busy serving the public to have time for such personal considerations. I will now light some incense and we will pray to Inanna to be a shield that protects your husband from all harm in the coming days, to save him from injury, and to give him valor and daring that he may defeat his enemies and return home safely to his loving and caring wife."

I reach into my satchel and remove a block of incense that I place into a bowl handed to me by a servant girl who instantly appears as Nagula claps her hands. The servant provides me with a brand of fire that I use to ignite the incense. I offer up a prayer to the war goddess inviting her to continue to watch over Naram and defend him from harm. When my supplication is complete, I produce a bundle of nuts and dates, which I offer to Inanna as a token of our appreciation for her strength and benevolence. The servant girl places the bundle on the table where the incense is burning.

Nagula lies prostrate on the ground in proper prayer position throughout the proceeding, and when I conclude our private ritual, I bend down and take hold of her hand to raise her back up. As our hands touch, I feel my heart quicken in my chest as though it might burst asunder. I also notice that Nagula's lips tremble slightly, and her unblemished cheeks blush in response to my own touch. I avert my gaze and assist her to her chair. I clear my throat and try to restore order to the chaos that has suddenly beset my mind.

"My lady, the goddess is pleased with our sacrifice and remains constant in her high regard for your husband's welfare. Continue to pray to her as often as you like, for she will heed you in this matter. I too will pray to her on your behalf." I smile and pause for a moment. "I am sure it will bring you comfort and relief to feel that your husband will return to you in good health and with great honor for the heroic deeds he will have accomplished on the field of battle."

Nagula manages to regain her composure during my summation and smiles gently as she acknowledges my words of comfort. "You are most kind, Ishme, and have restored me to harmony with your counsel and prayer. I don't know how I can thank you enough." She looks at me with so much gratitude, I fear I might melt like a pot of butter baking beneath the midday sun.

"I am delighted that I have been of some assistance to you, my lady," I manage to reply. "Please summon me again if your spirits sag, for I am ever at your service." I bow low and gather up my satchel. I am shown to the gate by the same young slave girl who assisted me during the prayer ritual. She is obviously Nagula's personal attendant.

I immediately return to the sanctity of my bedroom. I need a few moments alone to collect my wits before I begin to prepare for a contract negotiation later this afternoon with another wedding party. I collapse onto my bed and sigh deeply. I feel like a boat without a sail, or a miller without a grindstone, so unhinged has my sense of surety and purpose become after my visit with Nagula. I can't stop thinking about her trembling lips or experiencing the surge of happiness that follows this recollection, for could she not possibly share the same kind of attraction for me as I have for her? I know this is inappropriate and tell myself I must stamp out the joy that accompanies this realization that Nagula and I may long for each other. I am the high priest-elect in charge of matrimony; she is the dutiful wife of one of the most powerful soldiers in the empire. My duty is to administer to her spiritual needs; her duty is to wait patiently for Naram's return. I supposedly sublimated my sexual appetite when I became priest-elect, but now this uncontrollable fire that rages in my loins could endanger my best laid plans. I must grab the reins of my destiny and control this unholy craving that Nagula engenders in me, lest I ruin everything that I find sacred and fulfilling. The High Priestess herself has advanced my career of her own free will. I know that I can never disappoint her by violating my sacred trust to the community.

I fall to my knees and grasp my hands in prayer. I bow my head and call upon Inanna to breathe a frigid breeze upon my longing and freeze it, right here and now. I concentrate on my request so hard that I can feel my loins cool down and return to the blessed slumber that befits a holy man. I must stay pure and innocent, conscientious and practical, and above all, diligent in my duties as an ambassador to the gods. I thank Inanna for restoring my purpose and for helping me banish all covetous thought of Nagula from my mind. I am once again her priest and counselor and will focus on her spiritual welfare. I have responsibilities to tend to and a glorious future to protect and nurture. I rise, restored and relieved, exit my bedchamber, and head for the Temple of Union. After all, a priest's work is never done.

***

A few days later, Ada drops by the Temple of Union and politely informs me the High Priestess wishes to see me in her chambers. I go there immediately. Enheduanna has recently returned from a voyage upriver; she periodically travels north or south to visit other temples. She is working on a series of temple poems and needs to visit each site in order to invite the local deities to inspire her with verse. As I walk toward her rooms, I wonder if I am to scribe for her again. But when I enter her private chamber, she is sitting across from my old mentor, Kitushdug, who is busily taking dictation.

"Oh good," Enheduanna exclaims as soon as she sees me. "Your timing is perfect, Ishme. I need to take a break." She returns her gaze to her diligent scribe. "Kitushdug, why don't you come back after the midday meal, and we will pick up where we left off."

"Yes, Your Holiness," the scribe answers as he rises to obey her request. He bows to her and then nods to me, for we have been friends since my apprenticeship. He is too practical to be jealous of my abilities and recognizes that I am an asset rather than a rival. Given my relationship with Uri, I find Kitushdug's professional courtesy very refreshing. As soon as he leaves the room, Enheduanna points to the chair he has just vacated.

"Have a seat, Ishme. I want us to have a little talk."

"Yes, Your Holiness," I answer, wondering what it is she wants to talk about. I sit down and smile. "How was your trip upriver?"

"Wonderful. I went to the Ebabber Temple and paid homage to Utu, the sun god. I was only now recording the opening verses of my new song. I felt the sun god's presence, and he has encouraged me to sing his praises. As you know, he is the divine complement of Nanna, our moon god. He brings water and sunlight every year to help grow our crops and feed Nanna's cattle."

"I am confident that Utu will be well pleased with your verse when you have completed it. I thought you might be needing my services as your scribe, but clearly I am mistaken."

The High Priestess appraises me without expression before answering. "I want to have a conversation with you today about your work and your relationship with all of us here in the Temple." I suddenly feel very uneasy and worry that my struggle to control my instinctual urges may have somehow become a matter of public concern. "You have been a head priest-elect for over a year now and are well liked and accepted by our community of priests and initiates. I too am pleased with your competency and with the enthusiasm that you exhibit in the performance of your duties." She gazes at me with another of her penetrating stares that probes right to the very center of my being. "But are you happy with your situation, my friend? You are youthful and handsome, a man who can go and do whatever suits his fancy. Do you grow at all restless now that you have had sufficient time to become accustomed to your duties in the Temple of Union?"

Since being tempted by Nagula's beauty and her apparent attraction to me, I have wondered if I've chosen wisely in this matter. Do I have the proper constitution to advance from priest-elect to head priest and devote myself to a lifelong service to the gods? Do I have the discipline and will to control my baser passions? Are my abilities alone worthy of Enheduanna's high regard for me? These questions and considerations rush through my mind in the briefest of moments, but I know I have confronted and dealt with my feelings of lust and put them behind me. I have chosen wisely to become a priest. I've enjoyed my rapid advancement and success under Enheduanna's encouraging mentorship, and I definitely like having authority. I'm not about to abandon my career and return to civilian life. My younger brother is the arms merchant, set to take over my father's successful weapons foundry. I am born to be a head priest. This realization shows itself as clearly to me as the light that reflects from my mentor's eyes as I engage them and respond to her final inquiry.

"I am grateful, Your Holiness, for your satisfaction and confidence in me and my abilities." I articulate with careful deliberation. "I have never been happier than I am right now. I am at home in the Temple and am content to serve the gods as one of their representatives to the great City of Ur. I assure you that I have no other ambition than to continue on in my duties as the en-priest in charge of matrimony. I am confident that I have left my previous life and inclinations behind. I am fully committed to serving you and the Temple hierarchy to the best of my abilities for the rest of my life."

The High Priestess inclines her head slowly in acknowledgment. "I want you to be absolutely sure,

Ishme, for I will bind you by oath right now and in witness to Inanna that you will be celibate and faithful to her and all the other gods and goddesses that we hold dear at the Temple of Ur." She stares directly into my eyes. "Are you certain that the priesthood is the destiny you would choose?"

I straighten up and returned her gaze. "I am certain, Your Holiness."

"Very well then. Ishme, are you prepared to drop all ties, both familial and emotional, and commit yourself, once and for all, to priestly service at the Temple of Nanna in the City of Ur? Will you dedicate yourself to the gods and refrain from sexual union with humankind? Are you prepared to be a priestly ambassador between the immortals and the citizens of Ur, to live by the codes that are enforced in this Temple, and to obey the dictates of its hierarchy? Please consider these demands carefully and say yea or nay."

My mind is certain. "Yea," I reply, and by saying so I cross an invisible line that I can never uncross. I have sealed my fate with my word and have bound myself to Enheduanna and to the gods and goddesses she serves from this day forth.

"Thank you, Ishme. You have chosen well. I am delighted that you have decided to fully embrace your current position. You are a wonderful asset to me, and I look forward to our continued association as colleagues and friends. I will inform Uri of your decision to pledge yourself fully to the Temple life of a priest. Now, please excuse me while I rest before the midday meal."

I bow to her and leave her office uplifted. I feel relieved now that I have committed myself to her with all my heart and soul. I return to the Temple of Union, shedding the "elect" and commencing my duties as head priest in charge of matrimony. By giving my word to my mentor, I have been instilled with a new and deeper sense of holiness.

***

The next week passes quickly, for I am busy with two separate weddings. Spring turns to summer and the early crops reach skyward in salutation to Utu and his warming rays. Traveling merchants have brought word that the army has assembled and marched north to deal harshly with the unruly elements that have dared to oppose Sargon. Upon hearing this news, our Temple sacrifices a hearty cow in offering to Nanna and Inanna to enlist their support in the upcoming struggle. Uri cuts the beast's throat and I capture the blood in a large copper bowl that I place on the main altar. The High Priestess gives the blessing in support of her father's campaign to reestablish order in his kingdom. The Temple is filled with nobles and tradesmen alike. Many villagers come to show their support for Sargon and his troops.

One afternoon later that week I am walking back to the temple after visiting the home of a wealthy merchant who needed to discuss the guidelines he must follow in asking for a proper dowry for the hand of his oldest daughter when I spy Nagula shopping in the marketplace. She is accompanied by her servant girl and is chatting with her and fails to notice me at all. I watch her appraise a necklace that a merchant holds before her. Once again, I feel my heart jump in my chest like an excited dog that is greeting his master after a long absence. Like it, I am equally helpless to control my own reaction to her unexpected presence. I feel unnerved by my lack of control and turn away, so she will fail to notice me. I maneuver behind a stall and elude her altogether. I persuade myself that I am wise to avoid her and the attraction I feel for her.

At the end of the week, Uri summons me to his office to notify me that another young maiden is considering marriage and seeks my counsel. When he gives me her name, I recognize it immediately; Siduri was a bridesmaid in Nagula's wedding. She too is born of noble blood and heralds from wealthy stock. She is also one of the maidens I knew socially before I became devoted to the priesthood four years ago. I conversed with her at Nagula and Naram's reception and remember how impressed she was with my sudden rise to authority within the Temple hierarchy. Like Nagula, she is young and beautiful and is of an age where her parents would be eager to find a suitable mate. Uri insists that I visit Siduri this afternoon. He stresses that her family is a big supporter of the Temple and has earned our immediate attention.

Because this visit is of a counseling nature, I leave Grudea behind to prepare for the upcoming ceremonies that are scheduled in just a few days' time. The Temple of Union needs a thorough cleaning, as the surrounding fields are constantly sending unwelcome dust into our sacred spaces whenever the wind blows up. The last few days have been windier than usual. He can handle that chore while I attend to this new development. I go alone to Siduri's family estate that same afternoon.

It is smaller than Ninband's but still considerable in size and scope and has several out-buildings besides the main structure. I ring the warning bell and am soon guided by a young and attractive servant girl to what appears to be a guesthouse. The traditional structure is composed of mud bricks and has a slightly pitched, thick thatched roof. Although the guesthouse is inside the compound, it is situated well away from the main house. It has its own garden area with a small and tidy fishpond in its center. The place is very cozy and private. The servant girl opens the door for me, and I walk in. I startle when I see Nagula standing in the center of the room, all by herself. She smiles at my obvious confusion.

"Siduri has offered me the use of this guest house so that you and I may meet together in secret, Ishme. Her parents are away for a time, visiting her older brother and his family upriver in the City of Uruk."

"I don't understand," I counter, feeling very uneasy and completely off-course. "I'm supposed to be meeting with Siduri to counsel her on her upcoming marriage."

Nagula smiles again, obviously enjoying my discomfort. "Her marriage to Ishu has been set for the fall and is mostly agreed upon by both families. They will consult the Temple priests later this summer. Siduri sought your counsel only so that I could meet with you alone. Her servant let you in and has been sworn to secrecy. No one else knows except for my servant girl, whom I would trust with my life. We can meet here in the privacy of this guest house and be absolutely safe from prying eyes." She pauses for a moment so I can try to assimilate her words. "I must see you alone, Ishme, because I can't stop thinking about you."

I am cast adrift on a sea of conflicting emotions. I feel a rising tide of panic in my gut, for I sense that I am sailing a course that will grow less navigable as I proceed ahead, yet I also detect excitement gathering in my heart. I have never seen Nagula looking so beautiful as she does in this moment. Her head is uncovered, and her long, sable-like hair falls in shiny black rivulets about her shoulders. Her deep blue dress hugs her tightly and outlines the contours of her rounded breasts as they hide beneath the garment's neckline. Her collar is open, and I can see the silky softness of her throat. Her dark amber eyes blaze with a passion that radiates from her as a tangible force that I cannot escape. I experience a stirring in my loins that acts of its own accord, for I am desperately attempting to control my mind and willpower with every ounce of determination I can muster.

"Nagula, I am a priest and have just sworn my allegiance to Inanna and the Temple of Ur. The High Priestess has bound me by my word. I have dedicated myself to the gods and must remain celibate for the remainder of my life. I can offer you my friendship and counsel. Beyond that, I dare not go."

If Nagula is the least bit discouraged by my words, she hides it from my view. She only smiles again and reaches out to grasp my hand in hers. "Come, Ishme, and sit beside me, for I only seek your counsel." She gently leads me to a pillow-laden bed on which she sits, pulling me down beside her. She releases my hand and brushes her hair away from her eyes, then rearranges her dress so that her breasts appear above the horizon of her neckline. "You misunderstand me, my dear. I am a married woman and could never betray my beloved husband, even if his seed has yet to bear fruit with in me." She looks squarely into my eyes. "Naram desperately desires an heir, and yet his best efforts to produce one have failed miserably. I fear he suspects I am a barren field that yields no grain." Her dark and captivating eyes fill with tears and melt my heart with pity. I place my arm around her shoulder to comfort her and try to appease her unrest with my words.

"It is still early in your relationship, for *only* a year has passed since you and Naram first consummated your marriage. I know my parents were forced to till the soil of their union for three seasonal cycles before I came into this world. Besides, Naram could be hasty in his judgment of you. Is it not possible that the barrenness may lie in his seed and not in you at all?"

"He would never allow himself to suspect that his seed was in any way lacking, and he is not a patient man. No, I fear he may eventually declare me fallow and demand recompense from my father, as the law of matrimony allows." She is correct. A husband can demand a return of his dowry if his spouse fails to produce a child. Nagula looks beseechingly into my eyes. "I could never allow myself to be so disgraced. I would rather take my life than endure such shame." She buries her head against my shoulder and weeps deeply. Unfortunately, my counsel has failed to assuage her distress. I can find no more words of comfort and hold her gently instead.

At length, the tide of her despair abates, and she sits up to dab her eyes with a silk handkerchief plucked from her sleeve. Once she has regained her composure, she smiles demurely and grasps my hand in hers.

"You are kind to hear me out, Ishme, for I have no one else to turn to. My parents don't want to be saddled with my problems anymore. I am Naram's responsibility now, and my father would be very displeased if he was forced to return Naram's dowry. Alas, I am at my wit's end."

She appears so beautiful and vulnerable I want to seize her in my arms and reassure her that all will be well. I believe that Naram is probably too possessed by her beauty to ever abandon her. If need be, he can always impregnate a servant girl and claim her as a second wife—unless of course his seed is the issue. But I know that Nagula is too despondent to believe me, so I remain silent. I simply hold her hand and act calm and sympathetic. We sit in silence for a goodly while, holding hands and listening to the sounds of animals moving about the compound outside. Chickens scratch the ground looking for bugs and cluck incessantly as goats bray at each other and a milking cow moos in the distance. We hear children's voices laughing as they play in an adjoining yard.

Something strange and mysterious happens to me as we sit together in silence. I sense a subtle energy flowing from her hand into mine, enticing me like a sweet fragrance. My manhood lengthens beneath my robe despite my mental resolution to remain neutral and unimpressed. The scent of sweet perfume emanates from her lovely neck, tempting my senses and weakening my resolve. The simple truth is that my priestly stance and determination have begun to waver in her presence as my youthful vigor reemerges like a spring flood. I know I should release her hand, stand up, and move away at once—and yet I can't. I gaze at her downturned face and marvel at her loveliness.

Nagula raises her eyes to meet my own and whispers to me in her sweetest voice, "Ishme, I have a favor I would ask of you."

If a warning bell sounds somewhere deep inside my being, I heed it not. "What would you ask of me, Nagula?" I whisper, still holding her hand, for I am reluctant to let it go.

She gazes at me and gives immediate voice to her request. "Ishme, will you break your vow to Inanna and make love to me, today, right now? I need your seed to rescue me from my despair." She squeezes my hand. "Give me a child I can present to Naram as his very own. Will you do this for me?"

I cannot believe what I have heard. I expected her to seek an offering or a blessing to aid her in her distress, something that I could do willingly and in keeping with my role as her priest, but to break my vow of celibacy both to the goddess of love and war and to her earthly representative, Enheduanna, my mentor… This goes way beyond the reach of my imagination. I release her hand and stand up.

"Nagula, you ask too much of me. I am a priest. My vow is a sacred trust that I have forged with my Temple and my gods. To break it would be to violate the bond that unites me with them." I shake my head. "I cannot give you what you want. To do so would crack the very foundation on which I stand. I am sorry, Nagula, but I will not and must not grant you your request." I speak as slowly and deliberately as I can, which challenges me given the turmoil that rages beneath my priestly veneer. The thought of making love to her gnaws at my will like locusts devouring a field of grain. She is so beautiful and inviting, so in need of comforting, so vulnerable and so desperate for my seed. I cannot reveal this temptation to her, or I will surely fail in my resolve to remain celibate and holy.

When she hears my refusal, she collapses on the bed and bursts into tears. She sobs like a little girl who can't have her way. Her body rises and falls in rhythmic measure with her grief. I dare not comfort her but stand nearby and watch as she wails away. Eventually her sobbing subsides, and she sits up and pulls herself together using the same handkerchief as before.

"Of course, you are right to refuse me, for what I ask of you is both unreasonable and wrong. It's just that…" She stops to dab her eyes and blow her nose once more. "It's just that I have no one else to turn to, and I feel so helpless and alone." She seems so fragile and afraid that my desire to comfort her outweighs my need for caution. I sit down next to her and grasp her hand in mine.

"You must be strong, Nagula, and pray to Inanna for strength and guidance. I sense that you are not the one the gods have made barren. You are too young and fertile, too beautiful and loving for them to frown on you in this way. I think it is Naram who they dry up like a hot desert wind. Perhaps he has angered them somehow, and they would punish him in return."

Nagula smiles at me with gratitude for my supportive words, but then shakes her head slowly with sullen resignation.

"No, even if my husband is dried up, he would still blame me. He could never lose face with his uncle or his soldiers. He must fault me, Ishme, and I must accept his accusation as truth. I am therefore doomed. Unless…" She tightens her grip and looks deep into my eyes. "Unless you help me, Ishme. Please reconsider. If you won't, I don't know what I'll do." The scent from her perfume wafts over me and caresses me like a skilled masseuse. "Don't you think that Inanna would forgive you, Ishme? If you break your vow to preserve the reputation of Naram, Sargon's favorite general and Inanna's chosen warrior, and by doing so help maintain the harmony of his home and family? Surely the goddess smiles on Naram as she does his king, and if she did lead him to me as he professes, then she must want me to bear him a child. If Naram is incapable of engendering one, then you must stand in for him and gift me with new life. No one would know of your generous deed but myself, my best friend, and our two servant girls who would rather die than betray us." She clasps my hand tighter still and looks beseechingly into my eyes. "Please reconsider, Ishme. Can't you see how desperate I am and how helpful you could be?"

I feel my resolve leaking from me like wind from a mismanaged sail. "My vow is sacred, Nagula, and not to be trifled with. I would be disgraced if I complied with your request and was publicly exposed for betraying my word and trust. Inanna may forgive me given the desperate circumstances that you now face, but Enheduanna would never understand, nor would your husband. My career and my life could well come to an end. It is too much to risk, even if Inanna herself would turn her gaze aside and pretend to look the other way. Besides, Naram would know that there was treachery here by the count of moon cycles from the child's conception till birth."

"He has told me that this campaign will be short lived," Nagula informed me. "He believes he will return before this year's harvest is over. I will bed him at once and then later will pretend that our child has arrived early. He will never know the difference. I promise you that no one here will ever say a word against us. Our secret will be safe forever. I am sure of it."

She releases my hand and reaches up to softly stroke my cheek. She smiles at me sweetly and places her hand behind my head, pulling my face to hers. Our lips touch and I experience a surge of energy rushing upward from my loins and encircling my heart. Although I have flirted with other females, I have never before kissed or been kissed by a woman. To have Nagula initiate me in this subtle joining is like drinking the gods' own nectar for the first time. I sense a lightness settle over me as I release all my burdens and cares and focus on her presence. When our lips press together, I instinctively place my hand upon her breast. Her tongue penetrates my mouth, and I marvel at how serpentine it is as it darts about, caressing my own. Any notion I have of priesthood vanishes before an onslaught of pure, unadulterated passion, both primal and vital in nature. Her touch, her lips, her breasts, and her hands consume me in the fire of their embrace. Clearly, she is as enlivened as I, and the pent-up attraction we engender in each other now expresses itself in our mutual need for connection.

We remove our clothing and lie naked together on the bed. Her experience in lovemaking leads me to places I have never been and will probably never go again. My rod, which stiffened when our lips first joined, is now guided gently by her soft and reassuring touch into a sacred cavity where life itself begins. Her body thrusts and heaves with a regularity that induces a surging tide of lust to rise within my central core. The blending of rhythmic massaging and emotional arousal allows me to transcend mere physicality and reach a place of joy and happiness I have never known. As my seed finally explodes into her, I meld into an ecstasy that I wish would last forever.

Alas, it does not. Instead, it slowly subsides and leaves our two bodies, intertwined like vines, breathing heavily in love's embrace. We lie in silence for an indeterminate stretch of time, until an awareness of our nakedness begins to awaken in my mind. I suddenly feel very vulnerable and exposed. I pry myself from her embrace and reach for my priestly garb. Nagula immediately senses my discomfort and reaches for her own robe. We dress in silence.

"I must return to my duties," I say, speaking in a voice that sounds less sure of itself, younger and less established.

Nagula sits on the edge of the bed and stares up at me as she brushes her long silky black hair. "Thank you, Ishme, for your sacrifice on my behalf. I am forever in your debt. May Inanna forgive us both for what we did today and accept that we acted selflessly and with good intentions." If the young wife of the powerful and respected general is experiencing any regret over her own betrayal, it doesn't reveal itself in her tone.

I reassert my priestly authority even though my heart and head toil in abject confusion. "Yes, let us hope the goddess will understand our motive and forgive us for what we have done. I bid you good afternoon, Nagula." I sound more like myself again. I exit the guesthouse and am guided out of the compound by the same servant girl who greeted me earlier. She does not meet my eyes.

When I return to the Temple, I go directly to the altar under the domed ceiling in the main gathering hall and make an offering to Inanna on behalf of Nagula and myself. I sacrifice a small hare and plead for her forgiveness. I then go to the Temple of Union to inspect Grudea's preparations for the marriage ceremonies later in the week. I think it best for me to act as if nothing untoward has happened. Therefore, it's right back to work for me, even as I experience this profound sense of guilt over what I have done.

***

Over the next several days I slowly regain my composure and sense of purpose. It requires some time to purge my mind of Nagula's beautiful body and passionate embrace. The climactic release I experienced in her arms, the joining together of our hearts, and the incredible explosion of ecstasy to which I surrendered are impossible to erase, but with much effort, I return my focus to my responsibilities as a head priest.

The few times I am in the presence of Enheduanna, I feel less comfortable and assured. I know full well that I have betrayed my oath to her and in doing so have violated the covenant of our relationship. My guilty conscience prevents me from being as relaxed around her as I normally would be. But luckily, she is unaware of my discomfort, for she acts as friendly and supportive as ever. I think the goodwill that we have developed over the years blinds her from detecting my unease.

Uri, however, seems more distant and less approachable, which surprises me given how well we've been doing over the last several months. We were never friendly in our interactions, but we had developed a respectful and cordial relationship that felt workable at the very least. Now, since my visit to Siduri's family compound, his demeanor seems to stiffen and harden when I approach him about Temple business. I know he could not possibly have heard of my treachery given the secrecy that surrounds it, and yet ever since that fateful afternoon, he acts with a suspiciousness to suggest that he has. The few interactions I have with him are uncomfortable. I wonder if the wizened old priest has somehow intuited my betrayal, perhaps through the use of sorcery. I also wonder if my own guilt might be imagining the whole thing. At any rate, I try to act as I always do around him, but it is becoming increasingly difficult to be in the same room with him and his suspicious nature, so I only address him when it is absolutely necessary.

Word comes from the north that Sargon's army has engaged the rebel forces and is systematically destroying the opposition in one encounter after another. I'm not at all surprised. Sargon may be old, but he still has all his teeth. The known world has never before experienced a ruler who exercises such a brilliant grasp of military strategy. His empire, as vast as it is, remains firmly in his grasp, and I pity those who were foolish enough to challenge his authority. His troops are too professional and experienced to be outmaneuvered or bested on the field of battle. I also feel certain that Naram is adding new glories to his storied career. *Soon he would be marching home in triumph.*

One day leads to the next, and harvest time is fast approaching. Certain crops mature sooner than others, and luckily for the City of Ur, the benign weather patterns reflect the continued benevolence of the gods. It is provident that a fruitful harvest lies ahead for the farmers this season.

A complete moon cycle has come and gone since I strayed off course in Siduri's family compound. I am gradually feeling like my old self again. One warm sunny morning, I am summoned to Uri's chambers. When I enter his musty den, he informs me that Siduri has once again requested my counseling services regarding her scheduled marriage later in the fall. I hope that the old priest fails to notice my shock at being invited back to Siduri's compound for a second visit. I immediately assume that my previous intervention with Nagula has failed to be productive, and I pray my disappointment has not recorded itself on my youthful features. Unfortunately, Uri's stoic face rarely strays from its usual impassivity, so I cannot determine if he is aware of my emotional reaction or not. I thank him for notifying me of Siduri's request and take my leave.

Grudea has already been sequestered by Uri to assist him in preparing for the annual ceremony of thanksgiving for the upcoming harvest, so I don't need to instruct him as to his duties while I am gone. I leave the Temple complex directly and head for my supposed counseling session with Siduri. I am in no way surprised when the same servant girl ushers me to the same guest house where the one woman I fear and desire most of all is indeed waiting for me.

She stands up as soon as I enter the room. "Oh Ishme, I was afraid you wouldn't come! Thank you for returning. You see, I'm still desperate for your help. A month has passed, and I am without child. I just don't know what I'm going to do."

I figure that Nagula knows exactly what she is going to do, and that I will play a pivotal part in her plan. "I am sorry to hear that you are not pregnant yet, and I am disappointed on your behalf," I state as a matter of fact. "As you may already know, word has come that Sargon has successfully quelled the northern rebellion, and your husband will soon return to the loving embrace of his devoted wife." I see her face flush with shame at my biting words. I go on, nonetheless. "Perhaps the gods have turned their backs on you and do not smile on your best efforts to provide him with an heir." I'm sure her shame is further intensified by my unfriendly tone of voice.

"Be not unkind to me, Ishme, for I act only to increase my husband's happiness. The gods know this to be true. And yes, Naram will certainly return home to my loving embrace sometime soon." She stares boldly into my eyes. "That is why I have requested your presence once again. This is my last opportunity to create a blessed child to gift to Naram as his own. Since his arrival is immanent, our opportunity to manifest life is even more timely and will solicit less suspicion." She pauses before she addresses the real purpose of this meeting. "Will you bed me again, Ishme, for one final time, and plant your seed in my sacred garden?"

I know I should refuse her request and let the fates decide for themselves what will unfold between Nagula and her ambitious husband, but her beauty and earnestness have once again begun to corrode my resolve. My repressed manliness is already welling back up at the mere notion of engaging one more time with Nagula's divine form, and I can feel my heart begin to race with anticipation, but I dutifully make one last attempt to persuade her otherwise.

"I have only recently returned to feeling comfortable with myself, having forgiven us both for our separate betrayals: you to your husband, and me to the gods. I have moved on with my life. To commit another act of betrayal will undo all the progress I have made. Perhaps we should accept that the gods really do not smile on your plan. Maybe we should trust to their wisdom in this matter." I can see her disappointment and forge on even though I really want to comfort and embrace her. "I still believe that Naram will be more understanding than you believe, and that you worry overmuch about your failure to bring his child into this world."

"I know Naram much better than you do. I have little doubt that he will act swiftly and mercilessly once he decides that I am incapable of birthing his child. He needs to respect me if he would love me, and if I fail him in any way, he will renounce his claim to me and seek another wife." Her gaze hardens as she speaks. "I must succeed in this if I am to survive. *Only two moon cycles have passed since his departure. We still have time.* You are my only hope." She falls to her knees and grasps my hand. "Please bed me again, Ishme, for I am ripe and feel that I will bear an offspring for my husband, if only you would agree to join with me one more time." Her eyes plead as well as her words. They reach into my heart and move me to help her.

"Yes, Nagula," I whisper, "I will bed you one more time. But this is my final attempt, for I must honor my obligation to the gods and return for good to my priestly ways."

She kisses my hand in gratitude, then rises up and removes her clothes. I remove mine too. We lie together on the bed and rekindle our passion. Her lips meet mine, our lower limbs embrace, and our hands lovingly stroke each other in places and ways that encourage the complete and total reunification of our bodies, minds, and spirits. All the wonder and majesty of our first encounter is reignited, and my sense of ecstasy only increases as I finally, after what seems an endless period of delightful exploration, release my seed into her sacred container. For a few precious moments, our two hearts beat as one.

As we lie in silence afterward, letting our heartbeats return to their normal pace and rhythm, I wonder whether Nagula enjoys the same kind of emotional and physical sensations with her husband as she does with me? I decide not to seek an answer, for I have trespassed far enough into Naram's private world and can only inflict further harm by comparing myself to him in such a delicate and private matter. The gods, who see everything, will surely frown upon my attempt to do so. In their eyes, I have served as a tool to help facilitate a child for a barren relationship that may have died on the vine had I not sacrificed my honor to assist Nagula in her time of need. Such a vain comparison would only bring insult into the unique arrangement that I have made with the general's wife.

But Nagula addresses my secret musings as if she has heard my unspoken thoughts as clearly as her own. "Ishme, when we lie together, I experience a love so deep and profound, I feel like we are two halves of a whole. I have never approached such a passionate blending of energies with Naram, or such joy. I wish you were my mate, and that we could be together day and night."

My heart weeps as her words caress me like her kiss. Never in my life have I felt so completely at peace with myself and so connected to another. Nagula lies beside me, a perfect fit. Her body fills the contours of my own and makes us feel like one. I wish we could remain entwined forever. But we cannot. Gradually, the familiar sounds of domestic life invade the sanctity of our reunion. I feel my staff shrinking back to normal and my weight bearing down upon Nagula's tall and slender frame. I extract myself from her embrace and roll out of bed. I reluctantly pick up my robe and make ready to leave.

"Unfortunately, the fates have steered us down separate paths, and the time has come for us to honor their dictates and respect their will." Tears moisten my eyes. She lies naked before me, her eyes also welling with tears. "Our love can only bring ruin to us both. We can never meet like this again. I hope our joining will bear fruit this time, and that Naram will accept our child as his own. I will pray to Inanna to bless you with a son, and I will once more seek her forgiveness for both of us." Nagula weeps as my words wash over her like a cold breeze. She instinctively pulls a blanket over herself to hide her nakedness from my eyes.

"I will miss you every day of my life, Ishme, and will be eternally grateful if you have blessed me with a child," she replies so softly, I can barely hear her. Together we cry in silence. Then I leave the guesthouse and am shown out by the young servant girl who is entrusted with our secret.

As I leave the compound to tramp the dusty streets, I notice a tall, shadowy figure lurking in a nearby doorway. I instinctively wonder if he is spying on me. A bolt of terror strikes me and causes me to gasp for breath, but then a wave of relief soothes my fear when I see the hooded figure turn to knock at the door. He is just an ordinary man making a house call.

I return to my work at the Temple, determined to honor my word to Enheduanna and the gods. I am through with Nagula and her need to bear a child. Twice, I have acquiesced to her request and both times have experienced such joy and agony that I know I would go mad should I continue another step down this road of treachery and betrayal. My feelings are deepening for her, and I must now turn my back on her or face certain destruction. Her husband would make a formidable and merciless enemy, and I would be foolish to endanger myself any more than I already have. Our strong mutual attraction and love for each other will have to wither and die, for our destinies forbid our coming together. My mind knows it is time to move on. My reluctant heart will have to follow.

***

For the next several days, I focus on my work and my prayers. I have a rare late summer wedding to prepare for and some scribing to do for the High Priestess. Kitushdug has come down with a stomach ailment and will be unavailable for a few days. Working with Enheduanna helps to settle me down. I am soon returning to my old self, content with my work and with the various responsibilities entrusted to me.

A week later, a huge cloud of dust appears in the northern sky, signaling that Naram's triumphant army is marching home. Excitement builds throughout the morning as the soldiers gradually approach the city. When word arrives that the army has finally reached the outskirts of town, a huge crowd assembles along both sides of the road to welcome the hardened warriors back home. I join the throng of villagers with most of the other priests to witness the triumphant return.

When I see Naram riding in the forefront, elevated in his chariot, I feel a stab of disappointment pass through me like an invisible arrow. I am surprised and ashamed at my reaction, for I have been trying so hard to leave the memory of Nagula behind. Obviously, some part of me still craves her loving touch. As I watch my fellow citizens cheer the great general, I accept that I will never touch or hold his beautiful wife again. Naram is arriving home a hero and will undoubtedly couple with her that very night, perhaps even that afternoon; I know I would if I were he and had been away for such a long time. I, myself, will sleep alone in the company of the gods whose house I serve and will continue to serve for the rest of my life. It is for the best. Our destinies are carved in stone, and I am meant to sleep in solitude.

As before, Naram stares straight ahead and hardly acknowledges the riotous crowd that shouts his name in praise. He is a true hero, valiant and cruel. He is above the rest of us in power and influence. His uncle is the greatest king to ever reign in Mesopotamia, and Naram is like an incarnate god. His steely discipline and unmoving nature only serve to inspire the crowd with louder acclamation. I am truly impressed. His breastplate no longer shines with polish but is dented and nicked by the swords of battle. It is obvious he has faced and defeated many enemies himself, for he is a warrior as well as a general. The people love him for his courageous heart. I secretly feel ashamed that I cuckolded him and wonder at my audacity. I hope deep down he will never discover what I have done.

During the next moon cycle, the whole city clamors with celebration over the King's victory. Naram and his lovely wife are wined and dined at one estate after another, as he is feted as the heroic general responsible for the final victory. One afternoon, myself, Enheduanna, and several other priests are invited to a party held specifically in Naram's honor. Uri is also included, but he declines. He rarely leaves the Temple compound to expose himself to the light of day. The rest of us accept the invitation, especially since this particular event offers up a late lunch and a musical performance. It is hosted by Ninband and held in the same garden where the general and his beautiful wife were married more than a year before.

All afternoon long, I endeavor to steer my eyes away from Nagula, who radiates with joy and happiness. A healthy glow emanates from her skin, which encourages me to believe she may at long last have been blessed with new life. When Ninband proudly announces that his daughter is with child, I am probably the only person in the garden who isn't surprised by the news. The general and his adoring wife smile happily as the party guests applaud the announcement. Naram is obviously delighted that he has finally engendered an heir.

I, however, feel depressed. My seed has now contributed to the solidification of Nagula's relationship with her heroic husband, while I shall live a solitary existence in the service of divine entities that I can neither touch nor embrace but in my own imagination. I suffer from a deep sense of isolation and loneliness unlike any I have ever known.

"Why look so downcast, Ishme, when the entire room vibrates with so much joy?" Enheduanna startles me with her inquiry, for I failed to notice her approach from my right. "Have you eaten something disagreeable?"

"Perhaps, Your Holiness," I lie, "for my stomach is suddenly out of sorts. I may have feasted on too much fish. I found it hard to refuse."

"My conquering cousin must have refrained from overeating. Look how pleased he and his lovely wife are. Such happiness is to be envied, is it not?"

I make some effort to elevate my spirits. "Yes, he has much to exalt in. Word has it Naram led the final charge that sent the opposing forces into full retreat, and now he celebrates the news that he has gifted his wife with a child. His victory on the battlefield seems to have foreshadowed his present achievement in his marriage bed."

My mentor looks at me knowingly before she replies. "Perhaps one victory has led to another. Who can say? Yet, clearly, they have been blessed by Inanna, who watches over them both."

"Indeed, they have, Your Holiness." The High Priestess moves on to mix with a cluster of conversing nobles. I listen sullenly to the music that follows before making an early exit.

The next day, I am preparing for a negotiation ceremony in the Temple of Union when Grudea enters the chamber carrying a bundle of flowers that are to grace the altar.

"Uri requests your presence in his office, immediately."

"Really," I answer, "do you know why?"

"No, Your Holiness. He didn't say why." Something about Grudea's expression suggests that he might know more than he indicates. Maybe it is his eyes that look defiant even though his words sound respectful enough. I exit the Temple of Union and proceed down a long hallway before descending the stairs that lead to Uri's sanctuary in the basement. As usual it is darker and cooler than the upper rooms where I spend most of my time. Little daylight works its way into Uri's domain, and I wonder if he ever stops burning oil lamps and torches, even when he sleeps on the meager cot in the back of his chamber.

When I enter his subterranean world, I am surprised to see a familiar-looking military officer standing beside Uri's desk. I recognize him as one of the soldiers who stood up for Naram during his wedding.

"Ah, Ishme, Captain Agga is here to escort you to the army garrison. Apparently, General Naram seeks an audience with you." The old priest's smile makes me uncomfortable. It is far too ingratiating. There is nothing friendly about the officer who stands next to him. Captain Agga is a large, broad-shouldered officer who has seen plenty of action on the battlefield. The slew of scars covering his face and arms advertise that more than a few enemies have tasted the sharpened edge of his sword and not survived the encounter to wear similar scars of their own. The grizzled veteran looks down at me, for he is at least a head taller than I.

"The general requests your presence immediately, Your Holiness." The tenor of his voice is surprisingly high considering his massive appearance.

"Very well then," I reply, trying to sound as undisturbed by the situation as I can. "Let us leave at once."

Captain Agga bows politely to Uri and leads me out of the Temple and down to the river. He is dressed casually, wearing a simple gray tunic. A large dagger is sheathed and attached to a belt that encircles his generous waist. He wears cloth sandals with hard leather soles. Long laces wrap themselves upward around his thick calves. As I follow the captain's hulking figure, a host of concerns stampede through my mind. Why does the general seek an audience with me? Has he learned of my encounters with his wife? If so, how did he find out? Did one of the servant girls betray us? Did Uri somehow figure out that I was unfaithful to my vows of celibacy? I can feel a ball of fear forming in my gut as I contemplate the upcoming meeting, especially if Naram has indeed learned of my trespass into his most treasured possession.

When we reach the river, a wooden ferryboat is waiting for us. We board the vessel, which is carved from a huge cedar tree. It has plank benches in the middle where two to four passengers can sit. The bow and stern of the boat point upward toward the sky, making it look like a crescent moon. Two river men wait to maneuver the craft with long poles. We push off from the shore and head out into the brisk current. The river has been dropping all summer, but the City of Ur is close to the river's mouth, so it still flows smoothly between its banks. Clouds race across the sky, and a stiff breeze cools the late-summer air. I perch next to Captain Agga, whose hefty frame tilts the craft noticeably in his favor. We are soon poled over to a floating dock made of reeds woven and tied together in sections like a large quilt. It is attached by rope to timbers and air-filled animal skin sacks, which help to float the structure alongside the river's bank.

We exit the ferry and bob our way off the pier that rises and falls with every step we take. I lose my balance and almost fall in, but my escort grabs me from behind and steers me safely ashore. From there, we hike up a steep path to the top of the bank and approach the military garrison.

Except for the Temple itself, the military post is the largest structure in Ur. Four towering mud-brick walls surround a cluster of one-story buildings that house over three hundred soldiers. Sargon maintains a large army and has dispersed it throughout his empire. Since Ur is an important Sumerian city that guards the mouth of the Euphrates, our garrison is one of the largest forts of all. All told, the King can summon up to five thousand soldiers to march off to battle if the need arises. The rebels up north learned that lesson the hard way.

I follow Captain Agga through a wide-open gate and across a large courtyard to the administration building that contains General Naram's office. Soldiers mill around the yard, attending to various tasks and disciplines. Some sharpen swords and spears that have been nicked and dulled during the battle up north. Others practice their martial arts with each other, using sticks instead of swords to hone their skills. Still, more patch the walls that, like those of every other mud-brick structure in town, tend to crumble and turn to dust over time.

We enter the administration building, and I follow the captain down a long corridor, passing two opposing doorways along the way. *Several torches light the way.* Draperies hang across their openings, preventing me from seeing what transpires on the other side. My burly guide stops before a larger opening at the end of the hallway. He pulls one of two tapestries aside and silently gestures for me to enter.

I walk into a spacious office carpeted with woven rugs from all over the known world. Some lay upon the floor, others hang on the walls. It is obvious that Naram must enjoy collecting them. He sits at a long and wide table that is piled high with cuneiform tablets. They must have to do with the day-to-day operations of the large garrison. I am impressed that the general attends to these details himself, for he could probably have delegated them to other officers had he been less industrious.

He rises when he sees me come in and strolls around his desk to greet me.

"Ah, Your Holiness, I am delighted to see you." He salutes me formally, which surprises me, for he is showing me more respect than I have anticipated. He points to a chair that faces across from him. "Please come in and be seated." I bow to him and sit down while he returns to his own chair. Once we are both comfortably facing each other across the wide expanse of his crowded tabletop, the general smiles warmly. "I have asked you to come here today, Ishme, because I want to thank you personally for providing comfort and counsel to Nagula while I was away. She has told me that you helped her overcome her sadness and concern for my safety after I marched off to war."

"Yes," I confirm, "I did visit with her once, and we prayed to Inanna to watch over and protect you, Your Excellency. Our prayers seemed to bring some comfort to her distressed heart."

"Indeed, I give thanks for that. I felt the goddess standing next to me during the heat of battle and am eternally grateful that her mighty shield kept me from harm." I relax now that I realize Naram only wants to express his appreciation for my priestly intervention on behalf of his worried wife. "I see that you have grown and matured as a priest, Ishme. I must confess, I doubted your abilities when we first met in the Temple of Union." Naram smiles warmly again. "But, clearly, I was mistaken. You performed your duty well at our wedding, and since then have prospered in your role. My cousin, the High Priestess, has informed me that you have officially renounced your rightful inheritance and have instead sworn an oath of celibacy and devotion to the gods and goddesses of the Temple of Nanna."

"Yes, Your Lordship, I have chosen a life of service to Inanna and the other deities that watch over our Temple and protect our city. I hope I have chosen wisely, for I have much to learn."

"Well, I hope so too, Ishme, and I intend to discover if you have lived up to your vow as a servant of the gods." I sense the warmth draining from his countenance and feel the overall climate of this audience turning as cool as the first unexpected breath of winter.

"I don't understand, Your Excellency," I reply, trying to sound calm even as I seek to stay above the rising wave of fear that I experience within.

"Then I shall explain," the general answers in a voice that has now taken on an edge as sharp as a finely-honed dagger. "When I left Ur to campaign against the northern rebels, I enlisted certain agents to watch over my interests during my long absence. Upon my return, these same agents have informed me that my wife has had two additional meetings with you at a neutral location. To be more specific, I have ascertained that you and Nagula met privately in the guest house of her close friend, Siduri, who conspired to help arrange for these surreptitious meetings on her father's estate." He pauses and stares at me with the cold concentration of a snake holding its prey firmly in its constricted coils. "What was the purpose of these two meetings?"

Grudea's disdainful expression and Uri's ingratiating smile appear before my eyes, as does the shadowy form that stood in the neighbor's doorway as I exited Siduri's compound after the second visit. With the crystal-like clarity of a holy revelation, I see that Grudea has been spying on me all along, and I am certain that he and Uri are some of the agents enlisted to watch over Naram's possessions, including his not-so-loving-and-devoted wife. My heart is a stone sinking in an endlessly deep pool of water.

"As your wife's counselor and priest, I am compelled to honor her right for confidentiality, Your Excellency," I answer, somehow finding my priestly voice amidst the terror that reigns within my mind. "You must ask Nagula herself why we met secretly, not me."

"I would prefer that you answer that question, Ishme," Naram quietly responds. A long silence follows. We stare at each other until I finally find the courage to challenge his authority.

"And if I refuse?" I ask, feeling as trapped as a netted fish.

"Captain Agga has many unpleasant ways of persuading you to comply with my request. I suggest you tell me the truth, if you are capable of such a thing, for Inanna is watching us, and she too waits patiently for your answer."

He is correct. The goddess of love and war, the patron of Sargon and all his heirs, now waits for me to speak the truth, which she of course already knows.

"Your wife arranged for both our meetings in order to solicit my services regarding an extremely private issue that was disturbing her greatly. I assisted her to the best of my abilities."

Naram waits for me to continue my explanation, and when I stubbornly refuse to do so, he patiently inquires, "And what was the service that you provided for my wife?"

"Once again, I feel it would be more appropriate for you to ask your wife about that, for I am bound to silence as her priest and counselor."

"And once again, I insist that you tell me in your own words."

I hear the cold and level authority that resonates in his words, and quietly accept that I have finally run out of wiggle room. I tell him everything. How his devoted wife feared his disappointment and disfavor for not bearing him a child. How she persuaded me, against my better judgment, to assist her with the disposition of my seed. How I tried to assure her that her husband was devoted to her and would never return her to her father. How she refused to believe me and instead agonized over her almost certain disgrace. I refrain from disclosing the divine nature of our sexual union and the wondrous sense of unity we experienced together. Instead, I describe our relationship as a business matter, as if I was a stud offering my seed as an act of charity. At last I explain why we met on two occasions, the second visit being required due to the disappointing outcome of our initial attempt to create new life.

When I conclude my confession, we sit in an icy silence for several very long moments before the general clears his throat.

"Given your indiscretion, I must conclude that the child that grows within my wife's womb may not be the product of my own seed." His gaze turns inward. I watch his prideful mind wrestle with his conclusion. Can he accept the possibility that his seed is hallow? Will his love and attraction for his beautiful wife overthrow his inborn arrogance and sense of entitlement? Will he permit this child to enter his world? He pauses long enough to nod his head at someone or something behind me. Then he returns his gaze to me. "What is certain is this, Ishme. The child will be my heir, and no one will ever know otherwise."

His expression is as hard as the wooden floorboards beneath my feet. I hear footsteps approach from behind and begin to turn around when a large hand encircles my brow and yanks my head backwards. At the same instant, a cold, sharp edge cuts into my throat, slicing it open like a piece of fruit. I gag on my own blood and see the ceiling blur and fade from view as a veil of darkness engulfs my vision. I hear a whirling noise growing in my mind and feel myself rising up from the chair. I sense the darkness swirling around me as I spin with increasing force in the middle of some vast vortex that has no beginning and no end. I know it is limitless, endless and eternal, and that I might twirl forever within its grasp.

Then just as suddenly, I find myself ruthlessly sucked back into matter and am once again confined to the prison-like limits of time and space. I am staring at my own slightly distorted reflection in a bronze mirror. Much to my surprise, I find myself looking into the eyes of a beautiful, sophisticated female, and then I merge inexorably into my new image and am shamelessly admiring my own reflection. My awareness is the same, but my form has changed. I have become another person.

PART THREE

I am well preserved for my age. Both my sons are grown and gone, serving in separate legions on the Roman frontier. I married young, bore two children in quick succession, and raised them to respect their elders and the Empire. Now, at thirty-five, I am still attractive with only a few faint age lines around the corners of my eyes. I have only recently begun to dye my hair, hiding the few strands of gray that rudely invade my glossy black curls. I am grateful that my hazel-green eyes work proficiently and that I still feel young. I practice good habits, indulge with discipline, and, most importantly of all, control a robust appetite for food and for life.

And I have plenty to be thankful for—most importantly a wealthy and successful spouse, twenty years my senior but still active and capable. Together we enjoy good standing in the community, and fortunately for us, my Marcus is a very close friend to Emperor Vespasian. He has served him loyally for three decades and through many far-flung military engagements. As a result, we live comfortably on the Palatine, not far from the Imperial Palace. In fact, this very evening we are invited to a small private dinner with the Emperor, his mistress, and a few close friends.

Given that Marcus and myself both herald from the equestrian class, the lower of the two aristocratic orders here in Rome, we feel lucky to be on such intimate terms with the Emperor at all. We never could possibly have risen so high during Nero's reign, but Vespasian is a different kind of emperor than all those noble-born rulers of the Julio-Claudian dynasty that preceded him. Like Marcus and myself, Vespasian hails from equestrian roots. He worked his way slowly and surely up the hierarchal ladder until his destiny and his good standing in the military literally thrust him onto the throne.

And now, three years later, sanity and stability are restoring the Empire to its former glory. Nero's madness, which led to the dissipation of our Treasury, is at long last fading into the past as Vespasian raises taxes to rebuild the city's badly neglected and burned-out infrastructure. New temples are on the rise, roads are being restored, not just in the city, but also throughout the Empire, and a new sense of order is replacing the chaos that reigned supreme after Nero's suicide. Three different emperors rose and fell in the space of a year and a half, each one assassinated by his successor. All of Rome was beginning to come apart at the seams until finally the armies of the east and the north convinced Vespasian to claim the seat of power for himself.

As Marcus prophesied at the time, "At last we will have a real soldier in charge to clean up this mess and restore common sense to the people of Rome." Needless to say, my husband was biased by his long years of loyal service to his friend and commander, but now three years later his words are coming true. Rome is beginning to feel solid once again as new buildings and temples rise from the ashes of Nero's unstable rule.

"My lady, your husband has returned from the quarries." Adonia, my handmaiden, appears like an apparition in the reflection of my mirror.

"Adonia! You have startled me again. Do you delight in doing so?" I protest, placing my hand over my heart.

"I am sorry, my lady, I do not wish to disturb you when you appear so meditative," she answers, smiling meekly in response to my gentle rebuke. She has been sneaking up on me for longer than I care to remember and will continue to do so. It is a little game we've been playing for years. Adonia is a Greek slave, and despite her cleverness, I feel I can trust her with my life.

"Please remind Damaris that my husband must be ready to depart for the palace within the hour."

"Yes, my lady," she replies as her reflection withdraws as quietly as it appeared. Adonia and Marcus's man, Damaris, are married. He serves my husband with the same devotion she brings to attending my needs.

Marcus has spent the last few days in Tibur, a half-day's journey from Rome, cultivating a working relationship with a travertine quarry. He is preparing for the eventual construction of a new coliseum, which is to be called the Flavian Amphitheater. Vespasian has asked him to build it for the people of Rome. The Emperor has torn down much of Nero's ostentatious palace complex, the Domus Aurea, as a gesture of charity. The former emperor had built his private estate on the ruins of fire-stricken neighborhoods, thus stealing the land from the common people whom he was supposed to shepherd. Vespasian has decided to return the very same land back to the people in the form of a public amphitheater to be constructed where Nero's man-made lake once stood. That fiasco has already been drained in preparation for its new incarnation as "the Coliseum."

I've never seen my husband so excited about a building project. He hired the best architects in the city to draw up plans for what he insists will be the largest and most sophisticated amphitheater the world has ever seen. Meanwhile he is hardly home, he's so busy establishing connections with different quarries all over Italy. He is also spending a lot of his time with various engineers detailing the final plans for the amphitheater. Vespasian has instructed him to make sure that a proper sense of hierarchy be reflected in the new structure, so that every class of citizen will know exactly where they belong when they access and utilize the facility.

It is not surprising that the Emperor chose my husband to build his new coliseum. Over the last few decades, Marcus has built all kinds of structures for Vespasian, from siege towers to bridges, from aqueducts to roads. Marcus can build anything that's asked of him. As a result, we have become very well to do. Vespasian even offered to promote Marcus to the senatorial class, for my husband is wealthy enough to join the order, but Marcus respectfully declined. He is satisfied with his equestrian status, which allows him to be in the construction trades. If he were to become a senator, he would be restricted to owning and farming the land, which is about the last thing my husband would care to do. Marcus excels in engineering and building. The additional status that would accompany the title of "senator" is hardly sufficient compensation for the loss of his true calling. Besides, we already enjoy a special relationship with Vespasian, which counts for a lot now that he rules the Empire.

I behold my distorted reflection in the bronze mirror and apply some shading under my eyes using the new Egyptian mascara that has become all the rage. Adonia has already helped me dress. I am wearing a lavender linen stola that almost covers my white inner tunic. I plan to show off some of my finest jewelry this evening, precious gems encased in gold settings, around my neck and wrists. I am proud of the riches my husband has accumulated and am delighted that I can model our good fortune as part of my attire. Vespasian's mistress and constant companion, Antonia Caenis, is likely the wealthiest women in the Empire and will also be bedecked in all her finery. I want to look presentable to her as much as to Vespasian, as she will be the one to notice and appreciate the quality of the stones that I display.

Caenis is an interesting woman. Born a Greek slave, she was educated in her youth and served as secretary to Antonia Minor, the daughter of the great Marc Antony and mother to the late Emperor Claudius. Antonia Minor freed Caenis from slavery just before she committed suicide. She had written a letter to the Emperor Tiberius exposing the tyrannical treachery of Sejanus, his right-hand man. Antonia Minor had the heart of a real Roman. She knew she would pay a heavy price for her act of conscience, for Sejanus was an evil man. She took her own life and hoped that he in turn would end up losing his. As it turned out, he did. Tiberius was not pleased when he discovered the truth. Once everything settled back down again, the former slave, Caenis, adopted the given name of her dead mistress and became known as Antonia Caenis, a free woman of Rome.

She met Vespasian when Tiberius was emperor. It was during the latter part of his reign that Vespasian and Caenis fell in love and became youthful lovers. They were members of the court at that time, he as a young praetor, and she as an adviser already well accustomed to palace intrigue. After Tiberius's death, things became really interesting when Caligula inherited the throne of power. He was a rabid emperor whose nefarious nature ranged somewhere between hysteria and grandiosity. After his violent murder at the hands of his enemies, humble Claudius assumed the throne and restored order and decency to Rome, at least for a time. It was during Caligula's reign that

Vespasian, always the stalwart soldier and man of honor, married Flavia Domitilla the Elder, a fellow equestrian, and produced two sons.

Since her lover abandoned her to become a married man, Antonia Caenis quietly retreated into the background, but still remained in Rome. Despite her humble origins as a slave, she soon prospered as a respected lady of means. She had a shrewd head for business and was consulted often for her sage advice. Twenty years later, Vespasian's wife died. By then he was a powerful politician as well as a military commander, and he immediately resumed his relationship with his former mistress. Today, Caenis sits at his side as his closest confidant and adviser. Rumor has it she procures large sums of money for her lover by representing him in his financial arrangements. Like I said, she has a shrewd head for business.

Whatever else can be said about Vespasian, I see him as a loyal companion. First, he was faithful to Caenis, then, by necessity, he was faithful to this wife, and now he is once again faithful to Caenis. Contrary to accustomed practices, he never married for status or wealth. His one wife came from modest origins, and his live-in lover is a former slave. He's earned every advancement that has come his way by virtue of his accomplishments on and off the battlefield, and now, with a few timely connections here and there, he is an emperor who respectfully tolerates the noble and senatorial classes even though he owes his allegiance to his military backing. While he respects the Senate, he relies on his generals. In some ways, he is a plain man. His sound and humorous disposition seems more at home on the battlefield than in the corridors of the Imperial Palace. Yet here he is, hosting us tonight, where he will exhibit the same earthy qualities that endear him to men like Marcus who have served so long under his authority. I feel very fortunate indeed.

I open my jewelry chest and appraise what's inside. I select a heavy gold chain that boasts a large garnet pendant with multiple stones inlaid into it. I place it over my head and then select two golden bracelets, each with an assortment of small gemstones displayed in a random pattern. I open another drawer and slowly survey its contents before choosing two matching anklets crafted to resemble coiled snakes with shining emerald eyes. I slip on the bracelets and attach the bands to my ankles before checking the final effect in my bronze mirror. My hair has already been washed, combed, and pinned up by Adonia and adorned with a fine golden net to hold it in place. Adonia enhanced my features with cosmetics after my hair was styled, and I have dabbed just enough perfume on my wrists to entice my admirers without overwhelming them. My ensemble is complete, and I smile at my reflection.

Adonia arrives to notify me that my husband is ready to leave. My slave and I exit my apartment and cross through a central garden that opens up to the night sky. Vast assortments of stars blink on and off, keeping step to their own whimsy. It is cooling down outside, and I wear a palla over my dress to protect me from the fall breeze that stirs the evening *air*. My woolen cloak is a darker shade of white, almost gray, and blends nicely with my lavender dress. In the center of the atrium, a tiled fishpond stocked with a school of fancy goldfish is surrounded by an assortment of exotic plants from all over the Empire. Different types of palm trees, ferns, and flowers are tended by one of our many servants. Every winter we lose a few plants to freeze, but some of the heartier species have grown significantly over the years.

We moved into this domus two and a half years ago. We were encouraged by Vespasian to acquire this property, which had belonged to a senator who supported Vitellius, the previous emperor. Both were slain by Vespasian's troops during the changeover. We happily obliged our powerful friend and quickly moved from our previous residence on Capitoline Hill, one of seven hills in the center of Rome, bringing some of our favorite plants with us. Our former home was only a few blocks from the Temple of Jupiter. I have always believed that Jupiter, the god of good fortune and beneficence, smiles upon Marcus and me. Even though we moved away from his Temple, he still smiles upon us, for our new address is definitely a step up. It places us in an easy walking distance of the Imperial Palace, which is convenient for nights like this when we visit Vespasian.

Adonia and I proceed along the pillared walkway that fronts the perimeter of our inner garden. My husband's apartment is next to my own. Adjacent to us are the kitchen and servant quarters, which stand across from the grand living area where we eat and entertain our guests. Another inner atrium opens to a bathroom and several additional sleeping quarters for overnight visitors, including our two boys, whose visits are becoming increasingly fewer and farther between. I do miss them.

We enter the living area and pass through a grand room with several lounges and settees, all resting on wide woven carpets that spread about the floor and hang from the walls. The tapestries add color and pattern to the environment. A few large potted plants also help to fill in the large space. From there we stroll through a formal entryway, which opens onto the front courtyard. Not surprisingly, Marcus and Damaris are already there, awaiting our arrival.

My husband is a tall man with a full head of thick white hair. His florid complexion accents his bright blue eyes, which generate plenty of spirit. Even now in his late fifties, he seems vibrant and healthy. Unfortunately for us, the bloom in our own relationship has long since faded, what with two children to manage and his military career intervening constantly. I spent twenty years watching him come and go from one battlefront to the next. He was absent more often than not. Even when Vespasian retired for a while, my Marcus kept on marching in the service of one legionary commander after another, as his skills were highly sought after. But as soon as Vespasian was called back into military service by Nero to bring order to Judea, Marcus was quickly reassigned to his old friend's legion.

Once, a few years before that, I joined Marcus in Germania with our two young boys in tow so that we could all be together, but the experience was disappointing. He was still away most of the time building bridges. Since then, I have stayed in Rome or spent time during the summers at Herculaneum at our country estate overlooking the Bay of Naples.

Over the span of our marriage, our passion steadily waned. We have become more like friends or companions than lovers and rarely take our relationship to the bedchamber. I know Marcus has other sources that he utilizes, and I respectfully look the other way. I don't begrudge him his needs. I myself have access to whichever slave I would prefer, but I am too proper to allow myself such indulgences. After all, I am thankful for the comfort and stability that my husband has provided for me and our boys, who are now bravely following in their father's own footsteps, training in the military to be engineers just like he is.

My sons are alike in looks and disposition and have always gotten along. I could not have asked for a more stable and respectful brood. Both boys were eager to grow up and become soldiers in the army of Rome. With them grown and gone, I must admit that my life seems a little empty. I was a full-time mother, and now I am a full-time wife to a man who still spends more time away than at my side. I grow bored and need to find something new to liven up my existence. I'm just not sure what that something could be yet.

"My darling," Marcus calls out as I approach him, "the cool breeze is stiffening, so I have called for our litter." He pauses and adds, "You look as lovely as ever. I'm sure the Emperor will be dazzled by your beauty."

I smile as I stretch out my hand for him to kiss. "We both know that Vespasian will be far too gracious to drool over his good friend's wife. Besides, it's Caenis I am trying to impress. She will have a keener eye for the details."

"I suspect you are right, Lucia, but Caenis will be as kind as always, for she knows we are favored by Vespasian and always treats us accordingly."

"Yes, she does. But nonetheless, I need to show her my finest fashions. She appreciates it, just as I enjoy looking at what she is wearing." Marcus smiles and nods his head enough to convince me that he understands.

"How was your expedition to Tibur?" I ask in order to shift the focus back to him. "Are you satisfied with your connection there?" I am always interested in keeping pace with his wheeling and dealing. After all, I share in all his successes. For instance, I already know that the price of travertine has been rising now that the building boom in Rome is finally gaining momentum, and that two new temples are nearing completion near the Forum. Marcus's journey to Tibur will hopefully have established a fair relationship with one of the new quarries that has opened to keep up with demand.

"Well, as good as can be expected given the environment we're in," Marcus answers. "I am satisfied that my bid will be honored, for I have need of great quantities of the stuff and will be calling for it soon. The plans for the Flavian Amphitheater are complete, and that silly lake that Nero built is all filled in. Sometime soon the construction will actually start." He gently grabs my elbow and steers me toward the litter. "Unfortunately, I may need to widen and level the road between here and Tibur to withstand the heavy traffic once the deliveries commence. I plan to discuss this with Vespasian at his convenience. Large teams of oxen will be needed to haul the material and will definitely necessitate some widening of the highway. I'm certain he won't like the additional expenditures that such an expansion will require, but I see no other alternative."

As I duck my head and enter the litter, I sense my husband's excitement at the prospect of beginning the huge construction project. I envy him his enthusiasm.

"Do you have any idea who else will be present at this evening's get together?" I ask.

"I think Pliny the Elder will be invited. He has just returned from Gallia and will be in Rome for a while," Marcus replies as he joins me in the litter. Damaris closes the curtain, and our bearers hoist up the conveyance and depart from our courtyard. "Titus Flavius will probably be included as usual." Titus is Vespasian's eldest son and his right-hand man. Two years ago, he successfully completed the siege of Jerusalem and the destruction of their Temple. Since then, he has been at his father's side helping him manage the affairs of the Empire. "There may be others as well."

To say that my husband is one of the Emperor's closest friends is no exaggeration. They have known each other since they were young soldiers campaigning in Thrace and have managed to serve together on and off through the various campaigns in Germania, Britannia, and Judea. Even when the two friends were between military adventures, they always stayed close. Vespasian was a frequent guest of ours at our summer estate down south. We are hoping Vespasian will come and see us this next summer, but now that he is Emperor, it is more difficult for him to get away. His own estate is in Sabine Country, just to the north of us. We have visited him there a few times too.

As our fortunes grew over the years, so did our estate on the Bay of Naples. Our latest addition increased its size yet again, for we added a brand-new bathhouse and another more spacious guest room. Our summer home is far larger than our domus in Rome, and I really value the time I spend there. The grounds are spacious, and the views are sensational. Not only do we look upon the Bay of Naples, but Mount Vesuvius looms behind, providing us with another wonderful vista. Much of the wealth we have garnered over the years has been rolled into our summer home. When the hot weather descends on Rome every June, we pick up our family and servants and migrate south like everyone else that has enough denarii to do likewise. Some former emperors, like Augustus and Tiberius, had estates in nearby Stabiae, as did many of the most influential senators from our past, including Cicero.

Even though our home is half as large as some of the grander estates, we still manage a huge facility complete with orchards, vineyards, gardens, courtyards, and plenty of rooms to spare. In the coming seasons, considering the magnitude of Marcus's current construction project, we could easily afford another addition if we so choose. Now that the kids have ventured out into the world, they will someday establish families of their own, and we will expand our estate to meet their needs as well.

A sudden crash shatters the already boisterous clamor of the street and causes our litter to halt its forward progress. One of the carriers opens the curtain and reassures us that everything is fine. Apparently, a few roof tiles have fallen and smashed into fragments in front of us; they are already being cleared away by the other bearers.

"I swear by the name of Jupiter, these streets are more dangerous than the battle plains of Britannia," Marcus angrily mumbles as we wait. "Why, only last week one of our neighbors—I think I heard his name was Aulus Caelius, he was an equestrian and a centurion in the northern legion—anyway, he fought all over Gallia and

Germania and had only just retired to Rome, and he was *killed* a few blocks from here by a flower pot that fell from a second-story window!" Marcus glares at me. "Can you imagine that? He survives years of soldiering only to die so ingloriously on these very streets we travel daily."

My husband is right. The streets of Rome are hazardous, to say the least. They are crowded day and night now that so much building is occurring all over town. Our destination is only a few blocks away, so we shouldn't be too late. Before long, our progress resumes and we soon arrive.

The Imperial Palace stretches for blocks atop the Palatine and constitutes the center of our city. Began by Augustus, who grew up near here, the palace has been added to by each successive emperor and recently reached a ridiculous level of grandiosity when Nero constructed his Golden House down in the valley below, which is currently being dismantled to make way for the Coliseum.

Marcus and I exit our conveyance in a huge courtyard where several other empty litters rest on cobblestones nearby. Their respective crews mill around, talking quietly amongst themselves. Two Praetorian Guards, part of the Emperor's private legion, wave us through the main entrance, having recognized us as frequent visitors and close friends of the Emperor. We proceed through a series of public rooms, guided by one of Vespasian's personal attendants who's been waiting for us to arrive. We pass through one atrium after another, each surrounded by rows of columns, fountains, and a variety of statues, some of which were plundered during various campaigns abroad. We arrive at a doorway, where two more guards are stationed on each side. They also let us through, and we walk into another smaller atrium that is part of Vespasian's temporary quarters. He is remodeling another part of the palace that will serve as his permanent apartment, but for now, he has chosen to stay in the oldest section of the vast complex where Augustus once lived. It is surprisingly modest compared to the grandness of the public spaces we trekked through to get here.

We hear growing voices as we turn the corner and enter a spacious room where tonight's dinner party is being held. An assortment of couches, settees, and pillows surround three sides of a large square table in the middle of the room. A few guests have already arrived, including our hosts, Vespasian and Caenis, who lounge together on a settee. He waves when he sees us approach.

"Ah, Marcus and Lucia! Come in, come in. Caenis and I are delighted you could join us this evening." Caenis smiles politely and nods her head in greeting. Vespasian is a solidly built man with a plain and honest face. He has a high forehead, and his steady eyes always seem to be considering something important.

"I'm sorry we're late, Your Excellency, but we were delayed by some errant roof tiles that just managed to miss us," Marcus replies. "I swear, I told Lucia I felt safer battling the Dumnonii in Britannia."

The emperor laughs. "I know what you mean. Here in Rome, I have to beware falling tiles as well as discontented citizens. Believe me when I say my guards can no more protect me from falling debris than they can from the complaints of injustice and corruption that bombard me from senators and plebes alike. I too miss the relative safety and order one finds on the field of battle."

Another voice enters the conversation. "Well, you have yourself to blame, Your Excellency, when it comes to venturing onto the hazardous streets of the city." It belongs to Pliny the Elder, a friend and colleague to the Emperor who is well known as a man with an opinion on just about everything. He is slighter of build than his emperor, but handsome with an intelligent face. He is bearded and has curly hair that falls about his crown in some disarray. His eyes stare out from below a stern but contemplative brow. "All of your various reconstruction projects, which quite frankly amaze me now that I have returned to Rome from Gallia Narbonensis, are partly responsible for the chaos. Just try to cross the Via Apia during the middle of the day. You are as likely to be run over by a wagon filled with blocks of marble as a cart filled with produce destined for the marketplace. Just yesterday evening after the tenth hour I witnessed an accident where several large jugs of beer dislodged from their cart and tumbled onto the street killing a hapless old beggar who couldn't scramble out of the way. Lucky for the merchant, the jugs stayed intact and didn't spill their contents onto the busy thoroughfare. Imagine the chaos if that had happened!"

Pliny has just returned from an assignment as procurator to the southern coastal region of Gallia. He is a famous historian and writer, as well as a soldier and accountant. Marcus and I have known him for years, as they have served together under Vespasian's command in the past.

"Lucia, please come and sit by me," Caenis says, offering me the seat next to her. She is elderly and has an air about her that suggests she's both astute and aware. I smile, for I am fond of her. She reminds me of my late mother, who died from natural causes several years ago. She was an intelligent woman, like Caenis, who stayed abreast of my affairs right to the end. She encouraged my marriage to Marcus and was always ambitious in her expectations of how I should fare in life. My father was a loyal soldier and later a responsible procurator but was never a very wealthy man. He did love me completely and was ever dear to me. He died a few years prior to my mother's passing.

I dutifully lie next to Caenis while Marcus finds a spot on a separate couch on the other side of the Emperor. She smiles at me and leans closer so she can better be heard. "I like your pendant, my dear. The garnets are lovely."

"Thank you, my lady," I reply. "Garnets glow with a deeper red than rubies and are so much more available. Your sapphire necklace is breathtaking by the way. It must have cost you a small fortune!"

"It did," Caenis confirms without any hesitation whatsoever. "I am getting on in years and have little time for caution or modesty. I purchased it last week from a jeweler I trust in the Campus Martius. I'm glad you like it." Caenis is every bit as old as Vespasian, maybe even older, and must be somewhere up in her mid-to-late sixties. She seems a little tired to me, like she's seen most everything she needs or wants to and is now content to coast along in the company of her powerful friend and lover, who obviously values her company.

I look across from me and nod respectfully to an exotic foreigner who reclines on the other side of Marcus. I recognize him as Flavius Josephus, a Jewish historian and personal friend to the Emperor. He is often invited to the palace. He is a former enemy of the Empire who switched his allegiance from his native country, Judea, and became an ardent supporter of Rome. It is said that even while he was still in chains, having been captured by the soldiers of Rome, he prophesied to Vespasian, then the commanding legate, that he would soon become emperor. When the prisoner's prophesy became a reality, the Jewish captain's fortunes changed dramatically. Vespasian immediately granted him his freedom. These days, the state pays him a handsome fee to chronicle the Jewish War, which he is currently researching and writing for the glorious record of Rome.

Josephus appears to be about the same age as myself, although he seems much older to me. Maybe it is his long beard and exotic and colorful clothing, which is multilayered and billows about him like a sail at sea. I know my husband has a low opinion of the Jewish historian, as he did betray his own kind when he sided with us.

I hear footsteps slapping against the tiled floor and see two men enter the room. One is Titus Flavius Vespasianus, the eldest son of the Emperor. He is the Praetorian prefect in charge of the army of Rome. Like his father, Titus is a broad-shouldered and solid-looking man with a sincere, if not handsome, countenance. I fail to recognize the other man. He is of the same height but is slighter of build and quite handsome with curly brown hair, clear gray eyes, and a finely shaped nose that rests above his thin, tightly drawn lips.

"Ah ha, Titus and Decimus are here at last. Let us commence with the dinner," Vespasian announces to us and to his serving staff who immediately spring into action.

"I'm sorry Father, but the Senate ran over as usual. Decimus and I came straight over from the Forum," Titus says, sounding more matter of fact than guilty.

"No need to apologize, my son. Caenis and I are delighted you both have come to share our meal."

It is common knowledge that Vespasian and Titus are very respectful of each other and share much of an emperor's responsibilities between them, truly a unique situation for Roman leadership. None of the previous emperors were so fortunate. Augustus yearned for a son he could work with, but in the end, he had to leave his throne to his son-in-law Tiberius, whom he was not always so fond of. Claudius was forced to bequeath his power to a nephew who was too young to help him share the burden of command. Luckily for Vespasian, he has a son he can count on. When he was forced to leave his command in Judea to assume the throne of power, he left Titus behind to clean up the mess. Titus was in charge of the sacking of the Temple of Jerusalem and discharged his duty with a workmanlike capability. My Marcus took part in the siege of the city walls and told me later that it was a bloody struggle from beginning to end with many, many thousands of people dying while much of the city was laid to waste.

"Lucia, this young senator with Titus is Decimus Tulles Capito, a longtime friend of my son's," Vespasian says to me before he turns to my spouse. "I believe you know him, Marcus, as you served with him and Titus in the Judea campaign."

"Yes, Decimus and I are acquainted," Marcus responds, nodding to the handsome senator. Decimus bows politely to all of us and chooses an empty place on the couch next to Caenis and me.

Several servers appear carrying trays loaded with food and drink. They disperse and divide themselves into three separate groups, so that each side of the table will be served simultaneously. Before each of us is a large plate and a tall silver goblet. Wine is poured, and attendants pass by to dish up an assortment of appetizers, including fried oysters, pickled fish, boiled eggs, and a few other delectable items. As we sample the first course, the conversation bounces about from one guest to another.

"Tell me Marcus, how is your vast construction project faring?" Pliny inquires of my husband.

"As well as can be expected. Nero's lake is all but drained, and my crew is preparing the dry bed for some considerable foundation work. Meanwhile, I've just returned from Tibur, where I've set up some new connections for travertine marble." He turns to address Vespasian. "By the way, Your Excellency, I may need to widen the road between here and Tibur. It is too narrow and worn down in places to properly service the kind of oxen teams I have in mind."

Vespasian grimaces at the news. He is known to be a miser of sorts, which is ironic considering how much denarii he is expending to rebuild our vast and glorious Empire. In order to afford the massive reconstruction projects, he is heavily taxing the provinces, as well as the citizens of Rome.

"Come and see me when you have detailed the kind of expansion you have in mind," he replies before guzzling his fourth oyster.

"Rumor has it that this amphitheater will set a new standard in size and scope," Pliny says. "I imagine it will take several years for you to conclude the project."

Marcus swallows some wine and replaces his goblet on his tray. "I hope to begin work on the foundation in the coming weeks. After that, it should require at least a few more years to complete the structure." He smiles warmly at Pliny. "And your sources are correct, my friend. The Coliseum will be larger than any theater in the Empire to date. It will be a major tribute to the Emperor's vision of a newly restored Rome and a grand gesture to the citizens of Rome that he is a generous and capable leader."

"Well, he had to do something to compensate for the atrocious land grab that Nero managed to get away with," Titus chimes in. "Imagine stealing an entire district for one's private use! My father's generosity in restoring the land to the people for public use will not be forgotten for a long time."

"He is also restoring the Senate to its former size," Decimus adds. "It seems I see new faces at every session. Several of them come from the provinces, which I approve of, unlike some of the others. It broadens our overall representation and breeds trust among the provincials."

My Marcus often complained that the ranks of the Senate declined sharply during the year of the four emperors, which threatened our overall security. As a result, Vespasian and Titus appointed themselves to the Office of Censor and are busy refilling the empty seats as fast as they can. I've heard gossip to suggest that Caenis participates in the selection process and collects hefty fees for the Emperor's treasury as a result.

"You appear too young to be a senator, Decimus," I observe, giving him my most charming smile. I realize I find his lean and intelligent bearing quite attractive.

"Well my lady, I have served for more than a year and already I feel like a veteran, so many new replacements have followed on my heels. I've managed to gravitate from the backbenches toward the front of the chamber. Of course, my close connection to Titus hasn't stood in my way, either."

"Decimus and I schooled together as kids," Titus agrees. "He also served with me and Marcus in Judea, and he is now a valuable ally of mine in the halls of the Senate."

"Speaking of Judea," Vespasian says as he guides the conversation in a new direction, "how is your history of the Jewish War coming along, Josephus?"

The Jewish scholar straightens and turns to address the Emperor. "I have begun chronicling the early years of the revolt, Your Excellency, and my part as a captain of Galilee. I have detailed out how inexorable your troops were in bringing about the destruction of my command."

"As I remember it, we took almost a month and a half to breach the walls of your fortress at Jolapata," Marcus interjects. "I know this because I had a hand in the construction of the siege tower that prevailed in the end."

"Yes, Marcus is right, Josephus. You put up a good fight," the Emperor adds. "You were fortunate to have foreseen my future as emperor. Otherwise I would have crucified you as a necessary act of war."

"God be praised, for I was the sole survivor of that command," Josephus notes. "I am thankful for your mercy, my lord."

I glance at my husband and notice his jaw clenching as he tries to keep from uttering something contemptuous. He knows full well that Josephus refrained from killing himself only after the rest of his more dedicated comrades had already slain themselves in defiance of Rome. He apparently preferred to live on as a prisoner rather than die a zealot's death.

"I still marvel that so many of you willfully ended your lives rather than subject yourselves to Roman rule," Vespasian observes, shaking his head in bewilderment.

"Yes," the Jewish historian concurs, "the fanaticism of the zealots was unrelenting. Time and again my pleas for moderation fell on deaf ears."

"Speaking as a fellow historian," Pliny cuts into the conversation with a precision that always impresses me, "I imagine this history of the Jewish War may take you several years to complete."

"Yes, I believe it will. I have only just begun to record it and still have more research to collect and compile before I set down the details of the entire campaign." Josephus turns to address the Emperor. "Rest assured that you and Titus will be fairly treated when I have completed the project." He nods to them before sipping heartily from his goblet of wine.

"Well, be as accurate as you want, Josephus. I still regret the burning of the city walls," Titus laments, "and the Temple too. It would have made a suitable home for Jupiter and the other Roman gods. But alas, my soldiers got out of hand, which is ever a danger when caught up in the heat of battle. You Jews put up a fierce resistance and refused to surrender. As a result, the total destruction of the city was inevitable."

A silence settles over the room as we acknowledge the fact that the armies of Rome have recently leveled an ancient city. Meanwhile, the servers clear away the plates from the first course and replace them with clean ones.

"I have always found war to be messy and unforgiving," Vespasian confesses, breaking the silence. "No one seeks to be conquered, and many innocents die in the struggle. But alas, Rome is a hungry engine that must be fed by expansion and gain. Empires require fuel to feed upon; it is the way of the world we live in."

"The Roman world, for sure," Titus agrees.

Suddenly the aroma of roasted fowl fills my nostrils, and I watch as a parade of servers brings in the second course: a huge platter of roasted peacock followed by several platters of seafood and more scented wine. We happily fill our plates with the bounty and begin to feast on the delicious offerings. The conversation breaks into various circles of small talk. Vespasian converses with Marcus and Pliny, Josephus continues to discuss the war with Titus, while Caenis and I focus our attention on the handsome senator beside us.

"Tell me Decimus, why are you still a bachelor?" Caenis asks. "You are well past the marrying age. Do you not seek to have a wife and family? I judge you to be close in age to Titus and therefore far beyond the innocence of youth." The old dame is of an age and stature where discretion is no longer required unless so desired.

"Indeed, I am in my early thirties and have failed to attract a spouse to share my life. I have had a few opportunities to settle down, but in the end, I always manage to escape back into my lonely life as a bachelor." He smiles coyly. "Perhaps I have grown too used to my own company."

"What a waste," I proclaim, surprising myself and the others as well. "I mean, you are so handsome and self-aware, Decimus. You would make a fine husband and father, I'm sure." Caenis eyes me with curiosity before responding to my observations.

"Lucia is right, of course. You would make a fine catch for any Roman maiden lucky enough or deft enough to snare you in her web." She winks at him and smiles knowingly. "Perhaps you seek a mistress instead. Now that's a subject I know better than most, I can assure you."

"A mistress would not be out of the question, my lady," Decimus replies, "but alas, there too I have naught to show but an empty net." He turns to me. "But look at you, Lucia, close to me in age, and from what Titus has told me, you already have two offspring who are grown men serving their Empire abroad. I must say, you seem none the worse for wear. We have certainly chosen opposite paths, have we not?"

I feel my face flush at his unexpected compliment and look at my plate. Caenis quickly responds in my stead.

"Indeed, Lucia my dear, I must agree with Decimus. You have maintained your figure and your youthful complexion despite the ravages of time and parenthood." She pauses. "My one regret in life is that I could not bear any children of my own. As a slave and then a mistress, I had little opportunity for family life. I freely admit it gets lonely when one grows older. I was lucky to reconnect with Vespasian after his wife died. Otherwise, I would have faced lonelier dinners than I would have cared to." She looks squarely at Decimus. "I warn you my friend, you could suffer a similar fate if you are not destined to find a mate or lifelong companion."

The younger senator shrugs, as if he has already resigned himself to such a fate. "I will always have the company of men, for the Senate is full of them. And lacking the companionship of a wife or a mistress, there are always certain ladies that are available at beck and call. But your point is well made, my lady, and I shall take it to heart."

He looks at me and smiles, and once again I feel my complexion heating up. This time I look at him directly and reply, "Well, you still have time to spare, and I for one wish you good luck. As I said, it would be a waste for you to remain a bachelor forever." All three of us smile agreeably at my summation and then subside back into the prevailing current of mainstream conversation.

Once again, the servers sweep away our empty plates and replace them with a final set of clean dinnerware. Our goblets are replenished, and several desserts are presented for our pleasure. I select an assortment of small pastries and a clump of red grapes. The conversation comes back together when Vespasian's booming voice demands our collective attention.

"Now then Pliny, since you are back in Rome and I have you at my disposal, please tell me how your Natural History is progressing. I know you have been collecting taxes along the shores of Gallia, but I suspect that you have also been collecting research and are busy writing all the while."

Pliny smiles broadly at his good friend and supporter. "Ah, you know me all too well, Your Excellency. Yes indeed, I am always collecting information and making observations wherever I go. I can't seem to help it. I have completed almost twenty volumes to date and still have much more to do. I have piles of notes that I haven't had time to correlate and set down yet." He nods at his emperor and adds, "You keep me too busy looking after your tax assessments in the provinces."

"And I shall continue to do so for a while yet, my friend. I trust you, and that is a rare commodity indeed." Everyone laughs at the emperor's little joke, because we all know that most procurators have a tendency to skim off the top. It is the Roman way. Even provincial governors are prone to do the same. "Have you anything of interest to share with us," Vespasian continues, "now that I have your fine company at my dinner table?"

"Well, I'm working on a volume regarding the diverse fauna of this world. There are so many different types of animals to catalogue and describe. I am ever astonished by the stories I come across about the creatures that roam the wild areas of our Empire. It's a most fascinating subject."

"Really, do you care to tell us of one?" Caenis asks.

"Why yes, in fact I do," the ever-entertaining scholar replies. "I've just finished recording a story as laid down by the philosopher Demetrius regarding an unusual encounter between man and beast. He recounts the story of an old man, the father of Philinius, another philosopher, who was walking along a path in the forest. He came upon a panther, a rather large wild cat that was behaving in a most unusual manner. It was jumping about, as if trying to catch the attention of the old man who had come into its view. At first, Philinius's father was frightened by the beast and tried to retreat from its presence, but the large feline circled around him, hopping up and down, leaping about as if it were excited about something. Its behavior began to suggest that it might be seeking help from the human. At this point, the large predator approached the old man and actually reached out and caught his garment with its claw. It began to pull at it, trying to lead him in a certain direction. Needless to say, the old man was cautious of the animal's strange behavior, but even so, he allowed himself to be led off the trail and into the brush. Apparently, his curiosity had replaced his fear." Pliny pauses and gazes quietly about, suspending his narration for the briefest of moments before setting off again. The room is enthralled. "The large cat led him to a narrow ditch. The old man looked into the chasm and spotted a brood of small kits, which had apparently fallen into the ditch and were unable to escape their unfortunate circumstance. Obviously, the mother panther was unable to successfully intervene. He immediately lowered himself next to the ditch and lifted the little creatures out of their predicament. There was a playful reunion of mother and cubs, after which they happily escorted the good fellow back to the trail and then all the way to the border of the forest. The old man concluded his tale by saying that he was touched by their obvious joyfulness and gratitude."

The silence that followed on the heels of Pliny's tale was short and deep.

"I have heard of a similar tale about an escaped slave named Androcles," Josephus quietly informs the group, "who aided a lion by extracting a thorn from its paw. The beast befriended him as a result and helped to save his life later on. Perhaps that fable was based on a true event. Stranger things have actually happened, it appears."

"So it would seem," Vespasian concurs. "Let us not forget that our own founding fathers, Romulus and Remus, were suckled by a wolf. Do you discuss this in your compilation of natural observations, Pliny?"

"I address wolves as a species, Your Excellency, but the subjects of myth and legend must fall into another body of work altogether. There is some speculation, however, that our twin founders could well have been suckled by a "she-wolf", otherwise known as a prostitute in those times." He smiles at his benefactor and goes on. "Legends and myths that are based on hearsay are often difficult to discern and sometimes impossible to prove. I can only say that while it is possible for some basis of fact to underlie our various fables, none of them should be taken literally as a whole."

"Well, we will leave the origin of our legendary founders for another night's discussion," the emperor decides. "I grow weary and must excuse myself. My bedtime fast approaches." He smiles broadly. It is common knowledge that Vespasian is an early riser. We, therefore, agree that it is getting late and that it has been a marvelous dinner all around. Vespasian and Caenis slowly stand and nod to us all before making their way to an exit in the back of the room, where one of the imperial guards stands silently at attention. They pass through the doorway and disappear into their private chambers.

As we prepare to leave the palace, Marcus goes ahead to summon our litter. I manage to privately address the bachelor senator one last time.

"Decimus, my husband is often away for long periods of time, tending to his responsibilities regarding the construction of the new amphitheater. May I tempt you to fill in as my escort if the need were to arise? I am sure Marcus would understand, given the frequency of his lengthy absences." I smile and add, "I do so hate attending socials on my own."

Decimus nods his head slowly and replies. "I would be honored to stand in for Marcus, if he's agreeable, especially as I am currently available to do so given my thoroughly discussed bachelor status." We smile at each other and at Caenis's well-meant probing and stroll out of the palace the same way we came in. Marcus is waiting for me next to our conveyance. The night's chill has deepened, as some clouds have moved in during the evening's feast and blanketed the starry canopy overhead. We enter our litter and head home for a good night's sleep.

***

Two days later, Gaius, our youngest son, returns to Rome on a week's furlough away from his post in Germania. Marcus and I spend as much time as we can in his company, but he is a popular youth and has many friends to catch up with as well. A couple of days after his arrival, I notice that he is sometimes in the company of a young equestrian girl called Servia. She is poised, refined, and quite beautiful. I approve of her, especially since she is clever and amusing in her conversation. I can tell that Marcus is also quite taken with her, and his subtle yearning for her amuses me. It has been a long time since I felt him look at me with the same enthusiasm. Obviously, Gaius is smitten. I have never seen him behave so attentively toward another person before. Both Marcus and I hope she will remain available once our son returns to his military duties up north. Fortunately, she appears to be equally fond of him.

Off and on during the week, I catch myself thinking about Decimus, the handsome senator. Something about him, either his carefree manner or his penetrating intelligence, attracts my interest. A part of me would like to see him again right away, but I know this urge is foolish and I easily ignore it. Besides, I am too busy spending time and energy on my son, whose visit grows shorter with each passing day.

At last, the final day approaches. Marcus and I host a farewell dinner for Gaius the night before his departure. Many of his friends attend the affair, including Servia. She and I are comforted by my son's admission that his duty along the Rhine is mostly peaceful work. The major unrest in the region was settled three years earlier when Vespasian sent eight legions to Germania to subdue a major uprising involving a discontented Roman legion and a few local tribes. Gaius assures us that these days the Roman soldiers mostly patrol the area and maintain an already established peace.

We say our farewells the next morning and watch sadly as our son rides off to join his detachment. Our hearts are heavy, for Marcus and I are still adjusting to our boys' too sudden departure from the nest, yet we both agree that Gaius has clearly become a capable young man who is ready to handle his own affairs.

Marcus returns his full focus to his work, which he never fully stopped attending to even while Gaius was with us. He has been supervising the massive digging and trenching that has commenced at the building site of the Coliseum. Apparently, there will be a huge subterranean basement below its main floor, which will house multiple rooms and passageways where the combatants will stage themselves before accessing the arena above. There will also be caged areas for the various animals needed for the different elements of entertainment. Marcus explained to me that this area must first be constructed before the outer walls of the huge building can begin to rise. The foundation surrounding this basement level will be a massive elliptical ring of concrete. My husband has forewarned me that he will be leaving on yet another expedition to secure the required substances to manufacture the concrete needed for the foundation. He must procure large amounts of lime and rubble, there being plenty of the latter around the city from the vast destruction caused by the great fires of the last decade, and also large amounts of volcanic ash called *pozzolana* which, along with lime, is used to bond with the rubble and gravel aggregate. Marcus wants to head south and visit a few sites at the base of Mount Vesuvius where *pozzolana* is abundant. He plans to stay at our summer villa, even though we have already shut it down for the season. He will probably visit with Quintus, our foreman who lives on the property year-round.

Meanwhile, I return to my normal life, managing our household in town. I oversee more than a dozen servants who help to maintain our expansive complex. We also have slaves who carry our private litter and protect us from harm outside our own walls. Even on the Palatine, ruffians roam about, looking for easy prey. All eight of our litter attendants are armed with short swords to better ensure our safety. Our household servants clean and tend to our baths, cooking, and gardening needs. Adonia and Damaris assist in this process and act as my chief assistants in the day-to-day operations. Since Marcus is gone most of the time, Damaris serves as my procurator and manages other duties if he is not traveling with his master. He tends to supervise the gardeners and the outside attendants, while Adonia oversees the cleaning and cooking duties. Together, the three of us make a very efficient team.

Because Marcus and I are so well connected to the Emperor, we are now considered socially desirable. We receive invitations to wine and dine with many of the elite families in the surrounding community. Marcus is reluctant to venture out any more than is required, politically and professionally. We are amused by our situation because under more normal circumstances, our company would be far less desirable, as Marcus is directly associated with the building trades, traditionally frowned upon by aristocratic circles.

At any rate, the next month passes in the usual manner with a few dinners out, most at home, the daily acquisition of food, and the maintenance of the property. This includes a fresh whitewashing in the bathroom along with the replacement of several damaged tiles in the mosaic tub.

Marcus is so pleased with the progress of the digging at the worksite that he prepares to depart later today and head south in order to procure the necessary *pozzolana*. He will ride his horse and travel with a special contingent that Vespasian provides from his Imperial Guards to guarantee his safety there and back again. We share a lunch prepared for the two of us and then I watch as he rides off into the city. He says he will be away for fourteen days or more.

Moments after he and his martial guard disappear from view, my mind conjures up an image of Decimus. Not long after we met at the Emperor's dinner party, I casually mentioned to Marcus that I might invite the young senator out on occasion to serve as my companion when he is away on business. Marcus thought it was a fine idea, especially as he regrets that he has to be away so often. When I told him I found Demicus to be amusing in a dry, witty kind of way, Marcus said he didn't know him well but always thought him quite capable as a soldier and as a politician.

Now that my husband is heading south for two weeks, I am eager to spend some time with the handsome senator. I know that a new staging of *Phaedra* by the late playwright Seneca the Younger is currently showing at the Theater of Pompey, located in the Campus Martius near the Tibur River. I have always wanted to see *Phaedra* acted on the stage; I've heard that it is very heartfelt, but also very tragic. I head for my bedroom, sit at my desk, and write a note to Decimus requesting his company on the morrow as my escort should he be available. I ask him to arrive at my home near the palace an hour before midday so he may accompany me to the theater in my litter. I summon Adonia and send her to the Forum to deliver my note directly to him. I tell her not to return without his reply.

Later, I am delighted when she reappears with his response. It reads: "My Lady Lucia, I will be delighted to accompany you to the theater tomorrow and shall be prompt. I look forward to seeing you again. Your new friend and escort, Decimus Tulles Capito" I spend a lonely night dining by myself, after which I enjoy a long, languid bath before retiring for the evening.

The following morning crawls by as I prepare a multi-day shopping list for Damaris, whose company was not required by Marcus on his journey. I set about preparing myself for an afternoon of theater. The weather is sunny, but the air is brisk. A northern breeze cools the temperature, which means that the outdoor seating at the theater will require a few layers of clothing. After Adonia washes and dries my hair, she piles it in braids atop my head and allows a few loose curls to dangle causally along my brow and down around my ears. I also have her stick a few golden pins crowned with various seashells here and there to enhance the presentation. Next, she wraps a brassiere around my chest to help fend off the cold. I step into an inner tunic and then into a pale blue stola with long sleeves. Adonia drapes an olive green palla across my shoulder and down around the side of my back. With a pull here and a twist there, my outfit is complete.

At exactly one hour before midday, Damaris informs me that a senator has arrived and is waiting for me at the front door. I apply a last dab of rouge to my cheeks and head for the entryway where Damaris has arranged for our personal litter to take us to the theater. Decimus is waiting in the courtyard dressed in his white senatorial toga with a broad purple stripe cascading down his side, keeping with the ripples and folds of his garment. I notice that he too wears an inner tunic for the outdoor performance. The Theater of Pompey will be closed down for the winter season by the time Marcus has returned home.

When I approach Decimus, he smiles and bows graciously before speaking. "My lady, you look lovely. I shall no doubt be the envy of the theater crowd this afternoon." I see Adonia glance at Damaris, whose own expression remains impassive.

"I'm delighted you have agreed to escort me today, Decimus. I am so eager to see this play," I reply, ignoring his compliment for the sake of my servants, who are watching me like a hawk. "Marcus was relieved to hear that you would be substituting for him. He feels he is neglecting his duties toward me, but he is helpless to alter his busy schedule."

"I am pleased that he supports my new role as your escort, and I promise to protect you from thieves and suitors alike."

Damaris pulls back the door cover to our litter so we may enter more easily.

"Thank you, Damaris," I say before he closes the thick curtain. "I shall return *at dusk, if not sooner.*"

"Yes, my lady," the Greek slave replies.

Decimus and I lay across from each other on pillows while eight hardy slaves carry us down the Palatine to the flats below. The theater complex is near the Tibur and surrounded by a series of temples and monuments. Another theater, the Theater of Marcellus, stands nearby, and several bathhouses steam near the riverbank. The huge mausoleum of Augustus looms in the background. As we proceed slowly through the crowded streets, the litter sways gently back and forth with plenty of stops and starts along the way. From time to time, our carriers shout out roughly to clear a path through the crowds of Roman shoppers, merchants, and city travelers.

"I'm not accustomed to being carried around," Decimus observes as he stares at me with his keen and penetrating eyes. "It's somewhat confining, isn't it?" Thick winter curtains fall in folds around us, darkening the environment and adding to its closeness.

"This litter actually came with our house on the Palatine. Marcus and I had to get used to it too. Now, I rather enjoy the privacy. It seems so privileged."

"You and Marcus have done well for yourselves. Two sons to be proud of and a very close and intimate relationship with our emperor. You are the envy of the court. You must feel very satisfied with your situation."

I look at Decimus, considering his depiction of my life, and I wonder to myself why I don't appreciate my auspicious situation more than I do. "Oh yes, I do value our good fortune." I gaze at his smiling face and decide to be more honest. "But I do grow restless inside myself. My sons have left my care to forge their own destinies. As a result, I have more time on my hands than I know what to do with."

His smile widens a bit and he reaches over to gently grasp my hand. "Then I happily volunteer my services to assist you in filling up the empty spaces of your life." I feel a thrill pump through my heart at the touch of his hand, our first physical contact. I haven't felt so alive since I was a young maiden being courted by an older and far more worldly Marcus.

"I shall hold you to your word, Decimus," I answer as I slowly retract my hand from his. "But you are an active and important senator. Won't you be too busy to service the needs of a bored and restless housewife?"

"I am barely a midlevel participant on the Senate floor. Any real responsibility comes my way through Titus Flavius." He pauses to wink at me. "Like you, I have cultivated a close intimate relationship with the Imperial family. I am therefore free to come and go as I please, and only have to be present if any meaningful votes arise, especially around foreign policy where I assist Titus as much as possible. Many of the older senators are less progressive about opening up the opportunities for provincial participation in the halls of the Senate. I represent a new wave of younger and more forward-thinking politicians who are willing to expand real influence beyond the confines of our Italian borders. Currently, our military campaign in Northern Britannia requires our attention, and I am helping Titus encourage the Senate to authorize the funding of additional troops in that region."

"Well, lucky for me, no such votes require your attention this afternoon." Our litter stops suddenly, and our bearers shout obscenities at a crowd of shoppers blocking our progress. We hear a few unkind responses before our pace slowly picks up again.

At last, we arrive at the Theater of Pompey and are assisted out of the litter by the head bearer, who assures me that they will be here to take us home once the play has ended. Decimus and I climb the extensive steps that lead us to the long promenade filled with statues and vases from all over the Empire. We cross through a garden area where many other works of art are on display. I spot a few acquaintances, smile politely, and steer Decimus away from them to avoid any pleasantries. Even though it is not uncommon to be escorted by another man to such public events, I don't feel like socializing. I want him all to myself.

Our clay billets are collected as we enter the theater proper. The Temple of Venus towers above us, placed on top and at the front of the theater's roofline, closer to the realm of the gods. The great Roman Consul Gnaeus Pompeius Magnus, founder of this theater, worshiped her and had her shrine placed high above the complex. Venus is associated with beauty and fine art, so I'm sure she is very happy with her temple's placement. She is also a favorite goddess of mine, and I keep a private shrine for her in the corner of my bedroom. Marcus has always been a devotee of Jupiter and was reluctant to move to the Palatine, away from his god's temple that was adjacent to our previous dwelling. I'm not sure whom Decimus worships and make a mental note to ask him sometime later.

We choose two seats in the preferred section near the center that are far enough removed from the stage so we may observe the performers without being spit upon. The seats around us slowly fill up, and by the time the performance commences, the theater is about half full. Stage productions are not as popular as they used to be, the average Roman preferring more action-oriented entertainments like the gladiatorial games and the chariot races that occur constantly both in this city and throughout the Empire.

A hush falls over the arena as the first performer strolls onto the stage. The play's young male protagonist, Hippolytus, prepares for a hunt in the forest and invokes the support of Diana, goddess of the hunt. After that, the focus shifts to Phaedra, his stepmother, played by a male actor wearing a woman's wig. She confesses to her wet-nurse that she has fallen hopelessly in love with her husband's son. Her attendant tries unsuccessfully to dissuade her from pursuing her wild passion for the young man. The play swings back and forth between the two protagonists, one always chasing after the other. Phaedra vainly tries to bed Hippolytus, at first by seduction and later by the use of insults and slander. To her growing frustration, the young hunter remains steadfastly virtuous.

When her husband, Theseus, returns from the underworld, Phaedra induces him to believe that his son has forcefully seduced his wife. The outraged father prays to Neptune, god of the sea, and curses Hippolytus for his evil deed. As a result, the young man dies tragically when one of Neptune's pet sea monsters surprises his chariot along a coastal road, causing his horses to pull the slandered youth to his death. Phaedra regrets her actions, confesses her treachery to Theseus, and kills herself. In the end, Theseus forgives his falsely accused son and honors him with a proper burial, while refusing to do the same for his disgraced and deceitful wife.

Throughout the production, the actors are often forced to shout out their lines in order to be heard over the unruly braying and heckling of the unsophisticated audience, a vast majority of which sit in the upper seats where the plebs and foreigners congregate. After applauding the performers, some of which were heartily booed—especially Phaedra, the plotting adulteress—Decimus and I work our way out of the auditorium and find my litter still parked in the same spot we left it in a few hours ago. We climb inside, close the curtains, and are relieved to be on our own again.

"Not a very happy tale, was it?" Decimus offers. "Especially for Phaedra, who ends up dead and grave-less for all her troubles."

"Well, she couldn't control her romantic feelings for her stepson, even though she knew better," I respond. "She probably deserved her fate… But I can't help feeling sorry for her, nonetheless. She was so passionate and alive."

Decimus shakes his head back and forth as though he disagrees with me. "Unfortunately, Roman law is harsh about such displays of passion, especially when married women are involved. Inappropriate and unsanctioned sexual displays from a wife are legally considered to be committing stuprum, a charge that can lead to her death. She may indulge herself privately with her household slaves, but to engage in intercourse with a freeman of any rank and to be discovered…" He trails off, then smiles in my direction. "But I'm sure you are already aware of what parameters surround the behavior of a proper wife."

I find it exciting to talk about such issues with a man. I notice how well-proportioned his hands are as he speaks to me. He gestures with them to accentuate his points. His long and slender fingers are unusually delicate for a man, and yet he looks totally masculine and well balanced, as though he is completely comfortable with himself.

"It still saddens me that Phaedra should have to suffer such a cruel fate for having strong feelings for a younger man," I respond. "Some emotions are hard to reign in and control. Love can have a mind of its own. Look at our emperor. He managed to love two different women in a world where love and marriage are not always suited or paired with each other."

"Yes, but you must remember that Vespasian always enjoyed each woman in her own time and did not betray either one."

"He is fortunate to enjoy such a bountiful feast and still be so adjusted and down to earth. I envy him his sound judgment and warm heart."

Decimus considers my words before making his reply. "Yes, I do too. Titus is very fond of his father, happy to share his burden and not at all inclined to steal it away from him. How un-Roman is that?" Decimus says, alluding to the many mutinies that plagued the Julio-Claudian dynasty before Vespasian's rule and ended so unceremoniously with Nero's bankrupted suicide. He continues before I can respond. "You and Marcus appear to be well suited for each other. I realize he is quite a bit older than you, but he acts as though he were twenty years younger than he is. He's so active and engaged with his work and commitments." Decimus looks more fully at my face, which must be partially hidden in the fading afternoon light outside the privacy of our curtained environment. "Now that your boys have grown into stalwart citizens of Rome, your husband still has his occupation to demand his time and energy, while you are looking at a hole that you must somehow fill. Yet you and Marcus seem very respectful and accepting of each other. Are you happy in your marriage?"

Softness in the tone of his voice stirs something deep within. It is barely noticeable, like a faint whisper that can barely be heard. I gaze back at him and carefully consider my reaction. How honest can I be? How well do I even know him, and how far can I trust him with my true feelings? Recklessness rises up from within, and I decide to step off the cliff.

"I respect my husband. We have accomplished much over the years. He is a virtuous and capable man, a devoted husband, and a dedicated father. Together we have amassed a considerable fortune and have two wonderful estates to spread out in. Both of my sons have turned out well. I have nothing to complain of and everything to be thankful for. And yet…" I pause, for I am wrestling with my inner and outer selves. "And yet I am hungry for more intimacy and connection in my life. I feel like I am dancing on the surface of my being, and I want more. More touch, more passion. Yes, like Phaedra I want more passion, but unlike her, I don't want to risk my station and place in order to find it. Maybe I lack her courage, and I still resent that she had to die so disgraced for her reckless love."

Silence settles between us as surely as the dimming light of the setting sun. Have I gone too far in expressing my latent frustration and pent-up desires? As the silence stretches on, I suddenly feel exposed and foolish. Decimus must sense my anxiety because he reaches out to take my hand in his.

"You have been very honest with me, Lucia, and I am touched and honored that you would entrust me with such a sacred treasure." His words instantly melt my heart. "You are very beautiful and are at the peak of your powers. I understand your loneliness. You have no one to express yourself to fully and completely, except an older husband consumed by duty to his country and his emperor. Therefore, you can count on me to be your friend and confidante, for I too am lonely in the secret places that remain hidden from colleagues and acquaintances." He smiles sadly and speaks with a voice I can barely hear. "I also yearn for an intimacy that I may never realize with another person. I am not as cynical or dry as I appear on the surface of my social and political life. I have never found another person with whom I can communicate in the manner that would allow such a connection to arise." His eyes bore into my own. "At least not until now, my lady. And what chance have you or I to go where we would want to go, to share as we might seek to share, given our current positions and circumstances?" I feel his sadness in no uncertain terms and wipe the tears that seep from my eyes and run unimpeded down my cheeks. I can't remember the last time I felt such emotion and connection so purely, so unabashedly.

Decimus releases my hand and settles back into the darkness which crowds around us. We sit in silence and feel the gentle rocking of the litter as our bearers carry us home. The streets are crowded with city dwellers, many of which are packing up their wares and heading for their own residences. I can tell we are climbing the slopes of the Palatine by the subtle tilting of our conveyance. Before long, we reach the outer courtyard of my domus.

Damaris is there to greet us as we exit the litter. I have already wiped the tears away from my face with the corner of my palla and have managed to cool down my emotional nature to its more accustomed state. I turn and address my escort with a far more formal tone of voice.

"Thank you, Decimus, for taking the time to accompany me. I very much enjoyed both the play and your companionship. I would love to do this again sometime soon."

"You are quite welcome, my lady," Decimus replies, sounding very polite and respectful. "Perhaps we can go to the chariot races in a few days' time. There is an important contest coming up which everyone is excited about, including myself. I have been invited by Titus to join him in the Imperial box. Your presence would only enhance the occasion."

"I would love to go. It's been a long time since Marcus and I have been to the Circus Maximus." I try not to sound as excited as I feel beneath my cool exterior.

"Excellent. I will confirm our presence and send a message with the day and time as soon as possible," he adds. A small smile betrays his formal tone, and I know it is time to end our closely audited conversation.

"Goodnight, Decimus," I say with a slight nod of my head.

"Goodnight, my lady." He bows graciously before leaving the outer courtyard. I worry for his safety before remembering that his home is not far from my own; he resides in an apartment just on the other side of the palace. His is but a short stroll in probably the safest part of town. Praetorian Guards tend to patrol the neighborhoods close to the Imperial Palace as a general rule. After losing three emperors in the space of a year prior to his own ascension to the throne, Vespasian felt that a heightened atmosphere of security around his palace was a matter of common sense. Decimus, like Marcus and myself, took up residency in a home where the occupant was forcibly removed due to his close association with Aulus Vitellius, the previous emperor. My new escort's close friendship with Titus also facilitated his advantageous relocation.

I proceed with Adonia to my private chamber where I plan to dress down for another solitary dinner at home. The torches have already been lit and the shadows cast by, their bobbing flames seem to dance about my bedroom. With my servant's assistance, I peel off the layers of clothing I wore to the theater and slip into a comfortable robe with a matching belt that I tie around my waist. I ask Adonia to remove the pins from hair and untie my braids so my locks can hang naturally about my shoulders. I will bathe again after dinner. As she un-braids my hair, I chat with her in seeming idleness.

"Decimus proved to be a very capable escort. I felt very well looked after."

"That is good, my lady. Your husband would be pleased that you are being well looked after in his absence." I sense that she is reminding me that I am a married woman.

"Yes, Marcus feels very comfortable with Decimus and is pleased that he has agreed to accompany me socially from time to time." I turn to look at her more directly. "Since Marcus is so occupied with his big building project, I am beginning to feel neglected and almost like a widow. With both the boys gone, I need a little more distraction in my life. Wouldn't you agree?"

"Yes, my lady. How was the play?" Adonia inquires as she adroitly pulls my braids apart, loop-by-loop. I can tell she is deliberately changing the topic, which must be getting too uncomfortable for her. I am disappointed.

"It was very sad. Phaedra, the main character, loved too much and died in disgrace. Unfortunately, the audience was loud and boisterous and made it difficult to hear the performers. There were too many plebeians and foreigners for my taste, but alas, Rome is a worldly city these days and such crowds are to be expected, even at the stage performances." I hope my words might sting a little, given her Greek ancestry. When Adonia completes her task, I turn to address her more formally.

"Notify me when my dinner is ready. I will rest here until then."

"Yes, my lady," she replies with her flat, unemotional voice that years of servitude has trained into her. She bows and leaves me to myself.

For some reason, I am irritated with her. I really want to confide in her more deeply, but I don't trust her regarding this conflict that toils within me. Her loyalty includes my whole family. In her mind, I have ever concentrated on my duty as a wife and mother. I have taken pride in the accomplishments of my husband and on the willingness of both of my sons to follow in their father's footsteps. I have enjoyed great privilege and abundance. But at this very moment, I find myself feeling hollow inside, like a beautiful golden vessel containing nothing but empty space. My strong connection with Decimus has turned my world upside down. Suddenly, I desire something more than external recognition and reward.

Because he is so driven to achieve, Marcus has left me behind more often than not. Most of my marriage has been spent either as a single parent or as an abandoned wife. But more importantly, his prolonged absences have led to an ever-widening gulf between us. Yes, we maintain a working facade, a comfortable veneer in our relationship, but we hardly ever share our thoughts and feelings with each other anymore. We talk about things: our son's futures, our two estates, the Empire, his work. But we never share our own personal hopes and fears, our secret wants and desires. As a result, our sexual attraction for each other has waned steadily with the passage of time. Marcus is too busy to be bothered by such frivolous considerations as emotional issues, and I have too much time on my hands not to dwell on them, especially now that another man has managed to touch me so intimately with his hand and his heart.

I must be watchful of my emotions and hold them dear. Both Adonia and Damaris are too loyal to my family as a whole and to the longestablished trust that has underlined our hearth and home. My newfound feelings for Decimus can only endanger the stability of my privileged existence. I must tread lightly where I would so readily rush into this new and exciting realm where feelings mean more than accomplishments. I quietly resolve to be more cautious in cultivating my relationship with my new escort. He is to be a friend and companion to me, nothing more.

***

The next two days pass by in a flurry of activity. I attend the funeral of a good acquaintance, Aula Gellius Licina, who ate some tainted oysters and suffered a stomach sickness that eventually closed her eyes for good. Her shade hopefully strolls through the evergreen meadows of the Elysian Fields, for she was a good woman. She was mother to a son who spent many years schooling with my oldest boy, Publius. Marcus and I became friendly with her and her husband, who is a career magistrate with the Roman Treasury. It has been a few years since we've seen them; our sons drifted apart when their schooling ended. Their son focused on additional education to prepare for a life of public service while our Publius went straight into the military.

Her wake lasts two days, and I am required to show up for most of it as a sign of my connection to Aula Gellius and her family. On the second day, we proceed out of town in a traditional funeral procession, following behind a group of paid musicians. Once we reach the city limit, her remains are cremated. I can only assume that a coin has been placed on her forehead to pay Charon, the ferryman who will carry her shade across the river Styx to the shores of the Underworld.

During this time, Decimus sends a messenger, informing me that he has confirmed our invitations for the chariot races during the Ludi Plebii, a festival in early November honoring Jupiter. He will come by just after sunup on Saturn's day to escort me to the Circus Maximus, where we will join the Imperial family with an assortment of other guests. This time, he will provide the litter.

When that morning finally arrives, I am as excited as a young maiden going to a party. I rise before daylight and wash and dress for the races with Adonia's help. My local astrologer, Hippolyte, has advised me that this race day will be exceedingly auspicious. He said the weather will be benign, warmer than usual with a cloudless sky. Hippolyte also insisted that the gods were favorably aligned. Venus, my patron goddess, stands in good aspect to her father, Jupiter, the sponsor of today's festival. Hippolyte insisted that my fortunes for the day will be most beneficial. I dress accordingly, still choosing to wear an undergarment for I know the sun will require a few hours to chase away the early morning chill. I don a rust-red and forest-green *palla* over my beige *stola*. I will stand out without dominating those nearby. I wear a golden pendant set with a lovely, oval-shaped carnelian gem surrounded by a beaded wire band in matching gold. It blends nicely with my outfit. I eat some fruit and pastry to fortify myself, even though I know there will be plenty to eat; I've attended the races in the Imperial box several times before.

When Vespasian assumed power over three years ago, he invited many of his friends and advisers to enjoy the races with him and Caenis. Marcus and I were included in this company. At first it was fun, but Marcus soon grew tired of the spectacle, believing it to be a terrible waste of his time. We gradually became less available, and we have yet to go back since he began working on the Coliseum. I was disappointed because I have always enjoyed the pageantry and exhilaration that surrounded the contests.

Soon after first light, Decimus arrives at our outer courtyard in a large and luxurious litter. It is borne by twelve hefty-looking Nubian slaves. I confess I am impressed by the size and elegance of the sable-black conveyance. Silver fittings grace its exterior, inlaid around the doorway and hammered onto the four handles at the ends of the poles. Decimus, who stands before it, greets me with a big smile and a deep and sweeping bow.

"My Lady Lucia, I have obtained this magnificent litter for our use today. I hope you will approve."

"I shall be thrilled to ride with you in your shiny new litter! Where on earth did you get it?"

"Actually, Titus Flavius loaned it to me," he admits as a wide grin spreads across his face. "He has chosen to ride with Vespasian and Caenis as a show of public support." His expression becomes more serious. "There are rumors afoot suggesting that Titus intends to supplant his father any day now. Titus himself has confessed to me that nothing could be further from the truth. I guess some people just can't believe that he would actually respect his father and truly support him in his role as emperor. At any rate, he has decided to make good use of this, the final day of the Plebeian Games, to demonstrate his undying fealty." He gestures to the litter behind him. "As a result, we shall make quite a splash when we arrive at the Circus. Next to the Emperor's own litter, ours is the finest in Rome." He bows again. "Shall we depart, my lady?"

Damaris acts on cue and raises the drapes so we may enter the grand conveyance. Unlike my own, this litter contains opposing benches so we may sit more upright across from each other. It is curtained round with heavy drapes that can be tied back to allow in light and fresh air or can be kept closed to provide warmth and privacy during the colder times of the year. We choose to keep them closed, which darkens our environment, but also shields us from the uninvited gazes of the surrounding pedestrians. The immense contraption is hoisted and shouldered by our twelve bearers, and the litter starts to sway as we proceed out of the courtyard and onto the street that will lead us off the Palatine. The Circus Maximus sits in a long valley between the Palatine and the Aventine hills; it is but a short ride to get there.

"We shall arrive in time for the parade," Decimus informs me. "I'm sure a fine breakfast will be waiting for us when we get there."

"Who else is invited?" I ask.

"I know Titus will be there, and I believe Caenis is also attending. Beyond that, we shall have to wait and see."

"Good, I like surprises. Especially when they are bigger and nicer than what I'm used to," I tap the bench I sit on. "Tell me Decimus, now that we can speak freely with each other, which gods do you revere the most? I was wondering the other day where your fealties lie."

Decimus settles more comfortably into his seat and considers my question. "Well, my beliefs are going through a conversion of sorts. I have never been very religious by nature. My father was a man of learning and always pushed me to read the Greek philosophers. As a result, I have studied the Stoic philosophers, who seem to think there is only one intelligent god. I have looked at the new Christian teachings, which speak of one god as well, but more loving in nature. I have explored the Hebrew god, who also claims to be the only god, but he is far more vengeful than the Christian one. I do realize that these monotheistic teachings are not in favor with the more traditional factions in our society; therefore, I remain discrete about my beliefs. Lately, I have been exploring the Eleusinian Mysteries, of which I can say little, having been sworn to secrecy." He looks at me and suddenly seems mysterious and unfathomable. "This much I can say: I have a new appreciation for two gods of the Pantheon, Ceres and Pluto, who represent two crucial aspects of the new mystery teachings I am studying." His voice trails off into silence.

"I had not realized how philosophic you are, Decimus. You continue to surprise me."

"Well, I have too much time on my hands, being a bachelor, so I am inclined to study subjects that interest me. I must add that I usually keep my religious and philosophic inquiries to myself. Even Titus would be surprised if he knew I delved into the mysteries as much as I do. Politics and religion don't always mix, especially if one is attracted to the deeper truths that may contradict our more accustomed beliefs. Mine is an ever-active mind that may get me into trouble if I'm not careful. I will count on your discretion, my lady, as

I do feel compelled to reveal myself to you as honestly as I can."

"You needn't be concerned. I shall keep your religious explorations to myself." I pause to collect my own thoughts. "My beliefs are more conventional than yours. I have always regarded our Pantheon of gods to be sufficient for my needs. I honor Venus for all that is beautiful, and Minerva helps me stay on top of my management needs. I keep a special altar in my home for both of them. I also pray to my family deities, who help to protect my home and hearth. Marcus is drawn to Jupiter and Vulcan. They are gods he can identify with and emulate. Jupiter brings him success in his business dealings, while Vulcan inspires his engineering skills. He also has established altars for them in his private chamber. We allow that our destinies can be influenced in a positive way through our prayers, which help to obtain the benevolent consideration of these deities." I look at him closely. "I hope you can accept the simplicity of my faith and will not find me lacking in the world of philosophic discourse. I have always tended to more immediate and attainable outcomes of understanding."

Decimus smiles. "Lucia, I could never find you lacking in anything or in any way. You are fully alive and engaging, just as you are."

I experience the warmth and kindness of his words and smile graciously in return. Before I can say another word, our extravagant litter comes to a halt and settles itself on the ground. It appears we have arrived at our destination. The head bearer opens the curtain so we may exit our sanctuary. Once outside, my eyes adjust to the early morning light. The rising sun paints the outside walls of the huge arena with a soft golden hue. Deep shadows stretch away in the opposite direction. We have been delivered to the private entrance of the Imperial enclosure. Four Praetorian Guards stand at attention at the top of the marble steps that lead to a wide entryway, ready to prevent the uninvited from entering. Having recognized both our litter and my escort, they consult a scroll that shows our names and allow us access to the Imperial box.

We proceed down a dark corridor and up a surprisingly narrow staircase that leads to a large terrace fronted by a stone balustrade. Beyond it, I can see the rows of seats that face us from the opposite side of the enormous, oval-shaped racing structure. The entire building is over five hundred Roman paces long and another one hundred wide. Below us, a long sandy track encircles the interior of the open-air arena. I detect the faint scent of horses, probably coming from the stables adjoining the complex. A row of seats lines the front of the Emperor's enclosure, raised enough to see over the balustrade. Two throne-like chairs perch in the middle, no doubt for the Emperor and his consort. Several people have already arrived and are milling around a long stone table that is piled high with fine pastries, fresh fruit, shellfish, pickled vegetables, and a variety of beverages including wine, beer, and freshly squeezed fruit juices.

Decimus and I approach the table. I recognize Gaius Licinius Mucianus, an elder statesman and acquaintance of my husband's. He sees me approaching with my escort. I watch his eyes as he attempts to sort out who I am. Decimus appears to be even more aquatinted than I, for he quickly takes command of the situation.

"Gaius Licinius, let me present Lucia Vedia Drusa. I have offered to escort her on this fine day."

Mucianus smiles broadly. "Lucia, of course, I was momentarily confused. Where is Marcus? Off somewhere far away, I suppose?"

"He is down south near Mount Vesuvius procuring certain materials for his construction project. He has given Decimus his blessing to look after me in his absence. I was beginning to feel like a widow, he's been so busy of late."

"Well then Decimus, you are a lucky man." He turns to me. "Lady Lucia, please consider me a willing substitute if Decimus is ever unavailable. I would be delighted to stand in, if the need were to arise."

I smile accordingly. "Why of course, Gaius. I would be honored." Mucianus has only just retired as suffect consul of Rome, an honorary title bestowed upon him by Vespasian for his support and counsel during the time of the four emperors. Mucianus was governor of Syria when Vitellus assassinated Otho and became the third emperor in the turbulent year following Nero's suicide. Mucianus convinced Vespasian to seize the throne for himself and helped him manage his eventual ascension to power. Now as we converse, I can see that time and age are quickly catching up to the older statesman. He seems tired and drawn, as if he is suddenly drying up inside.

Several other senators and their wives are also in attendance, none of whom are familiar to me, but Decimus is acquainted with most of them. We mingle and partake of the food and drink. The sun rises above the eastern side of the arena and begins to fill the enormous enclosure with its cheerful radiance.

Before long, we hear voices coming up the stairs. Two Praetorian Guards enter and stand to the side. The Imperial family has arrived. Vespasian appears with Caenis, who holds on to his arm. Titus follows behind. I notice how slowly Caenis mounts the last few steps and become aware that she, like Mucianus, is also showing signs of advanced aging. Her shoulders stoop, and a sense of fragility surrounds the slow and tentative pace with which she walks. And yet, her eyes remain as sharp as cat's claws. She immediately notices my presence and nods to me as she draws nearer to the group. I bow to her and the Emperor.

Caenis nods her head to the assembled guests as a matter of formality before she settles into her elevated throne next to Vespasian's. I notice that several of the Senate wives nod back politely but remain distant. A few others ignore her completely. The fact that Caenis used to be a Greek slave may taint their opinion of her, but they are foolish to look down upon her. After all, she is one of the wealthiest and most powerful women in Rome. She turns to me.

"Lucia, I am delighted you are here, and I love your carnelian pendant. It matches your gown perfectly." She smiles wearily, then sighs. "My goodness, those steps grow steeper with every visit."

"Thank you, my lady. Your emerald broach is absolutely stunning. Is it new?"

"Oh, no. I've had it for a couple of years. It is a gift from the Governor of Hispania. I aided him in his rise to office. It was a token of his appreciation." She smiles knowingly. "How could I refuse?"

I laugh. "Your presence here is most welcome, my lady, for I am not well acquainted with the rest of your party, except for Mucianus, of course, who is well known to many people."

"Oh yes, Gaius has an open invitation to these events." She glances at him as he chats with her protector and my escort. "I suppose he too must be feeling his years. He looks somewhat worn around the edges." She shakes her head sadly. "I am always amazed at how fast one can come apart in the end, my dear. Suddenly, I am experiencing all my years of servitude and freedom piling up behind me like a heavy chain that I must drag from one event to another." She holds me tightly with her gaze. "I've always sought to be at the center of the storm, but now I grow tired and yearn for a solitude I may never find." She looks at Vespasian as he laughs at some story Mucianus is spinning. "He counts on my companionship and counsel, and I could never leave his side. We have seen so much together and will do so till the end." She shrugs as if to say she is resigned to her destiny, then looks about the room. "I understand that Decimus, our handsome young senator who prefers his own company, has agreed to act as your escort to this event?"

I am not surprised that Caenis already knows about my relationship with Decimus. I suppose there is little that goes on in Rome that escapes her attention.

"Yes, my lady. He has consented to escort me to certain events while Marcus is away on business. My husband has approved the arrangement, of course. He knows I grow tired of staying at home. Decimus is very charming and amuses me. I am delighted that he is available to accompany me now and again. We recently saw *Phaedra* by Seneca at the Theater of Pompey."

"I know the play, very depressing as I remember." The aging consort looks at me. "It's no fun being alone so much, is it? I remember when Vespasian left me to marry Flavia Domitilla. Even though I understood his need to marry a woman of patrician birth, I was still devastated. I had to wait a long time before he came back to me. A long time indeed."

Before I can respond to her confession, which has touched my heart, the crowd that's been gathering in the Circus Maximus all morning long lets out a loud cheer that drowns out the possibility of further conversation. The parade has finally reached the arena and is slowly approaching the Imperial enclosure. Vespasian strolls over to Caenis, gently takes her hand, and raises her up. Together with Titus they walk to the front of the enclosure so they can be more easily seen by the masses. The eager spectators roar with approval, for they always appreciate the Emperor's presence at the races. The fact that Titus stands proudly with his father is a clear signal that all is well. The rest of us surround them on both sides.

The elaborate procession started at sunrise in front of the Forum and proceeded through the avenues to the Circus Maximus. The presiding suffect consul leads the parade, followed by the charioteers and their teams of horses, which joined the procession only after it entered the arena. There are sixteen teams in all. Each of the four racing clubs that sponsor and support the separate stables is represented by four different teams, with each charioteer wearing the colored jersey that corresponds to their stable. The colors are red, white, blue, and green.

"Which stable do you root for?" I ask Decimus.

"I grew up supporting the Whites," he says. "I think Ajax, their lead driver, is one of the best there is."

"Well, we shall see," I respond, smiling. "I have always supported the Blues, and I believe that Belen is the most skilled charioteer in the world."

"Would you care to place a bet on the first race in which they both compete?" he asks, pulling his purse from his sleeve and shaking it enough for me to hear the tinkle of coins banging together.

"My my, aren't you the wealthy gambling man?" I quip. "Too bad I forgot to bring my change purse. I might have taken some of that off your hands." The truth is, I forgot to bring it because Marcus always carried his and bet for the both of us. While gambling at the Circus is forbidden, everyone does it anyway—even in the Emperor's box.

"Oh, what a shame. I was hoping to tip the litter bearers with the earnings I made off of you, my lady."

"If we ever come back here again, I will be sure to be better prepared." I wonder if we ever will.

A group of colorful dancers and musicians follow behind the racing teams. The crowd cheers loudly as the dancers execute cartwheels and daring spins and turns to the processional music. Several priests bring up the rear leading three single horse-drawn chariots, each with its own statue of a god or goddess to watch over the Ludi Plebii races. Today Jupiter, Juno, and Minerva—the Capitoline triad—are honored. The parade passes by and circles the arena. The race teams disappear through an exit to our right, where the twelve starting gates encompass the entire side of the complex.

Vespasian, Titus, and Caenis return to their seats and settle down for the first race. Decimus and I, along with the other guests, do likewise. Soon afterwards, a long, drawn-out trumpet blast alerts the two hundred and fifty thousand spectators that the first race is about to commence. Two magistrates in an adjoining box each drop a large white handkerchief. Twelve chariots drawn by two horses apiece explode out of the gates and charge toward the center divider, called the *spina*, which runs down the middle of the sandy track. A large obelisk, a gift from the Emperor Augustus many years ago, marks the western end of the *spina* closest to the starting gates. The stampede of chariots passes beneath our enclosure, and the drivers begin to align their rigs for the initial lap. There will be seven in all. The first chariot to cross the finish line in front of the magistrates' box will win the event. Each of the four racing factions enters three chariots in every race.

"Neither of our favorite charioteers are participating in this race," Decimus observes. "These first few contests are using the less experienced drivers to warm up the crowd. Belen and Ajax will show up later when they switch to the four-horse rigs that will dominate the remainder of the races."

It is easy to spot which team belongs to which stable. The charioteers wear colorful tunics that clearly show their allegiances. These long-sleeved jerseys are covered by corsets made up of separate bands of leather, which help protect the drivers from impact. The horse on the left is trained to help steer the vehicle, and its reins are held firmly in the driver's left hand. His right hand holds the whip used to encourage the beasts to strive hard throughout the race. The pulling reins are tied around the middle of the charioteer's waist, where the banded corset is attached. He also wears a small leather cap on his head for additional protection. A long, curved knife is strapped to the driver's side; he must use this blade to cut himself free if his rig is compromised in any way. Many drivers have failed to execute this procedure and ended up dragged behind their upturned rigs at a great cost to their physical welfare. Chariot racing is a dangerous and often deadly enterprise, which is why these drivers are extremely well paid. They are also the most popular athletes in the Empire, even surpassing the great gladiators both in earnings and praise.

This first race is less than thrilling. The Reds position their most experienced young driver in the lead from the very beginning and successfully block any of the other factions from passing him by. The absence of any pileups also disappoints the booing fans. The second, third, and fourth races are more exciting, in that there are a few lead changes and a couple of minor collisions. In one event, a Green driver is forced to abandon his chariot and manages to cut himself free, but only after he is yanked for a considerable distance along the sandy surface of the track. A couple of attendants rush over to assist him out of the arena. His arms appear to be badly skinned and are bleeding noticeably; the leather bands which cover his arms and legs provide inadequate protection if they are subjected to too much abuse. The crowd respectfully applauds his exit. He will no doubt be back again some other day.

After the fourth race, there is a long intermission. The dancers and musicians reappear to entertain the crowd. We join the Emperor and his consort at the table, where warm sweetened wine is poured into our goblets. We also partake of some fresh oysters and pickled eggs along with tasty roasted dormice and stuffed sausages. Titus joins us as we enjoy our snacks.

"Decimus and Lucia, are you enjoying the races?"

"Not as much as we enjoyed riding here in your extravagant litter, your lordship," my escort replies. Titus greets this response with a hearty grin. Although his features are plain, I can easily detect his intelligence and grounded sense of humor. He reminds me of his father, a dependable and confident man.

"I am delighted to help my closest colleague in the Senate try to impress his lovely guest on this occasion," Titus says as he bows to me.

"You are most kind, my lord," I answer. "And yes, I am very impressed, not just with your magnificent litter, but also with your kindness and generosity."

"Well, in all honesty, my lady, I didn't need it as I am spending the entire day in the company of my father. I feel that my gesture of support is being properly received by the masses. Would you agree, Decimus?"

"Indeed, I do, judging from the tremendous ovation you and your father received earlier this morning. I think everyone but your worst enemies are relieved to see you support your father. The people are enjoying the stability you both bring to the Empire, and rightly so."

"Yes, I am sure our enemies are disappointed that I have not attempted to overthrow my father. After all, they all assume I will do exactly that, the fools." His expression darkens for a brief moment but then regains its former buoyancy. "This next race promises to be a good one. I expect all of the top charioteers will participate. I'm rooting for Evander and the Greens. I expect him to thoroughly trounce your Ajax, my friend. What say you?"

"I believe you are sadly mistaken, my lord. Perhaps we can put up a few coins to back our different persuasions, say one hundred sestertii should one of our favorites wear the wreath at the end of the race?"

"Agreed," Titus states. "My lady, would you stand as witness to this wager, should the need arise?" Titus plays with me, knowing full well that both men are good for their word.

"Indeed I shall, my lord. My only regret is that I forgot my own purse. Otherwise I would join the wager and win it all on the back of my own champion, Belen of the Blues."

This brings a huge smile to Titus's already cheerful expression. "Well spoken, my lady. I, for one, am relieved that you did not bring your purse. Belen has been most fortunate of late and that lead horse of his, Dragon Fire, has also been dominating." He looks at a group of senators who are engaged in a vigorous conversation. "I must move on and mingle with my other guests. I need to garnish support for my father's policies at home and abroad. Alas, a politician's work is never done." He bows to us and proceeds toward the designated group of potential allies. Before long, another trumpet blast alerts us that the fifth race is about to begin.

"My sources confirm what Titus believes," Decimus informs me. "This next race is the one to watch. All the lead drivers will be in it, including our two favorites, and the best horses too. They want to utilize the track before it gets too torn up."

"I am looking forward to it," I confess. "I can feel my old enthusiasm returning now that I'm back here at the Circus again. I forgot how excited I get during the big races like the one coming up."

"Well, don't get overly excited, my dear. I don't want you to be too disappointed when Ajax wins his 534th race."

"Oh, I won't be at all disappointed. After all, Belen will be wearing the victory wreath when all is said and done." We smile playfully at each other. It's fun rooting for our separate drivers. Marcus and I always cheered for the same color, and therefore lacked the amusement of competing against each other. I find I prefer the tension that comes with supporting different colors. We settle back into our seats and wait expectantly for the magistrates to drop their handkerchiefs. This they do, and the twelve gates are hoisted up. Horses and their attached chariots blast out onto the track. This time, four horses pull each rig.

"Look, Ajax has Thunder Clap in the lead!" Decimus exclaims. "He's the best horse in the Whites' stable." He studies the chariots as they vie for position along the far side of the central barrier. I reluctantly notice that the two front-running teams are both Whites. "Titus is right," Decimus continues. "Belen has Dragon Fire as his steering horse. Together they should give my Whites a good run for the finish."

"I certainly hope so!" I shout, for the crowd is now fully aroused and the entire arena vibrates with enthusiasm.

"Look! Evander of the Greens has moved into third place, and Boden, the best of the Reds, follows him in fourth!" Decimus shouts back. The chariots race for the first turn. As the horses rush forward at full speed, a few of the chariots in the rear are forced to the outside and as consequence lose precious ground on the first turn. I am always amazed by the sharpness of the turning radius that these vehicles can execute around these turns. A driver's true ability is measured by his skill at maneuvering his team around the two ends of the spina. I watch Belen as he cleverly cuts off the number-two rig of the Green faction and moves up into the fifth spot. Meanwhile, Decimus's favorite, Ajax, is comfortably in front as he guides his steering horse on the far left around the second turn and completes the first lap. Brutus, his teammate in second place, is successfully blocking his nearest pursuer from passing him by.

"Ajax is well positioned, Lucia, I like his chances early on," Decimus says, leaning into me so I may hear over the crowd's cheers.

"The race is still young," I counter, hoping for the best.

Every time Evander tries to move up, Brutus prevents him by using his whip to keep the advancing Green leader at bay. There are no rules in chariot racing. The drivers are allowed to hit, whip, collide, bite, and do whatever it takes to cross the finish line in first place. The four different stables act in unison, usually placing their best team in the lead and then using their second- and third-tier chariots as defenders who will do any and everything possible to prevent the other factions from advancing beyond them. The twelve teams draw lots before the race begins to determine which starting gate they have. The few gates in the middle provide the best chance of reaching the spina first. Since the race lasts for seven full laps, some charioteers deliberately hold back and save their horses for the last few laps. Too fast a pace can wear a team down. It is not unusual for a blocking chariot to deliberately crash his vehicle into an onrushing competitor in order to preserve his lead driver's victory. Blood and death are not uncommon in the Circus Maximus. Crashes are frequent occurrences, and the crowd enjoys nothing more than a good catastrophe. It is human nature to anticipate and hope for collisions and even injury and death—as long as their favorite faction isn't involved. When I see blood, I only worry if the Blue team is involved.

Meanwhile, the front-runners continue in this order for a couple of laps, the Whites maintaining their lead. One of the Blue teams in the rear is forced to pull out of the race when his horse on the far right comes up lame and almost causes a crash. The driver quickly guides the chariot to the right side of the track and pulls on the reins vigorously, forcing his horses to slowly come to a standstill. Attendants with blue tunics come to lead the chariot off the track and out of harm's way. The other teams somehow avoid colliding with the disabled rig, much to the disappointment of the more bloodthirsty fans. Since he is a Blue, I am relieved he survives unscathed.

"Look, Lucia, Belen is making another move!" Decimus points toward the chariots, which have now made six half-turns around the sandy track and are nearing the halfway point of the race. Evander is so occupied with Boden of the Reds striving to pass on his right that Belen, my favorite, surges ahead and cuts inside both of them on the seventh turn. He has forced his way into third place, just behind Brutus. Evander is completely caught off guard by Belen's bold and daring maneuver. When he attempts to compensate for his carelessness by steering his team back to the left, he overreacts and catches his left wheel on the base of the spina, causing his entire rig to lean dangerously to the right before flipping over and ejecting him right out of his chariot. At the same time, Boden is forced to rein in to keep from charging into the errant chariot that bounces about in front of him. As Evander flies through the air, he pulls his knife out and slices madly at his reins. He is dragged along the track for a few terrible moments before he successfully cuts himself free. Somehow, the teams following behind manage to avoid him and his toppled chariot, which his horses have already pulled toward the stands and out of harm's way. When Evander jumps to his feet and runs after his team of horses, the entire stadium gives him a standing ovation. Given the circumstances of his sudden and terrifying crash, he is fortunate to be unharmed.

"By Jupiter, he is graced with the god's own blessings to have survived that mishap," my escort shouts in my ear, "and look who has managed to slip into third place!"

I smile and nod, feeling a mounting anticipation welling up inside of me.

"Dragon Fire may be the best horse in the business," Decimus adds. "Did you see how he stole his way through that turn? And the speed that Belen's horses have to power past the other two teams… That is a masterful piece of driving. Brutus will be hard pressed to keep him in his rear."

Indeed, Belen switches his reins to his right hand and takes his whip in his left, urging Dragon Fire to pass Brutus on the outside. Both drivers lash at each other on the straightaway, mostly missing, but suddenly the tongue of Belen's whip bites Brutus above his right eye, forcing him to lose focus for the briefest of moments as he wipes away the blood pouring into his eye. Belen whips his team and surges past the second-place chariot to deftly angle into the eighth turn, cutting inside Brutus and forcing him into the third position.

"Unbelievable!" Decimus shouts as the crowd explodes with cheers and moans, depending on which color they're rooting for. "We're down to a two-man race!"

Ajax, the lead driver, has managed to pull comfortably ahead while his pursuers were so violently preoccupied with each other. Belen has at least three chariot lengths to make up in his effort to catch his one remaining rival. The next two laps see both of them gradually pull away from Brutus, Boden, and the rest of the pack. Slowly, Belen inches his Blue team closer to the White team ahead of him. By the twelfth turn, he has Dragon Fire practically bumping into the rear of Ajax's rig. Belen is content to remain a hand's breadth behind his rival for the second-to-last lap, but at the start of the final straightaway, he pulls out to challenge Ajax on the right. Both Decimus and I are filled with exhilaration. The two teams are pressing each other, and all eight horses must be close to exhaustion. Their coats glisten with sweat in the cool November air. The drivers are lashing their teams as vigorously as they can. Belen's rig advances steadily, and as the finish line approaches, both chariots are head to head. At the very last moment, Dragon Fire and his three cohorts pull in front by the slimmest of margins to grab the victory from the sagging White team that has run its course.

"I win, I win!" I shout, grabbing Decimus's hand with both of mine and shaking it up and down like a pump handle.

"Too bad you forgot your purse," he reminds me, laughing at my obvious excitement. "You could have paid for our dinner!"

"Oh, are we to dine together then?" I ask as I release his hand, conscious that I have unwittingly touched him in a public place.

"I have a surprise, but you will just have to wait and see what it is. Especially now that I must taste the bitterness of defeat while you exalt in the sweetness of victory." I smile and watch as Belen parades his horses around the arena in his victory lap, both to receive the crowd's joyous acknowledgment and to cool his four beasts down gradually from their tremendous performance. He will stop before the magistrates' enclosure to receive his palm branch and laurel wreath.

"Well," I reply, "I shall bask in my exaltation and enjoy Belen's victory. After that, I will patiently await this evening's surprise."

"An excellent idea, given that we have at least seven more races to watch this afternoon. Come, let's have some more wine, shall we?"

"Certainly," I happily agree.

The rest of the afternoon rushes by with the speed of a racing chariot. Our favorite lead drivers return for a highly anticipated rematch in the ninth event. Dragon Fire, Thunder Clap, and the other celebrity horses that ran in the fifth event are off duty for the rest of the day. Each stable is equally deep in the number of well-trained racing stock, and they produce fresh horses for all twelve races. During the summer months, the number of races can easily double, given the extra hours of daylight. It would seem that Roman spectators can't have their fill of them.

The ninth race is a disappointment, lacking in drama and excitement. This second encounter with the world's best charioteers produces an entirely different result. Evander of the Greens wins easily. Once again, Ajax of the Whites is second. I am dejected because Belen of the Blues comes in sixth. His team lacks the same depth of heart without Dragon Fire in the inside position.

By the end of the last race, I am feeling a little giddy from all the wine I have consumed during the day's ongoing festivities. Vespasian, Caenis, and Titus have already departed, having reached their fill of food, drink, and fun by the end of the ninth race. Mucianus also left at that time. I suppose that a full day of celebration and competition can catch up with those who have reached a certain age. I wonder when my Marcus will begin to slow down. He still exhibits plenty of vigor, even in his mid-fifties. He is eight years younger than his good friend Vespasian. But time leaves no prisoners, and he will soon begin to show his advancing age. I have no doubt about that.

"Well, Lucia, the day darkens, and the races are done. Let's depart. Our litter should be waiting for us near the exit, and we have a prepared dinner to attend to."

"I must confess, I am more hungry than thirsty," I answer. "I have had enough wine for the time being. My head swims with its effect." I pause. "I may have to alert my household staff that I will be returning after the evening meal, so they can alter their plans as necessary."

"Not to worry, my lady. We will be able to address that issue when we arrive at where we are going." He smiles and adds, "And you will just have to wait and see where that is."

I return his smile. "Very well then, I will not pester you with my inquisitiveness, which I must admit is very much aroused."

"Excellent. I hope you won't be disappointed."

We wind our way out of the Circus Maximus. Once we reach the street, the Circus's mass exodus engulfs us. Thousands upon thousands of spectators are also exiting the arena, probably with the same intent of finding an evening meal to sop up the wine of the day. Plenty of public eateries will be doing a brisk business this evening, as many people will not be inclined to hassle the crowded streets in order to prepare supper hours later when they arrive home. I wonder if Decimus has reserved us seats at a restaurant nearby. We manage to shuffle to our litter, which is easy to spot; it towers above the crowd even when it rests upon the ground. We enter the sanctuary of its magnificent interior. Since Decimus says nothing to the lead bearer, I assume he has already informed him of our next destination. We are lifted up and begin to crawl our way along the busy avenue. I close my eyes, suddenly feeling tired and drained. Decimus also seems weary, and the two of us sit comfortably in silence for a while. The momentum of our conveyance is halting at best. Shouts and curses surround us on all sides, yet I am content. I drift into an easy slumber, and the next thing I know, we have picked up our pace and are heading uphill. The evening's darkening mantle has enveloped our litter, and

Decimus sits in shadow. I can hardly see his face in the darkness.

"We shall soon arrive at our destination," he offers. "The crowd is thinning out as we climb the Palatine. Did you have any dreams?"

I take a moment to find my voice. "No, I did not. Have I been asleep for very long?"

"For a while," he answers. "It was slow leaving the Circus. We stood at a standstill more often than not due to the congestion. It appears that half of Rome attended today's Plebeian Festival. It is a holiday, after all."

I notice that the shouting has abated, and I smell cooking oil mixed with the scent of spices wafting onto the street from adjoining homes. The swaying of the litter is comforting, almost like a child's crib rocking back and forth. Before long, our progress is halted, the litter is grounded, and our entry curtains open up.

"Come, Lucia, we are here." Decimus exits first and then assists me. We stand in front of a small courtyard that fronts a large oaken door. Decimus talks briefly to the lead bearer just out of my hearing, and then gently grasps my arm and leads me to the door.

"Welcome to my humble home." He turns and faces me. "I have asked Martus, the lead bearer, to notify your head servant that you will arrive home after you have dined with me."

"Thank you, Decimus. So, this is where you live. We're not very far from the palace, are we?"

"No, it's just around the corner. We're only a few blocks from your own residence. The Imperial family likes to have its closest friends share the hilltop with them." He bangs a bronze knocker. We wait briefly before the door is opened. A tall blond manservant dressed in a plain brown cotton tunic bows to us and steps aside so we may enter.

"Duratius, this is Lady Lucia. She will be joining me for dinner this evening."

"Yes, my lord. Everything is prepared and awaits you as planned." Given his accent, I discern that he hails from Gallia. He bows again and leads us through a small entryway into a large room that is lit with several torches. Three different seating arrangements are spaced around the room, each with a couple of settees and an assortment of pillows to sit upon. A variety of tapestries hang from the beige walls. Their patterns indicate that they come different corners of the world. A collection of exotic spears and shields hangs between the various tapestries.

"You are a collector, I see."

"Yes, my lady, it is a hobby of mine. Much of this I purchased when I was serving in the legions. Since I lack a family to support, I indulge myself with certain artifacts I find appealing."

I notice the terra cotta tiled floors are also covered with larger rugs. "Your room is lovely, Decimus. Very masculine."

"I admit it lacks a woman's touch, but I am comfortable here. We will be dining through that archway."

I see a heavy square wooden table that is lit with candles and has two place settings at one end. We will recline on the same couch.

"Would you like to wash up, my lady?" Duratius inquires. I say yes and am led to a washroom, where I gratefully relieve myself. I splash my hands and face with scented water and attend to my hair and outfit, both of which need some straightening up and rearranging. It has been all day since I had a decent look at myself. When I am ready, I join Decimus at his table.

I recline on the couch next to him, resting on my left side, so I may use my right hand to more easily serve myself from the table. Decimus rests upon his right side, meaning he will have to eat with his left hand. This small gesture of chivalry is not lost upon me. As if on cue, Duratius appears followed by a female servant, both carrying trays loaded with food and drink.

"My chef has worked all day so we may dine in style, my lady. Like Duratius and Cailin here, he is from Gallia and therefore specializes in northern cuisine. I hope you will be satisfied."

"Oh my, I am sure to be," I respond. Cailin pours red wine into two goblets and places them on the table within easy reach. Duratius sets a red ceramic plate in front of me and serves up our exotic appetizers. Snails chopped up with mushrooms and garlic and sautéed in red wine have been stuffed back into their very own shells. I must use a special stick to extract the delicacies from their natural containers. They taste so delicious that I devour several in quick succession. I sample fried oysters that have been rolled in a fine herb batter and fried in olive oil before being covered with a creamy goat cheese sauce. They too are delectable, and I am very impressed.

"Be careful not to overeat, my dear," Decimus counsels. "We have an excellent main course heading our way shortly."

"I can assure you that I am up to the challenge. I have worked up a healthy appetite as a consequence of spending the day with you at the Circus. I'm still reveling in Belen's marvelous victory in the fifth event."

"Well, please don't forget that my Ajax did best your hero in their rematch, even if he came in as a runner-up for the second time in row."

"I have little recall of that race and soon hope to erase it completely from my memory." I sample the wine. My thirst has returned now that his chef's exquisite flavors have graced my palette. I notice that this wine is less watered down than usual and exhibits a healthy, robust bouquet. Meanwhile, Duratius clears away our appetizer plates and replaces them with a clean set. He disappears into the kitchen and leaves us to digest our first course.

Decimus also sips from his wine goblet, then addresses me directly. "Tell me, Lucia, do you miss your husband now that he has been away for over seven days?"

I stare at him, quietly wondering why he would need to remind me of my husband in the middle of our private dinner. I consider his question carefully before I answer it. "Marcus has traveled frequently for long periods of time ever since we were wed. He was a soldier more often than not and spent much of his life away from Roman soil, building war machines, bridges, and the like for Vespasian, or whomever he served under. Now that he has retired from active duty, he still labors for his emperor as a highly valued engineer and building contractor. Marcus would die of boredom if he wasn't involved in some enterprise somewhere." I take a sip from my goblet; the wine is so good I must taste it again. "Do I miss him? No, I do not. To me, he hasn't been gone all that long. I know he will return in a week's time, and I will no longer require your services as my escort. That saddens me, Decimus. I enjoy your attention, and I will miss you." I look down at my hands and feel a little embarrassed by my admission. He gently strokes my cheek.

"I shall miss you too, Lucia." He almost whispers, he speaks so gently. "I feel my heart opening up to you in a way that is foreign to me. I think of you constantly, my lady, and find myself yearning for your company when we are apart." He places his hand under my chin and lifts my face so I must gaze into his eyes. "I believe I am falling in love with you, and I'm not sure I altogether enjoy the experience. I feel quite unmanned at times. You have conquered me in a way no other woman has, and to be frank with you, I am yours to do with as you please."

I am moved by his words, and the passion and honesty with which he utters them. I have strong feelings for him too, which I am helpless to control. I've spent my entire life behaving according to the rigid laws of Roman society. I have reined in my passion like one of today's charioteers forcing his magnificent team of horses to slow and eventually halt progress altogether. Now that I am falling in love, I find that I am disinclined to restrain myself in any way whatsoever. Marcus suddenly feels old enough to be my father. Over the years, the gap between our ages has widened. Now that I am enjoying the attention of a man whose appearance and inclinations match my own, I am reluctant to renounce them. But before I can say or do anything in response to my host's confession, Duratius and Cailin reenter the dining room, bearing the second course. Decimus and I straighten up as we prepare for this evening's main attraction.

"Tonight, you shall enjoy stewed hare, my lord, basted and cooked with apples and carrots," Duratius announces, obviously feeling very confident that we will approve of the chef's creation. A round loaf of baked bread is also presented with the main course. Our wine goblets are replenished, and our plates piled high with the delicious-smelling fare. Decimus and I devour our portions; I sense that our hearty appetites reflect the rising tide of our mutual attraction for each other. Before long, our plates are empty of everything edible and littered with the bare bone remains of our sumptuous feast.

"Dessert, my lord?" Duratius politely inquires. Decimus looks at me, and I shake my head from side to side.

"I am completely stuffed," I say. "The hare was excellent, and I couldn't refrain myself at all. I have no more room and can barely breathe, l am so full."

"We will skip desert, Duratius, and will instead retire to the great room. Please bring our wine goblets and then leave us undisturbed until my guest must depart for her own residence."

"Yes, my lord," the servant replies. We stand up. Decimus takes my hand and guides me into the large living room and over to one of the settees. We settle into it. We receive our goblets, which are refilled probably for the final time and placed on the table in front of us. My senses have clouded a little from the intoxication of the largely undiluted wine. The servant bows and withdraws from the room. We are alone again, filled with food and drink and quite content to sit together and digest our wonderful dinner.

A silence settles over us like a warm and comforting blanket. Decimus reaches over and lightly takes my hand. He holds it carefully while he places his other hand over mine and massages it slowly. We are facing each other. I look into his eyes. He looks into mine. I feel his soft caresses. My heart beats a little faster. A tender sensation wells up within me. I am experiencing a blending of desire and happiness. I wish it would last forever. We have transcended the need for words. His simple touch is far more eloquent.

He removes his upper hand and places it on my shoulder. He pulls me toward him, and our lips join together. A surge of exquisite energy rushes up and down my spine, quickening my heart and filling me with a desire so intense, I wonder if Venus herself has not touched me with her divine presence. I simply melt into his arms and disappear. I am gone, swept away by the connectivity that embraces and uplifts us. What happens after our first kiss is beyond compare. I will confess that I experience lovemaking in a way that is deeper and more exhilarating than anything I have previously tasted with my husband. Decimus opens my being and unleashes a passion I can't possibly describe. He exercises a discretion that protects me from bearing any unwanted fruit, and for that carefulness, I am grateful. I was too engaged in the heat of the moment to consider such precautions.

When we are done, I lie in his arms and cry, both joyfully and mournfully. I know I have violated the sanctity of my marriage, and yet I am too intoxicated to fully regret my action. We embrace each other in silence and slowly allow our passion to subside. After a while, Decimus raises himself from my arms and stands upright. He adjusts his toga and smiles down at me.

"I am reluctant to bring our evening to an end, my love, but wisdom counsels me to send you on your way. You should not arrive home too late or you will arouse more suspicion than is prudent with your servants."

"Yes, you are correct," I acknowledge. He helps me up and I adjust my stola, which is in complete disarray. He claps his hands, and Duratius appears instantaneously, obviously having been stationed close enough to have heard everything that transpired between Decimus and me. I am not concerned. Duratius is bound to secrecy and would be executed on the spot if he were to betray the confidence of his master. Such discretion between owner and slave is inviolate, or the very fabric of Roman society would be torn asunder.

"We must get together again, my lady," Decimus suggests as we follow Duratius toward the front entryway that leads to the outer courtyard.

"I agree. I will contact you in a day or two when I have determined what our next engagement will be," I reply.

"Wonderful, I look forward to it." He takes my hand and squeezes it behind his servant's back. Titus's immense litter awaits me outside the front door. I am ushered in and taken home, a short ride through the Palatine. Damaris and Adonia are there to greet me when I arrive at my own courtyard.

"I trust my lady enjoyed herself today at the races?" Damaris politely inquires.

"Indeed I did, Damaris. Belen of the Blues won his first race. It was very exciting."

"I am delighted to hear that, my lady." Damaris and Adonia are well aware that Marcus and I support the Blues. "Is there anything you will require from the kitchen?"

"No, I have dined well this evening and am content to retire."

"Very well, my lady." Damaris bows and disappears toward the back of the house where he and Adonia reside. She accompanies me to my bedroom to assist me with my disrobing and toiletries.

"I have had a long day, Adonia, and feel the need for a hot bath."

"Yes, my lady. I have prepared your tub already."

"You always amaze me, my dear. Sometimes I wonder if you know me better than myself."

"I simply knew you would be tired and in need of cleansing after such a vigorous day, my lady."

"And you are absolutely correct. Will you place some lavender in my tub? I desire its fragrance this evening."

"Certainly, my lady." We remove my jewelry and various garments and pin up my hair so it will remain dry in the bath. I put on my robe and lead Adonia to the bathroom, which is adjacent to the kitchen. I disrobe and settle slowly into the mosaic tub that is set into the tiled floor. The tub displays an ocean motif with dolphins and mermaids swimming along the sides and a large conch shell design lying on the bottom. Damaris has probably just added boiling water to warm its contents. They have no doubt been keeping it temperate for me all evening long. I am thankful, for I need to wash myself, both from the dust that blows about the Circus Maximus and also from my encounter with Decimus. I know full well that I have violated a sacred trust by committing stuprum. According to Roman law, such adultery can lead to my death. I do feel vulnerable… but at the same time, I feel fulfilled. I'm like a plant that has suffered a lifelong drought and has suddenly experienced its first summer rain. I am nurtured and refreshed. I am in love.

Adonia returns briefly to drop lavender petals into my tub. She adds some more boiling water and then withdraws. I enjoy the new warmth that settles around me and think about Decimus. I wish to see him again immediately but know I must wait at least a couple of days. I need to arrange our next meeting. I remember that Pliny the Elder recently sent Marcus and myself an invitation to a preview presentation on his ever-evolving *Natural History* in three days' time. Decimus and I could attend that lecture and have dinner at his house again. I decide to send him an invitation tomorrow morning. Having determined our next tryst, I relax more fully into my bath. I almost drift off. I rouse myself and retire to my bedchamber, where I fall into a deep and satisfying sleep.

\#

The next morning, I send Adonia off with a written invitation for Decimus then attend to my normal routines. Adonia returns with a note from Decimus confirming our get together. I lunch out with a few old friends and we, as usual, talk about our grown children. Later on, I write and send a letter to Publius, my eldest son, catching him up on his father's activities and how much we enjoyed seeing his younger brother recently. I inquire as to his plans and wonder if he anticipates a visit back to Rome sometime soon. I entrust this correspondence to Damaris, who will deliver it to the legionary headquarters near the Forum. Eventually, the letter will find its way into a courier's pouch and make its way to Britannia where Publius is stationed. He has been over there for two years, and I sense that he may be given leave soon to visit family and friends. I hope so. I dearly miss him.

The following day I receive correspondence from Marcus, delivered by a private courier whom he dispatched a couple of days before. My husband informs me that his trip is proceeding well. He has successfully lined up several shipments of *pozzolana* to go by sea at a reasonable cost to the Roman treasury. He reports that Quintus, our caretaker, is taking excellent care of both the summer home and himself. Marcus also says that he should be returning home as originally planned in another five days' time.

I experience sadness, which I can't entirely explain. My old and familiar self is relieved to discover that Marcus is well and will return home as planned, but my newly discovered passionate self is disappointed that he will be back in such a short time and that I will have to refrain from seeing Decimus until Marcus ventures off on another business trip. My despondency may have to do with the fact that our marital relationship will never be the same again. The normal flow of our marriage will seem empty and hollow, and I will ever yearn for Decimus and the heartfelt connection we share.

The next two days flow by in the usual manner. I go shopping with Damaris and Adonia along with a couple of household slaves and stock up on basic staples for the next week. We buy kitchen goods and select a pretty bolt of woolen cloth for a new winter garment. Adonia and I will design and fashion a new stola for the cooler weather.

The morning of the third day finally arrives, and I am excited at the prospect of visiting with Decimus one last time before my husband's return to Rome. An hour before his scheduled arrival, Cailin, his female servant, appears in his stead. Damaris brings her to my bedchamber where Adonia and I are preparing myself for my escort's expected arrival. I am surprised to see her here in my domus. The servant girl bows before me, then speaks haltingly with a heavy Gallic accent.

"My lady, my master departed for Britannia. He not to see you. He very sorry."

I am shocked. "He what? He has left for Britannia? But why?"

"I not know. Soldiers come and soon he leaves with Duratius and two trunks. He sends me to tell you he go away for long time."

"Did he write a letter for you to give to me?" I ask, hoping for more of an explanation of his sudden and alarming departure.

"No, my lady. He left in such big hurry."

I am stunned. I dismiss the girl and tell Adonia to show her out. My thoughts race from one corner of my mind to another. Why would Decimus have to depart so suddenly for such a distant frontier as Britannia? I know how far away it is because Publius's letters take weeks to reach me. And why would my escort be forced to leave now, just when our relationship is establishing roots in our respective hearts? Has politics intervened and demanded his participation? Has some crisis occurred that requires his intervention? Have Vespasian and Titus enlisted his service in some secrete enterprise? Or, has our budding relationship placed him in harm's way? Has my own adulterous encounter somehow been discovered? Am I also at risk? Am I to be put to death for betraying Marcus, a close friend and associate to the Emperor? But if so, would I not be more at risk than Decimus? Why would he be sent away? These questions haunt my mind and cause me to pace back and forth in my chamber like a caged beast, wringing my hands with anxiety. I feel totally and completely alone and abandoned. The anticipation and excitement I felt as I was dressing for today's date has instantly turned into sorrow and fear. What can I do? How can I discover what fate has befallen my new lover? The face of Antonia Caenis appears before my mind's eye. Yes, she knows everything that transpires in Vespasian's court! And she is my ally. I like her, and more importantly, I trust her. I will approach her and discover what she knows about Decimus's sudden departure to the distant shores of the Roman frontier.

I sit at my desk and reach for my bamboo pen and a piece of parchment. I write a brief note requesting an immediate audience with the Emperor's consort. I roll up the scroll and seal it with wax. I stamp it with Marcus's seal and summon Adonia. I dispatch her directly to the Imperial Palace.

An hour passes by before Adonia returns with Caenis's written response: *My Lady Lucia, you may visit me this afternoon during the seventh hour. I look forward to your visit. Your respectful friend, Antonia Caenis.*

When I depart for the palace comfortably before the designated hour, the weather is cool and breezy. Because it is so close by, I forsake my litter and choose to walk there instead. I have Adonia accompany me. When we arrive at the main gate, I display my correspondence from Caenis and am granted entry by the Praetorian Guards. A messenger is sent to notify the Emperor's consort that I have arrived. I stand with a large group of citizens who have shown up with petitions for the Emperor, though only a few will be lucky enough to address him in person. The messenger returns and requests that I follow him to the consort's private apartment. Adonia and I walk through a series of wide corridors, past a host of statues and a couple of open-air gardens, and finally arrive at an arched doorway with another guard stationed beside it.

He nods to me as I pass through and am met by a female servant who is to usher me to her mistress. I instruct Adonia to wait for my return at the doorway and follow the servant down a smaller corridor that leads to a private living area with several seating arrangements. An abundance of ceramic pots filled with flowering plants is scattered about while several beautiful tapestries hang from the walls. A few marble busts also beg to be noticed. I recognize one of Antonia Minor, the consort's former mistress.

I see Caenis sitting on a couch in the corner near a fireplace, which is alight with a few burning logs. She smiles as I approach her.

"Lady Lucia, I am delighted to see you. This is indeed a pleasant surprise. Please, come and be seated." She points to a chair next to her couch, and I sit down.

"Thank you, my lady. I am so grateful that you have allowed me to visit you this afternoon. Your apartment is lovely and well appointed. I recognize the face of Antonia Minor, and perhaps also that of Vespasian as a younger man?"

"You are very observant, Lucia. I also have a bust of Emperor Claudius, who supported Vespasian's early career. They remind me of how long I have been involved with the ruling families." A servant appears carrying a tray of small pastries and two cups of steaming spiced apple cider. "Please help yourself, my dear. I find the air is cooling down and thought some hot cider might help to keep us warm."

"Thank you, my lady. The pastries look wonderful." I take one as a gesture of gratitude, even though I have little appetite due to the nervousness I am feeling under my polite and gracious veneer.

"Now then, Lucia, are you here to talk of pleasantries, or is there something more specific you would like to address?" I am caught off guard by

Caenis's directness, but I shouldn't be. It is not the first time I have witnessed this attribute in her.

"Yes, my lady, there is a matter I would discuss with you. If I may?"

"Of course you may. As you already know, I am very fond of you and am honored that you would approach me for my counsel."

I nod to her with respect and proceed directly to the point. "I have been notified this very morning that my new friend and escort, Decimus Tulles Capito, has suddenly departed for Britannia." I pause to consider briefly how to express my concern for him. "Today we were to attend Pliny's latest lecture on his ever-evolving *Natural History*. My concern is that Decimus was required to leave so suddenly on this expedition. He did not even have time to write to me and inform me of the reason for his hasty departure." I take a breath and calm myself a little. "I am worried for him and wonder if he has somehow violated his trust with the ruling family?"

Caenis' face remains constant throughout my confession. She reaches for her cup and sips from it before she responds to my question. "Yes, I am aware that Decimus has been posted to Britannia as senior tribune to the legionary commander in Wales. His predecessor there was wounded in battle and is returning to Rome. Vespasian and Titus selected Decimus for this position based on his experience in Judea. His sudden departure was due in part to his need to board a vessel that was set to disembark this very day." She looks at me with a growing tenderness that causes me to be somewhat wary. "I also encouraged Vespasian in making this decision, but unbeknownst to him, for reasons that concern you, my dear, and your husband Marcus."

"Me and Marcus?" I ask sounding more surprised than I really am.

"Yes Lucia, you and Marcus. You see, your husband is one of Vespasian's closet allies and dearest friends. He is currently entrusted with a huge responsibility. The construction of the new Coliseum could well be Vespasian's greatest legacy to the people of Rome. As I have previously expressed to you, Vespasian's welfare is my primary concern. Should one of his closest friends be subjected to scandal, it would have a very negative impact on my protector's sense of well-being. I cannot allow such an ill-favored event to occur." She pauses to take a sip of cider. I remain silent. I can sense the ground beneath my feet turning to sand. "I have seen you and Decimus together on two occasions, and I detect the infatuation you share with each other."

"But my lady, Decimus and I are only friends and—" I begin to respond, but Caenis raises her hand to cut me off from any further comment.

"Please Lucia, let me finish speaking. I insist." Her tone of voice hardens, and I acquiesce immediately to her demand. "I have seen the attraction in both of your eyes, and I know full well where your relationship will lead you." She stares at me with her sharpest gaze. "If you have not strayed there already?"

I remain as stone faced as possible, for I realize that my survival depends on my next reaction to her inquiry. An icy silence pervades the space around us. We each remain as still as the statues that stand stoically around the room. She finally relents and backs off.

"I will assume your innocence in this affair, but I cannot permit you to pursue it any further. You and Marcus are too intimately connected to the court, and I will not allow you to jeopardize that privilege in any way." Her expression softens. "I am not unsympathetic to your situation, Lucia. I know what it means to fall in love only to lose the relationship due to outer pressures. I've felt that heartbreak myself. There is no greater pain, no greater suffering than to have to surrender a true love to the cold necessity of our societal requirements. But I had no choice, and neither do you. I am so sorry my dear, but I must insist." She carefully considers my reaction to her words. "Do we understand each other, Lucia?"

I remain silent as I struggle with her ultimatum, yet I must finally give in to her will. "Yes, my lady, we have an understanding. I will no longer ask Decimus to serve as my escort. I will leave him be."

"Thank you. Your choice is difficult, but wise. I will write to Decimus and tactfully encourage him to do the same. Neither Vespasian nor Titus need be advised about this matter, and I can only assume that you will refrain from informing your husband about the whole affair."

"Marcus need not know any more than he does already," I reply.

"Very well then. Thank you for coming to see me on your own and know that I still consider you my friend and ally."

"Thank you, my lady. I am grateful for that." I bow to her and exit the palace as if in a trance. Adonia and I return to my domus. I retire to my chamber to be alone.

I am completely devastated. This morning, I was in love. This afternoon, I am bereft. The one man who has touched me deeply, who has caused my heart to sing, is now sailing away from me forever. I sit in front of my imperfect mirror and gaze at my sorrowful reflection. Unchecked tears stream down my cheeks. I can utter no sound to express my grief, for Adonia must not discover my great loss. I can only watch my face weep silently before me.

I sink into my own despair... Then suddenly I am violently and inexorably pulled downward into a rotating, swirling well of darkness. It is as if I am yanked from my stool and thrown into a vast whirlwind that thrashes and tugs at me from every direction. All sense of time and place vanish into a void and I am aware of an emptiness that surrounds and embraces me. Then, the very next instant, I am incarnate again and am staring out of the eyes of a young boy who is looking at his reflection in a bathroom mirror, and I don't like how I look at all.

PART FOUR

I inspect my chin closely, hoping my beard is finally coming in, but all I see is the usual fuzz. I'm disappointed. I'm in a hurry to grow up. One of my best friends, Jerry, is already sprouting a real beard and will be shaving with a razor soon. My beard isn't coming in as fast, even though we're both thirteen years old, and I don't think it's fair.

"David, your session with Angus is about to start," Bernice, my birth mother, alerts me from the kitchen. I glance at my crystal watch and see that it's already almost 10 a.m.

"Thanks, Bernice!" I shout as I exit the bathroom and head outside. I run across the grassy commons to the learning center. It is in one of the newer buildings and looks like it's made out of glass. It is a large, globe-shaped structure built with specially formulated building blocks that are composed of layers of glass compounds. These contain gasses and fibers that help heat or cool the building and supply energy for the appliances and communication devices that operate all day and night. It's really cool. Jerry told me how it works. He's really into that kind of stuff.

I enter a large room with a sloping blue ceiling that looks like a sunlit sky even when it's really cloudy outside.

Jerry and Erin, our other best friend who rounds out our trio, are already reclining in the big comfortable chairs specially designed to allow for extrasensory perception. We call them "space chairs" because we can travel forward and backward in time. Wave frequency nodes are installed in the cushions that surround the body on all sides. These nodes are responsive to mental commands and can be programmed by the instructor without the need for manual control. I quickly settle into an empty chair next to Jerry. Angus, our instructor, smiles warmly at the three of us.

"Well kids, today we are going backward in time. I want you to see how the Before Times came and went over the last few hundred years. It's time for you, young ones, to view a little history of how and why we progressed to our current state of affairs." He pauses, looking at each of us in turn. "We almost didn't make it."

Angus is tall and lean with thick white hair that always needs brushing. He has a red, slightly wrinkled face that doesn't look all that old, even though he just celebrated his 120th birthday. He is totally healthy, mentally sharp, and wise like an old owl. He stands to our side; he likes to pace around the room as he lectures to us.

"You all know the routine," he says. "Lay back, close your eyes, and simply allow the images to appear. Here we go."

I close my eyes and relax. I can feel the chair tingling with energy. Before long, colorful moving pictures sprout in my imagination, clear as the day outside. It's like I'm dreaming while I'm still awake. I'm flying over a small city where wooden houses line the streets. There are lots of tall sailing ships anchored offshore next to vessels with smoke stacks belching long plumes of smoke into the air. Many more ships are tied up to a row of piers and are being unloaded by a slew of workers. Long black wires attach to wooden poles and drape everywhere. These wires connect to many of the buildings that sit alongside the hilly roads and alleyways. There's something really messy looking about the wires, like they were thrown up after the fact. Meanwhile, small farms surround the town, and beyond them large ranches stretch away in the distance.

"What you are seeing is a town as it existed a few hundred years ago called San Francisco. These images show what it looked like fifty years after it was founded. Notice all the ships unloading their cargo on the docks? Their wares include food, clothing, building materials, and beverages of all kinds. Already in just a half-century, this city has moved beyond a subsistent relationship with its environment and must depend on trade and commerce with other cities around the world. Notice all the ferries crossings the bay to connect the bustling town to other communities in the area. Since its inception, the town's population has doubled and then redoubled many times."

"What are all those wires for, Angus?" Erin asks.

"They carry electricity—a relatively recent invention at that time—to light up their homes and workplaces. They probably connect to an old oil—or coal-burning power plant outside of town. What you are witnessing is the burgeoning impact of what's called the Industrial Revolution. Do you see the few early-stage motor vehicles mixed in with the horse-drawn wagons and carriages? The age of the automobile is in its infancy. You can also see several steam or coal-powered ships in the harbor. They will eventually replace the sailing ships. Trains are the main form of cross-country land transportation."

I see rail lines running crisscrossing the town in all directions. All kinds of rail transportation carry people around the city.

"Notice the cable cars that climb up and down the steep hillsides of the city," Angus continues. "Large cables are installed beneath the streets and actually pull these quaint little cars up and down the avenues. It was a unique form of transportation and would help to define San Francisco as one of the great tourist cities of the world."

"What's a tourist?" Jerry asks.

"In the Before Times, people would travel about the world and visit other places for the fun of it. They called themselves tourists."

I'm struck by how crowded everything seems. The streets are teeming with people walking about or riding on horses or in wagons. Certain streets are even more crowded than others. I wonder what it would be like to walk in a crowd so thick that touching strangers becomes inevitable.

"One last thing I want you all to be aware of is how much farmland still surrounds this small city. We are about to jump ahead one hundred years. Please observe what happens to these open spaces. Okay, here we go."

The pictures of old San Francisco disappear for a moment and are replaced by new images of a much larger community. I recognize the bay, but it appears smaller than before, and there are hardly any ships at all. A few ferries steam about, and a handful of large cargo ships lay at anchor offshore. There are bunch of small sailboats all over the bay. Several impressive bridges connect opposing shorelines. Many moving vehicles crowd the roadways. I detect a few clumps of large buildings that group together on both sides of the bay and soar into the air.

I realize that most of the farmland has vanished. Instead, houses have sprouted everywhere and stretch away toward the horizon. The horses and wagons are also gone. There are still plenty of wires, but they appear less obvious and more organized. Huge roadways lead in every direction and are all swarming with motor vehicles, large and small. I am amazed at how populated the whole area is, even more so than before. Homes crowd each other everywhere just like the automobiles people drive. Only the ridge tops are left alone, and even some of those are filling up with homes and roadways.

Angus's voice slowly crowds out the silence that came with the newer images. "You are now experiencing this same city at the end of the second millennium, around three hundred and fifty years ago. Please note how much growth has occurred in the century that followed on the heels of your first view of old San Francisco. Back then the town barely exceeded 300,000 citizens. These newer images show a city that has more than doubled in size. When you add the additional increase that has taken place in all the surrounding communities, you now have millions of residents living where only thousands had lived before.

"By the year 2000, this surge in population had occurred all over the earth, on every continent and in every nation. Most forms of subsistent living and producing for one's own personal needs had given way to a global industrial production of food, clothing, transportation, and energy by huge corporations, requiring the subsequent need for marketing on a truly massive scale. As a consequence, almost everyone purchased these necessities with money or currency. Most people were required to labor in occupations not always best suited to their talents in order to acquire the wages necessary to sustain themselves and their families."

Suddenly, I see people working next to each other assembling motor vehicles. I see more people producing funny looking shoes with lots of rubber on the soles. I see huge rooms filled with people sitting at individual tables and staring at glowing screens, talking to no one. I witness lines of workers toiling in a huge field, extracting cauliflower heads and placing them in plastic tubs. In each scene, I observe the same thing. Nobody looks happy. Everyone appears lonely and unconnected.

"You're right, David," Angus says, startling me out of my reverie. I'm always taken aback when Angus reads my unspoken thoughts, though he's not alone when it comes to reading other people's minds. Many of our residents have advanced intuitive abilities because they meditate a lot and have spiritual practices. Angus is one of the most advanced souls in the community, and the most loved. "Survival needs outweighed joy and happiness back in the Before Times. Most people were slaves to their jobs; the acquisition of money was their driving force. They no longer mentored occupations for their children, but instead sent them out to institutions to be trained by strangers. Not only were people disconnected from their families and the earth they lived upon, but their spiritual needs were largely ignored, too. Unfortunately, the human race had completely lost touch with nature and spirit and ended up paying a severe price for it. But that's another story, which we will explore in our next session." The images suddenly vanish, and I find myself staring at the blue ceiling overhead. "Now, you young ones go on out and tend to your chores. It's too nice a day to be sitting inside."

"Yes, sir," we eagerly reply as we spring out of our chairs and head for the door. An hour has passed by in the learning center, but it feels like a whole lot more than that. I am intrigued by the images of how life looked in the Before Times. So many people lived on top of each other. I can't believe how crowded together they were and how little they cared about each other. Nobody looked happy, and it seemed obvious they didn't get along so well back then. Nowadays everything is shared everywhere, nothing is wasted, and every community is self-sufficient and trades freely with other communities both close by and far away. Peace is a basic right. I've heard about wars, but they no longer exist on this planet. There were a lot of wars during the Before Times which were one of the causes that led to the Bad Times. Lot's of people blew themselves up, I guess. Lots of people starved in the Bad Times, too.

"Hey David, I just heard this morning that tiger tracks were spotted out in the Wild Lands," Erin tells me as we head for Old Town. Jerry has already gone in the opposite direction to the lab where he works.

"No way," I answer. "Who says?"

"Max was out collecting herbs this morning and came across a mostly eaten deer. He took a look around and said he'd never seen such large cat tracks before. He thinks they belong to a big male tiger." Erin is crazy about animals and always has been. She studies veterinary medicine and works down in Old Town where all the farm animals are kept.

"Wow, that's cool," I reply. "Have we ever had a tiger pass through here?"

"Not according to Max," Erin says. "He thinks they may be expanding their territory."

According to Angus, tigers of all stripes came close to extinction in the Before Times, but when the global civilization came apart at the seams, many zoological parks turned their animals loose rather than let them starve to death. As a result, our wilderness now contains animals that originally came from other continents. The Wild Lands are home to lots of exotic species like elephants, tigers, lions, zebras, and much more. Since we have so much forest where we are, we attract animals that prefer that type of environment. Lions and zebras prefer the open grasslands and have ended up far to the east where the plains open up to the horizon. Tigers like the forest. So do leopards and jaguars. None of them are common, according to Erin, but every now and then reports of these big cats reach our compound. This is the first tiger to come our way though.

The path we follow forks into two. The left-hand trail heads toward Old Town, while the other path winds down to the Garden Patch where we grow a lot of our food. "I'll see you at lunch," Erin says. "I've got something I want to talk about with you and Jerry."

"Okay, see you in an hour." I have a hunch what it is she wants to talk about. I bet it has to do with that big cat. I suddenly feel a clutching sensation in my stomach and know that I am scared of that tiger. I sense it deep down in the pit of my memories. I search for the source of this and recall an early nightmare of mine. I was attacked by a male lion and woke up screaming under my pillow. It was just a dream, but even so, that big cat scared the hell out of me. I shake off the memory and take the right-fork trail down to the gardens. It's time to go to work.

When I get there, my supervisors Mark and Betty are busy picking lettuce and other vegetables for today's lunch. I join in and help them harvest. All our food is grown on the compound. Over 250 people live in our community, so food is a big deal. There are two different growing areas and four separate neighborhoods in the Park Lands, which is what we call our settlement. It's like four towns all living next door. Jerry, Erin, and I live in North Park, although Jerry walks over to West Park to work and study at the lab. East Park has more residences and a large manufacturing facility where we make the glasslike blocks used for new construction. South Park has still more residences and another growing area with more orchids for our fruit production. There's also a big section over there that's left wild with nice hiking trails for those who don't want to venture off the compound into the Wild Lands.

Erin and I pretty much stay in our neighborhood. We like the older stuff like fields and barns. Each section has a separate community center, but people cross over to work and party. The Park Lands cover around 400 acres of land. That includes all the living areas, communal areas, greenhouses, farmland, factories, and public parks. There is plenty of room to get around, enough food to eat, lots of stuff to make and trade, and everybody gets along. And though we are completely surrounded by the Wild Lands, the entire compound is enclosed by a twenty-foot high-energy fence to keep us safe. There are lots of wild animals out there—and after the Bad Times, there were bad people, too. That was a long time ago though, and now some of us like to venture out to harvest and collect nature's goodies, or even just to explore. Lots of people hike out in the wilderness too, but they always take a stun gun to ensure their personal safety. The stun gun doesn't kill, but it sure can discourage any-sized creature from getting too close. You have to be fourteen years old to go out on your own, which means that Jerry, Erin, and I have to be escorted out there for another year, which really stinks.

Before long, Mark, Betty, and I fill four good-sized tubs with a hefty amount of vegetables and greens. We load them onto the bed of our hydrogen-motored pickup truck. I get to deliver the cargo to the four community centers because my supervisors let me drive the thing. There are several motorized vehicles on the compound for hauling stuff around, but most people walk everywhere. There's also a single-track rail system that passes through the Park Lands and each of our four neighborhoods and connects us all to a huge collection of smaller and bigger communities everywhere else in the world. The rails go everywhere by land, and large transport vessels connect the different continents by sea. There's plenty of wilderness to surround it all. Nature rules here, and we coexist.

The freight train is really neat. It runs on autopilot and is fully automated. It looks like a big black box with a window in the front and has a programmable computer inside to navigate it about. Every community helps maintain the system, and it's constantly coming and going. There are a lot of look-alike trains running around. Apparently, the rail system links communities world round. The Park Lands specialize in a few products to trade. The glasslike building blocks are a big hit, and we make antique furniture, which trades well too. We trade with other villages for all sorts of stuff that we don't make ourselves. It's even-steven, as Mike, my birth dad, used to say. The tracks were laid about twenty years ago. Every community helped to build the entire network.

Mike's gone now. He just disappeared. He was out in the Wild Lands collecting plants and never came home. Search parties couldn't find him either. Just gone. I was six when it happened. I still miss him sometimes. I remember him being a lot of fun. But to be honest, I have several dads around to help me out. In this community, everyone shares in the parenting. No one gets married anymore and not everyone has kids, either. It's kind of a group decision. A lot of parents don't even live together, and kids get to choose which one or both to live with. Some kids stay with people who aren't their birth parents. It's not unusual. Like I said, everyone helps out.

I arrive at the community kitchen door and unload one of the tubs. I carry it to Bernice, who is working the lunch shift today.

"How was your session with Angus?" she asks.

"It was great. We got to see images of old San Francisco. Wow, there were a lot of people in the Before Times, weren't there?"

"Yes, there were," she replies. "Everything was way out of balance back then. I'm sure Angus mentioned that to you?"

"He did. He's gonna show us what happens to San Francisco tomorrow. I can't wait."

"Well, it isn't pretty, David, but it was necessary to pave the way for a more essential relationship with everything around us." She looks at me and smiles. "But enough said. Angus will explain it all much better than I can."

"Okay. I have to make the rest of my deliveries. See ya later."

"Drive carefully," Bernice advises me. I ignore her and climb back into the truck cab. I never go faster than Mark and Betty showed me. I'm not about to risk my driving privileges by behaving recklessly. I'm just not that stupid.

A little while later after I've made all my deliveries, I meet up with Jerry and Erin in the dining hall for lunch. My two buddies couldn't look more different. Jerry is the tallest of us, has blue eyes and blond hair, and always wears a smile on his face. He looks friendly enough, but he's not afraid of anything—or anybody, either. He's also a real techie, spends a lot of time in the lab and is really into the new glass building technology that is catching on all over the place. He loves all sorts of gadgets and is crazy about communication tech too. Erin is shorter than me, but still tall for a girl. She's got mixed blood, which is more common than pure nowadays and accounts for her darker hair and skin. Alice, her mom, is part black and has some Jewish ancestry as well. Erin's got dark brown eyes and seems a lot more serious than Jerry. She loves archery, animals, and music. She wants to be a vet someday. Even though she is the smallest of us, she makes up for it by being more of a leader than Jerry and me. I guess I could safely say she's a real Tom Boy. There's something tough about her that makes you want to go along with what she has to say. All three of us have been best friends for as long as we can remember.

We devour our soup and salads like we're starving to death then grab a few cookies and head outside. We have some time to kill before our afternoon training sessions. We decide to hang out under a huge bay tree. The summer sun is really starting to crank up the heat.

"Listen up, you guys. I have a plan I want to share with you," Erin informs us, sounding like some kind of general or big shot.

"Yeah and I bet it has to do with that tiger that's out there somewhere," I snap back, pointing toward the Wild Lands which pretty much surround us on all sides.

"Actually, it does." Erin smiles broadly. "I want us to sneak out and see if we can track him down. I want to snap a few pictures of him if I can."

"Sounds like fun to me," Jerry excitedly responds. "You're gonna use that 3D image maker your birth dad gave you?" Jerry is very envious of that camera and wishes he had one too.

"Yep, I thought it would look great to have a real tiger hanging out in my room with me." Her camera produces a 3D image that can actually move around. It really is pretty cool.

"How are we going to get out of the compound to even track that thing?" I ask. I'm less excited about Erin's plan than Jerry is. "We're not allowed out there without an adult, and you know it too. Are we going to ask Max to help us?" Max often leads outings into the Wild Lands. He knows the surrounding wilderness better than anyone.

"Hell no," Erin exclaims. "We're gonna sneak out like I said, tomorrow afternoon after lunch. We have a free afternoon and we'll have a few hours to mess around with. I've got it all worked out." She looks over at Jerry. "You've gotta figure out how we can get through the energy fence, okay?"

Jerry grins at her. "No problem. I'll steal a gate-opener out of the lab. I know where they're stowed. I'll scope it out later today and grab one tomorrow right before we leave."

"Great," Erin replies. "Can you get a stun gun too?"

"Sure. They store them in the same place. We can't go outside the gate without one."

"Nope, we can't. Okay then, are we all in or not?" Erin asks, looking directly at me.

"You bet," I answer.

"Good. Between now and tomorrow I'm gonna talk with Max and see if I can find out where he spotted the tiger's tracks, so we have a better chance of finding it." She looks at us and adds, "Nobody else hears about this, okay? It's our secret." Jerry and I nod our heads in agreement. We all shake hands to seal it and then head off to our various training sessions.

Once again, Jerry goes west to the lab in West Park. Erin and I walk down the trail to Old Town, her to tend to the livestock and study medicine at the animal clinic next to the old barn, and me to work in the furniture factory where I am learning the art of woodworking. I like using my hands to make things, and our shop can build just about anything we want out of wood.

The Park Lands actually began in Old Town about 150 years ago. The fields down there have been growing food for a long time. The soil is rich in nutrients. We use plenty of animal manure and table leftovers to keep it that way.

All of the wooden buildings down in Old Town are well preserved. Big porches surround the original homes and every apartment opens out to some kind of porch upstairs or down. Erin lives in one of them with her birth mom, Alice, and Rick, Alice's companion. Rick works in the furniture factory and is one of the foremen who run the whole operation. He's taught me a lot about the craft.

Jerry and I live up the hill in the new section of town. The structures up there have more glass and stone in them. They also feature heating and lighting systems that have been innovated over the last hundred years.

I head to the furniture factory and spend a few hours working a lathe and making table legs. The lathe has been preset by Rick, so I am basically reproducing the same table leg over and over again, but I still have to concentrate, or I could screw one up, which would be wasteful. After that, I go over to the Garden Patch and harvest more produce with Mark, Betty, and some other volunteers. Like I said, food is important. I like working with stuff that can make you feel good, and organic vegetables and fruits are good for you. That's what my mom says, anyway, and I believe her. Besides, I like growing and harvesting plants, and I love having so many tasks to do. It makes me feel like I'm a contributing member of the community, even if I am only thirteen. We grow up fast in the Park Lands.

When I'm done picking vegetables, I go home and shower. During dinner, I see Erin sitting next to Max. They're talking to each other, and I realize she's probably getting more information about that tiger's location without giving away our secret plan. My stomach starts clutching again, and I'm disappointed with myself for being such a scaredy-cat about that big predator. Once again, I try to shake it off. That night I sleep okay. I'm usually pretty pooped by the time I go to bed.

***

I wake up early the following morning and go to Chapel as usual to sit quietly and feel gratitude to the Source of all that is. Then I have a small breakfast with Bernice in our kitchen before it's time to put on my gardening hat and go out to do my landscaping chores around our building and the residence hall next door. I have a shack, more like a closet really, where my gardening tools are stored. I pull some weeds, deadhead some flower gardens, rake up the mess, and haul it to a compost pile nearby. After that, I wash up and get ready for my session with Angus at the Learning Center.

Today, I get there before anyone else. I select a space chair and wait a couple of minutes for the others to arrive. Angus shows up next. For some reason, he seems older all of a sudden. He walks slower and is more bent over. Maybe he's been like that all along and I didn't notice it before, but today I sense something frail about him, and it worries me. Angus is like everybody's grandpa. If he goes, the Park Lands lose our oldest and most popular resident, at least to my way of thinking. He bends over and coughs up a storm. Maybe he's coming down with something.

"You feeling okay, Angus?" I ask, sounding as worried as I feel.

"Oh yeah, I just picked up a little something since yesterday's session. I'll be fine."

Erin and Jerry enter the room and select their space chairs. Angus slowly clears his throat and gazes out in our direction.

"All right, yesterday I showed you images of how San Francisco appeared around the year 1890 and then again around 2000. We saw how the city prospered during that time. Today, I'm going to jump ahead another hundred years, and you will see what befell the cities of the Before Times during that span of time, using San Francisco as a typical example. Now, settle into your seats and relax, and we'll get this show on the road."

I close my eyes and calm my breathing. Before long, I'm flying over San Francisco again. I sense that something's different. The city itself seems smaller. I notice that the bay has eaten up some shoreline and that the city has been forced to build a bunch of seawalls to keep its low-lying sections from being flooded. I spot some neighborhoods that have already been abandoned to the rising waters, which is why the city seemed smaller at first glance. I also see that some other parts of the city are damaged with buildings toppled over and streets all torn up and impassable. There are fewer cars and less people about.

"As you can see," Angus says, "San Francisco has not prospered over the hundred years that followed the passing of the millennium. Several factors contributed to the problems that plagued this city and all other cities around the world in that time."

Angus stops and coughs up another storm. After he manages to clear his throat, he continues. "Now, the rising waters are due to changes in climate. All those motor vehicles that you saw one hundred years ago, along with a heavy reliance on coal-burning power plants, helped to create a phenomenon known as global warming. All these carbon-based technologies emitted too much carbon dioxide into the atmosphere and created a greenhouse effect that literally warmed up the planet's overall temperature. This subsequently led to the melting of the polar ice caps, which in turn engendered all the oceans to rise. The warming temperatures also led to an increase in destructive hurricanes and tornadoes. The massive deforestation that occurred all over the planet at that time also contributed to an increase in the magnitude of destructive windstorms. The damage to San Francisco that you are observing was caused both by the rising of the seas and a great earthquake, which disrupted the entire area." Angus grabs a glass of water and takes a sip before going on. "What you see here are the poorer neighborhoods that have not yet been rebuilt. At the same time, severe food shortages and a drastic decrease in drinkable water are beginning to have a negative impact on cities everywhere. A dependence on petroleum-based chemicals and a factory-style management of animal and food production have poisoned the underground aquifers and severely decreased the amount of serviceable water worldwide. Without water, people couldn't grow produce, and unfortunately most of the chemical-based food had already lost much of its nutritional value, creating lower birth rates and higher exposure to all sorts of sicknesses that began to pop up everywhere." He pauses to emphasize his next point. "You may have noticed that there are less people around. When nature is abused, all kinds of unpleasant consequences will occur—and did occur during the latter part of the twenty-first and beginning of the twenty-second centuries. Let's jump ahead another fifty years and see how well San Francisco is doing." He almost sounds like he can't wait to get there himself.

The pictures of San Francisco vanish and then reappear. There is a big decline in almost every aspect of the city by the bay. I see far less people. Large areas are totally abandoned and in ruins. The same is true for the highways that have collapsed in places, making them useless. I also witness areas where residents have banded together to create walled-in communities. I see narrow pathways or roads that connect these smaller communities together. I see that one of these communities is nestled close to the bay, and that a pier is still in use where a ship is tied up and being loaded with trade goods. The separate communities all have large fenced-in gardens and seem to contain different types of businesses attached to their complexes. I also notice satellite dishes and radio towers in each of these communities, which could indicate that they are connected to each other by some kind of communication network. Large areas of devastation and ruin surround these small islands of survival. The farther from San

Francisco I look, the farther away these communities are from each other, but I sense they continue on in every direction. Big cities are clearly dying off, and small communities are on the rise. A huge drop in population must be happening all over the place.

"Once again you are intuiting correctly, David," Angus says, again reading my thoughts. "By 2150, a major shift has occurred on the planet, and the global civilization of the Before Times has gradually ground itself down to almost nothing."

"What happened to all those people, Angus?" Erin asks.

"Most of them died off. Starvation, armed conflict, a few nuclear events, and a rash of natural disasters all led to a sudden and drastic reduction in the human population. Water shortages due to industrial contamination along with a series of prolonged droughts in key farming areas negatively impacted food production and, since most of the people had lost touch with the land and instead depended on commercially produced foods, they had nothing solid to fall back on when the whole system collapsed. Those who foresaw the coming Bad Times were better prepared. They began building separate communities off the governmental and corporate grids and developed a self-sustaining relationship with the earth. They accepted that the planet was a living entity in her own right, that spirit surrounded and imbued everything that is and that a balanced and independent relationship must be forged with the environment if they were to survive and flourish into the future." Angus erupts into still another round of coughing, which seems to go on forever.

"Are you sure you're okay, Angus?" I ask when he finally stops hacking into a white handkerchief, which he quickly stuffs back into his pants pocket.

"Sure, sure, I'm fine, boy. Just caught a little something. It'll pass."

"Angus, there must have been lots of killing during the Bad Times. How many people escaped alive?" Jerry asks, apparently not as worried about the old man as I am.

"Thankfully, some made it with good preparation and luck. Unfortunately, roving bands of outlaws desperate for food and water destroyed many small independent communities. But others managed to defend themselves or were just plain lucky and were left alone. There were visionaries on every continent, and some community compounds were already pretty well established by the time the situation really came unglued. They knew what was coming and were well prepared for the worst-case scenario. Also, plenty of additional communities were established during this difficult period as certain groups assumed personal responsibility and took matters into their own hands. The Bad Times lasted for many years, but eventually wore itself out. After that, it was rebuilding time. In the end, enough people were around to keep the race alive, and not only that, but to hold on to much of the scientific gains that had been achieved during heyday of the Before Times. We now prosper in the Park Lands because our ancestors had a share in this vision of a balanced and respectful way of life. Today, we continue to manage our population and birth rates. As we have seen, too many people lead to too many problems."

"How many people died during the Bad Times, Angus?" Erin asks.

"Well, let's just say a huge majority of the world's population did not make it. Over ninety percent perished."

A hush surrounds us as we try to realize how big a loss of life that really was.

"For centuries upon centuries," Angus continues, "mankind expanded itself without proper regard for its environment. A ruthless consumption of natural resources combined with a rising disregard for the sacredness of any and all forms of life paved the way for human civilization's rapid decline. And it wasn't the first time. Many such civilizations have come and gone on this planet. Luckily for us, enough of our species managed to correct our mistakes and retool our thinking so that today we can develop and actualize our inherent capabilities." He stops talking and sits in his chair. He gazes at us with a calm expression. "It's really kind of simple when you boil it down. We need to respect and honor Mother Nature and the Source of All That Is at the same time." He smiles at the three of us. "We must live in harmony with the natural world and give thanks to the spiritual reality that encompasses everything." A short silence surrounds the four of us as his words sink in.

"Okay, that's it for now," Angus says. "Oh, and by the way, San Francisco has survived the Bad Times as a few large communities, all independent and self-sufficient, one of which serves as a transportation port for our trade goods that are shipped overseas." He smiles again. "Our goods have global appeal. Okay then, time for you three to go out and tend to your chores. Tomorrow I'm going to take you back to ancient Rome and show you how their civilization leaned heavily on the backs of those they conquered. Have a great afternoon."

The three of us explode out of our chairs and run outside.

"I'll see you guys at lunch," Jerry yells as he heads over to the lab. Erin and I walk down to Old Town to tend to our chores.

"I'm worried about Angus," I comment to Erin. "He doesn't sound so good."

"I know. I don't remember him ever coughing like that before."

"He said he caught something. He sure looks old all of a sudden. I hope he gets rid of it soon."

"Me too," Erin agrees. "He's the best teacher I've ever had. He's always seemed so invincible and alive, especially for his age."

"Yeah, I know," I respond. "I hope he heals up soon." We say goodbye and separate as usual to tend to our different jobs.

Later at lunch, we select a table off to the side of the dining room so we can conspire together out of earshot of our elders.

"Did you get what we need from the lab, Jerry?" Erin asks.

"All set. Everything was right where I thought it would be. I grabbed what we needed and hid it all in my room. We're good to go."

"Great," Erin replies. "I talked to Max at breakfast and found out that he spotted the tiger tracks south of here in the Big Meadow. So, get what you need from home right after lunch and meet me on the far side of South Park near Spruce Grove. We'll go through the fence there, okay?"

"Okay," Jerry and I both agree.

All three of us have been out in the Wild Lands plenty of times, but always with someone to supervise us. We know the territory that surrounds the compound and we've explored the wilderness for a few miles in every direction. But this will be the first time we sneak out on our own. Instead of excited, I feel uneasy. It's dangerous out there. It isn't called the Wild Lands for nothing; there are lots of wild animals just as dangerous as what we're seeking. That's why we need the stun gun. It'll stop anything in its tracks—not kill it, but definitely keep it from coming any closer. That will be Jerry's job: to protect us from the wild things.

It's not like us to break the rules like this. Keeping your word is a big deal in this community. But with the tiger wandering so near to us, and with Erin wanting to us to sneak out on our own and with Jerry agreeing with her, what else can I do but go along? After all, they are my best friends and I don't want to look like a scaredy-cat in front of them. So, when I finish eating lunch I go back to my room and collect my knife, put on my hiking boots, and apply some sunscreen. Then I grab my water bottle and backpack and make my way to Spruce Grove.

I take a series of trails and shortcuts to get there. I pass a playing field in the center of the compound where I see a few kids kicking a soccer ball around. Since our community is so small, I know everyone who lives here. I wave to some casual friends but head on toward South Park. I pass the orchids on my right and cut through a section of designated parkland before arriving at Spruce Grove. It was planted a couple of generations ago, and all the different kinds of spruce trees have grown pretty big by now. I pass under the dark canopy of branches and aim for the fence line that borders the southern end of our community. I spot Erin hanging out next to the fence. I sit down next to her.

"I got a water bottle for us," I tell her.

"Good thinking," she answers. "It's really starting to heat up. I brought one too." Our compound is located in what used to be central Oregon in the Before Times. What Max calls "evergreen land" surrounds us. The Cascade Mountains lay to our east. The trees are a mix of fir, cedar, pine, and hemlock with some leaf-bearing trees and bushes underneath like alders, maples, elders, oak, and willows. There is a network of meadows, streams, occasional ponds, and some marshland, but tall evergreens pretty much dominate the surroundings. It's early summer, and it's starting to heat up all right.

"Here comes Jerry," Erin points out. I look left and see Jerry approaching through the spruce. Like both of us, he's carrying a backpack. We stand to greet him.

"Looks like it's all clear," Jerry announces as he joins us. "I didn't see anybody else around here."

"Good, let's use that gate-opener you've got and go find that tiger," Erin says. I can feel her excitement and see Jerry's by looking at his sparkling eyes. I wish I felt as eager as they do. Though I've tried to shake the nightmare, I'm still uneasy about the whole scheme.

Jerry yanks off his pack and reaches in. He pulls out a slick-looking gadget with a bunch of buttons and a small computer screen above them. He presses one of the buttons to turn the thing on then walks to the nearest fencepost. The energy fence is pretty weird looking. It's all fence posts with no wires or fencing between them— at least none that you can see with your eyes. Instead, high frequency energy waves are transmitted from post to post, which will shock the hell out of anything or anyone who tries to pass through it. And I do mean shock. The harder you push it, the more intense it gets. Every kid in the compound, including me, has touched it just to check it out. Once was enough.

Jerry inspects the post carefully and finds a number on it. He punches it into the gate opener then puts in a command code that programs the opener to work. A crackling noise, kind of like fire, erupts and then dies; a high-pitched buzzing sound comes and goes really quick too, and at the same moment that section of fence shuts down like it doesn't exist anymore. We cross over to the other side and Jerry reverses everything and puts the fence back up again.

"We'll take the southern trail out to the Big Meadow," Erin says, "but if anybody comes along, we have to hustle off the trail and get out of sight."

"Good idea," Jerry agrees. He replaces the opener into his pack and pulls out the stun gun. He snaps something and it turns on. I hear a faint droning noise coming from it. "I'll take the rear position."

"I'll go first," Erin announces. That leaves me in the middle. We follow along the fence line heading west for a short while then cut into the woods to intersect the southern trail before it reaches the South Park Gate. When we get there, we case out the trail. Everything looks clear, so we hop on it and trot south toward the Big Meadow.

Tall fir trees surround us on all sides. Shafts of sunlight filter through the branches giving us some light to see by, but not a lot. It's dark and smells dank inside the forest. I hear birds chirping at us, but I can't see any unless I stop to look for them. Erin sets a good pace while keeping a sharp eye out for any oncoming traffic. This foot trail will eventually wind up at Coopersville, another small community that lies about fifty miles south of us. It's rare for someone to actually trek all the way from one community to another, but it can happen. Since every community is self-sustaining, not a lot of visiting occurs between them. People usually stay in touch by using the communication technology that allows for two-way viewing. Some people who like to travel around will hitch a ride on the train where a few seats are available in the pilot room, but most folks are happy to stay put in their own community where everyone has ongoing responsibilities. We're pretty isolated where we are. There are some communities that are much larger than us, and they are located in areas where they are closer to each other. They're what remain of the large urban centers that existed during the Before Times. Those places probably have more direct interaction with each other.

Jerry once told me about a new technology that someday will move goods through molecular displacement, allowing for an instantaneous transportation of objects from one place to another. It's still in an experimental stage and may be years away from working, assuming it will work at all. If it does, he says maybe even people could dematerialize and re-materialize someplace else. It would really be something if that ever comes about.

We keep our ears open for any human voices or animal sounds, but everything is quiet. Every now and then we pass weird-looking structures of concrete that have been covered over with moss and plant life. They are the visible remains of the Before Times, mostly broken-down sections of old roadways that were abandoned centuries ago. Most of the homes and other types of buildings are either completely overgrown or have turned to dust. Nature is pretty relentless in reclaiming what's hers. Before long, the path climbs upward, and we come to a couple of small ridgelines that separate the valley of the Park Lands from the valley that we call the Big Meadow. It's actually a whole series of meadows that are linked together by a good-sized creek that eventually flows into a large river farther west. We switch back and forth as we climb up and down one ridge and then another before we finally descend toward the Big Meadow.

Suddenly we hear voices up ahead. Erin quickly turns off the path and we follow at her heels. We duck behind some large trees and peek out at the trail. My knees shake with excitement. A few seconds later, we see two people approaching. I recognize Max and another guy named Peter. They are carrying bags that hang from their shoulders. It looks like they were collecting herbs and are now returning to the compound. We let them get out of earshot before we dare to speak.

"Whew, that was close," Jerry says. "Thank God we heard them before they could see us."

"Must be our lucky day," Erin answers, smiling. "It's a good omen." We rejoin the trail and keep heading down the sloping pathway. I detect more daylight up ahead and know we are almost there. Moments later we walk out from under the forest canopy and into the bright sunlight of the open meadow. We scan the horizon and fail to see any other people, though we do spot a large herd of elk in the distance. Some tall mountains range to the East of us.

"We need to follow Ray's Creek to our right for about a mile, according to Max," Erin informs us. I look at my watch.

"It took us an hour to get here," I say. "It's almost two o'clock."

"Great, we have plenty of time to play with," Erin answers.

"Well, we have another hour," I reply, "if we plan to make it back in time for our chores."

"That ought to be enough if we get lucky. Tell me when it's three and we'll head back then."

"Okay." I pass around my water bottle and all three of us take a swig. It's warmer out in the open.

"Let's find us a tiger!" Erin says, taking the lead once again. I fall in behind her and Jerry follows with his stun gun out and ready for use. We leave the southern trail and use a small animal path that appears and disappears like it can't make up its mind if it really wants to be a trail at all. The ground's soft underfoot, and our boots are quickly covered with mud. It makes for harder walking, but we keep moving steadily ahead. We slow down as Erin begins to focus on the ground next to the creek, looking for tiger tracks and the deer carcass. Jerry and I do the same. There are big clumps of willow and alders growing along the bank that separate us from the creek except for an occasional clearing where the trail runs next to the flowing water. Because it's early June, the creek is swollen with the spring runoff from the Cascades, which we can see in the distance.

Just as we walk by another large willow, a deep growl catches us off-guard. My heart leaps into my throat at the terrible sound. I turn to see a huge grizzly bear standing no more than fifteen feet away. Since we are upwind of the creature, it is as surprised to see us as we are to see it. It looks like it's at least ten feet tall. Unfortunately, its surprise quickly turns to anger, and it roars at us exposing a healthy set of fangs. Its claws are the same size as my gardening shears. Panic grabs my heart and steals away my breath. I freeze up like concrete. I want to run like hell, but I can't; my legs have turned into stone slabs. Luckily for me, Jerry keeps his cool and uses the stun gun. I can't see him fire it because he is behind me, but I hear it go off. It sounds like an electric razor. At the same time, the bear's snarling changes into a groan like it's been kicked in the gut. The force of the gun's discharge knocks the huge predator back a few paces, causing it to tumble sideways into the creek. It splashes around for a few hectic moments trying to right itself then charges across the creek and up the opposite bank. I can't believe how fast it moves. It hustles behind the thick bushes that crowd that side of the creek. I can hear it crashing through the underbrush after it disappears from view.

"Wow, this gun really works!" Jerry shouts, filled with adrenaline. "He's not going to bother us again. I had it turned all the way up. God, he was big, wasn't he?"

"He sure was," Erin agrees, gathering her wits. "Nice job, Jerry. Way to stay on top of it. That was close, huh?"

"No shit," Jerry answers. "I didn't have time to think. I just aimed and pulled the trigger. It really vibrated when it went off."

"David, you okay?" Erin asks me.

I try to find my voice. "Yeah, I think so. Man, that thing scared the shit out of me. I couldn't run even if I wanted to."

"Well, good thing we didn't have to thanks to Jerry," Erin replies. "If we had ran, that grizzly would have caught up to us in a few seconds. They can really haul ass when they want to." She pauses to cast one more glance at the opposite bank where the bear just disappeared. "I agree with you Jerry, he'll probably leave us alone. But you better keep your eye on our rear in case he changes his mind." Erin looks at me. "You and I can focus on the trail. You take the right side and I'll take the left, and let's see who can spot the tiger tracks first. Look for a deer carcass too, it will be easier to find because of the smell."

"Okay," I answer, more than happy to put some distance between us and that grizzly, even if it means we may soon bump into a real live tiger.

The three of us continue to follow along the north bank of Ray's Creek. I carefully study the ground to my right, both hoping and dreading to see tiger tracks. I start to feel like I'm wasting my time or that maybe I missed them already, but then I spot a dead animal partially hidden under an elderberry bush.

"Erin, there's something under that bush," I announce, pointing to my right. She sees it too, and I can tell she's disappointed that I saw it first. We pull it out. It's the carcass of a black-tailed deer. It looks like a full-grown doe—or what's left of one, which isn't much. It feels strange to see how dead and gone it really is. Life's a lot tougher out here in the Wild Lands. We snoop around and discover a set of large animal tracks in the soft dirt, leading away from the bush. We follow them as they head east along the creek. They are easy to follow because the tiger's pads leave deep marks, and they are clearly the prints of a large cat, having four smaller pads in front and one big pad behind them.

After a short while, the beast's tracks veer off the trail to roam through the tall muddy marsh grasses, apparently headed for the forest that surrounds the meadow on all sides. Sure enough, its tracks lead straight into the trees. When we enter the woods, our task becomes more challenging. The forest floor is covered with thick undergrowth, smaller fir trees, maples, alders, and all sorts of bushes and shrubs. Ferns and moss cover everything, adding a bright green coating to the shaded darkness of the forest floor. Unfortunately, there is plenty of poison oak around too. I pull off my pack and pull out some balm I always carry with me made from boiled down acorns. I spread it on my exposed skin and have my buddies do the same. It really helps to keep the itching down. Plenty of fallen trees lay about slowing our progress from time to time. It's much harder to follow the trail. We even lose track of him a few times and have to hunt around in a circle in order to pick him up again. Eventually, the tracks lead down into a steep gully with a small stream running through it.

"Hey, look at this guys! The cat took a drink right here. See how its tracks tripled up?" Erin points to a spot along the bank where the tiger's prints seem bunched together. "Then he headed down stream," she adds, pointing south. "Come on."

I look at my watch. "It's 2:45, Erin. We'll have to turn back soon."

"Shit, it took too much time tracking him through the woods. Well, let's hope we get lucky," she replies and takes off. Jerry and I follow close behind. After about ten minutes, the tiger's trail strays away from the stream and climbs up a steep forested slope. When we reach the top of the hill, we notice a rocky ravine down below. We also see a cave-like opening in the rocks. The tiger's trail leads in that direction. We follow it to the opening of the cave.

"His tracks lead in and out of the cave in several places," Jerry comments.

"The tiger may be using this place as a home, or at least as a temporary hang out," Erin observes.

I look at my watch again. "It's 3:05, we have to head back to the compound, or we'll be late for our chores."

"Not before we check out this cave," Erin insists. She pulls a flashlight out of her pack and looks at Jerry. "You ready?"

Jerry pats his stun gun. "Hell yes, I'm ready."

I envy them their courage. They enter the cave, side by side. I follow behind. I feel my heart beating faster, like it's in some kind of hurry. The cave is only about twenty feet deep. Erin's light covers the area and comes up empty. No tiger. I feel my heart slowing down immediately. There's a close, musky scent inside, which smells like rotting mushrooms. There are a few bones lying in one corner.

"He's not here," Jerry says, "but he's definitely been here."

"He may be out hunting. Let's get out of here," Erin answers. I couldn't agree more. We leave the cave and retrace our steps to the Big Meadow. We hike back to the southern trail and hang a left and go north. Our pace is much faster going home. When we near the South Gate, we leave the trail and cut through the trees until we reach the same section of fence we used earlier. Jerry disconnects it and we enter the Park Lands, safe and sound but without the 3D photos that Erin hoped to get. Jerry reactivates the fence, and we hurry back to North Park. It's almost five o'clock.

When I finally arrive at the Garden Patch, I join up with Mark and Betty and a couple of other volunteers and help pull up some weeds that are infiltrating the rows of vegetables. I'm so relieved to have made it back without getting caught that it takes me a while to notice something's not right. The mood is too quiet, and everyone seems kind of down.

"Why is everyone so glum?" I ask Jane, a girl about my age who's into gardening like I am.

"You mean you haven't heard about Angus?" she answers.

"No, I've been down in the park hanging out with Jerry and Erin," I look up, starting to sense that something terrible has happened.

"He died this afternoon. I thought everyone knew by now."

"He died?" I answer. "But I just saw him this morning. He was coughing a lot, but said it was nothing to worry about."

"Well, he died in his sleep. They say he caught some kind of bug, and it killed him just like that." She shrugs her shoulders. "Maybe it was because he was so old."

I feel a huge hole open up inside me, like some part of my self has disappeared, never to return again. I've felt that same feeling before when Mike vanished into the Wild Lands. Now with Angus gone, just like that, I experience it again. He was so wise and comforting, so understanding and available. It will be hard to imagine life around here without him. I'm sure I'm not the only one who's missing him. Everyone loved him.

Death is such a rude awakening. Our community is so well maintained and well managed that people tend to live long lives. Accidents are rare and disease is discouraged by our healthy lifestyles. I sometimes forget that life doesn't go on forever. The dead deer reminded me earlier, and now with Angus' sudden passing, I realize once again that this world I exist in is truly temporary. Someday, I will die too.

At dinner I sit with Erin and Jerry as usual. "Too bad about Angus, isn't it?" I say as I settle into a chair across from them.

"He didn't look too good this morning, did he?" Jerry replies. "He sure was coughing a lot."

"Jane told me he died in his sleep while we were out and about. She thinks his old age caught up with him and killed him with a common cold."

"Weird, isn't it?" Erin says. "I mean because of how fast it happened. One day he's fit as a fiddle, and the next he drops dead with a cold."

"Well, he was 120 years old. I guess his number was finally up," Jerry figures. Leave it to him to think of death as a number.

"Yeah," I say, "but just yesterday he looked so happy. Who'd have thought he'd be dead within a day's time?"

That night, the whole community gathers in the central amphitheater to pay homage to the old history professor. I find out he was also a botanist, piano player, chaplain, and a woodworker like me. It seems he taught everybody something at some time during the last seventy or eighty years. Because the Park Lands are a spiritual community, people don't think that Angus is really dead and gone. He's simply shed his body and returned to the other side. Angus was about as good as they get. Never once did he say anything mean or nasty in front of me. He was definitely an old soul. Wherever he went this afternoon, I wish he would come back and visit me every now and again. I sure will miss him a whole lot.

***

The next morning, his body lies in state in the chapel, and probably everybody in the community drops by to pay Angus one last visit. Jerry, Erin, and I join the line after breakfast. We slowly parade by his body, which lies in a beautiful pine box that is filled with ice. Someone has dressed him up nicely in a purple shirt and a black pair of slacks. Since he is to be cremated later in the afternoon, they leave his body alone. The Park Lands stopped pickling bodies a long time ago. The amazing thing about his corpse is that it doesn't really look that dead. Yeah, maybe it is a little gray looking, but his expression is so calm and peaceful, I almost want to pinch his hand just to make sure he isn't sleeping. I see some tears sneaking out the corners of Erin's eyes. I'm not sure I'd ever seen her cry like that before. I feel a little guilty that I'm not crying too. I'm not at all surprised that Jerry's eyes are dry like mine.

Later in the afternoon, his body is burned in the crematorium behind the chapel. Black and gray smoke belches from a tall dark chimney and rises in a series of clouds toward the sky before breaking up and dissolving into nothing but thin air. As I watch the smoke burn itself out, I feel as though Angus is gone for good. I detect a lump in my throat and wonder if I'm coming down with the same cold that Angus had, but it goes away in a few minutes. I realize that I really wanted to cry too, and the lump came because I wouldn't.

After dinner, Jerry, Erin and I meet under a towering Douglas fir outside the dining hall to check in with each other. It's one of our favorite meeting places. All three of us haven't had a chance to talk about much because of all the activities regarding Angus's passing.

"I don't feel like leaving the Park Lands tomorrow," I admit. "I'm too upset about Angus to go after that tiger."

"Me too," Erin agrees, "Besides, some weather's heading our way according to my mom. We can't go out there anyway."

"Won't be the same without Angus, will it," Jerry comments. "He was one of a kind. I wonder where he is right now? Does he even still exist?" Jerry is the least spiritual of the three of us. He's more down to earth and into how things work in the everyday world.

"Well he's not in his body anymore, that's for sure," I offer.

"He probably adjusting to his new circumstances, whatever they are?" Erin says as she scratches an itch on the top of her shoulder. "I suppose he's operating at a higher vibration than we are, and I bet he's looking and feeling much younger than 120 years old."

"I bet he's not at all disoriented," I add, "he's so wise".

"He may not have to incarnate anymore. Unless he wants too," Erin observes. "My Mom's kind of a philosopher and she tells me we eventually work out our stuff and move on from Planer Earth School. If that's true, Angus could be graduating out of here."

"Well, I'm in no hurry to leave this place," Jerry states with conviction, "I like it too much. There's always something new to figure out."

"Well, wherever Angus is, I wish him well. And I hope I get to see him again, sometime, somewhere. I miss him."

"Me too, hey let's go to bed, I'm bushed," Erin says before she yawns like she means it. Jerry and I agree.

The next couple of days fly by like a hurricane. Well, maybe not a hurricane, but the day after Angus is cremated, a large wind and rainstorm slams the Park Lands with the full force of a real temper tantrum. Trees fall down everywhere. Part of a roof blows off one of the older residences down in Old Town. Luckily for Erin and her mom, it isn't their building. Some of the orchids are damaged along with all our beanpoles in the Garden Patch that we just installed a couple of weeks ago. The whole community grinds to a halt and everyone chips in to help clean up the mess. Big storms like this have been fewer and farther between over the last hundred years, but every once in a while, they happen. Even Mother Earth can have a bad day, I guess. I keep busy cleaning up a lot of fallen branches and hauling them to our waste area behind the Garden Patch. I help replace the broken beanpoles. Erin has fences to mend before rounding up escaped livestock all over Old Town. Meanwhile,

Jerry helps reconnect the energy fence where it's been damaged by falling trees. Several fence posts got taken out by the storm. Eventually, the whole mess is cleaned up.

One morning at breakfast, Erin announces to Jerry and me that tomorrow during our free afternoon she wants to trek over to the tiger's cave and see if she can get lucky and snap a few photos this time.

"Sure thing," Jerry replies. "I'll get the necessary gizmos tomorrow morning. Count me in."

"I'm in too." I say, following on Jerry's heels. "Same time and place as before?"

"Yep, one o'clock, behind Spruce Grove," Erin confirms.

That night, I have a dream where I'm standing in front of a big cave. I hear a deep growl coming out of it, and I feel my feet turning into cement. I wake up sweating. The next morning, I say nothing about it to my friends during breakfast. I don't want them to think I'm scared of that tiger. Besides, it's just a dream.

Our history session at the Learning Center is canceled due to Angus's passing. Bernice tells me they have to choose a willing replacement, and several people have already volunteered to take over the position, including Angus's oldest son, Henry. I head over to the Garden Patch to work. I spend the morning with Jane transferring starter-tomato plants from the greenhouse into the garden. We end up planting a couple of rows, putting them into the ground and tying each one to its own stake. I like Jane. She's a little older than me, but she's friendly and easy to talk with. She's my height and has light brown hair, blue eyes, and a bunch of freckles around her nose. She has a nice smile too. She's a hard worker, like I am. Until recently, I haven't been interested in girls romantically at all. Sure, Erin's a girl, but we've been best buddies for so long I never think of her as any different from Jerry or me. But when it comes to Jane, lately I've been noticing how pretty she is. She used to be real skinny, but all of a sudden, she's filled out and looks womanlier. I've seen Jerry stealing glances at her in the dining room too.

"How did you like the memorial service for Angus?" I ask as I dig a hole for the next tomato plant.

"I liked it," she answers. "I sure will miss him though. He was so kind and open. I loved his history classes more than anything. I wonder who'll replace him?"

"Probably Henry," I reply. "He's a history buff just like his dad was." Henry is in his nineties. He's in great shape like Angus was and is still very active in the community. Nobody really retires in the Park Lands. They are already doing what they want to, so why retire? "Angus just showed me and my friends what happened to San Francisco," I go on. "We saw it during the Before Times and then during the Bad Times too. It was really something to see how everything fell apart."

"I saw New York go through the same rise and fall," Jane says. "I couldn't believe how fast that city grew over the years and how big it got, and then how fast it fell apart too. By the end, the city was under so much water, the whole place was completely deserted. All these tall building rose out of the water like gravestones." She drops another plant into the hole I prepared, and I tamp the soil around it with the back of my shovel. We put in a stake and tamp it into the ground too, and then she ties the plant to it. We move on and I dig another hole. We have a good rhythm going and cover a second row before we hear the lunch bell.

We walk to the dining hall together, and I decide to sit next to her during the meal. She doesn't seem to mind. I see Erin and Jerry smiling at me from across the room. I ignore them and chat with Jane and some of her girlfriends. After lunch, I go to my room to collect my pack and water bottle. Bernice drops in to say hello.

"What are you up to this afternoon?" she asks when she notices that I'm getting all my stuff together.

"Jerry, Erin, and I are going to fool around over in the park," I reply, lying through my teeth.

"Well, have a good time," she answers merrily. I hate lying to her. It's so unusual and against everything I believe in. Angus taught me that deceit and deception went away with the Bad Times. Before that, he said it was really common for people to lie and cheat. He said even governments lied in the Before Times, along with the major corporations that ran all the business stuff. Apparently, a lot of people paid lip service to words like honesty, truth, and integrity. He said there was a ton of corruption around the planet in the old days, especially toward the end. Anyway, I hate having to tell lies to Bernice who really trusts me. It makes me feel like I'm rotten inside.

I leave the apartment and amble over to South Park. When I arrive at the meeting place, Erin and Jerry are already there.

"Hey, here comes Mr. Romeo," Jerry wisecracks to Erin. "We were wondering if you were going to skip out on us and spend the afternoon with your new girlfriend."

"She's not my girlfriend, and you know it," I answer smiling. "And I'd never skip out on you guys anyway."

"Let's go find that tiger," Erin says, letting me know that she could care less whether Jane and I are into each other. She isn't interested in boys yet, at least not that she's told us. Jerry, on the other hand, has kissed a few girls. Or so he says.

"It's one o'clock," I announce. "We have four hours to find that tiger and take some pictures."

"At least we know where to go," Erin says. "I hope he's there this time."

"Me too," Jerry agrees. I nod my head but keep my mouth shut. After my dream last night, I'm not sure I want to meet that tiger at all. Jerry disconnects the fence and we sneak off the compound.

We hurry and trace our steps all the way back to the cave. Along the way we see the same heard of elk out in the Big Meadow, but we see nothing of that big grizzly bear, which is fine by me. When we begin to close in on the cave, we slow down and approach the opening as quietly as we can. Once again, Jerry and Erin enter the cave side by side with me right behind them. Jerry has his stun gun ready to fire, and Erin holds her flashlight in one hand with her camera slung over her shoulder and ready to go. But a quick look around finds no tiger at all. There is a fresh pile of bones in the corner, which means that the big cat is still hanging out in this area of the forest.

"What should we do now?" I ask.

"We could just stay here and see if he comes home," Jerry suggests.

"No, it doesn't feel safe getting trapped in here by a big tiger," Erin replies. "Let's go out and find a spot where I can get some good photos of him if we get lucky." She looks at me. "What time is it?" She points her flashlight at my wrist so I can see my watch.

"It's almost 2:30," I answer. "That gives us about an hour to hang out here before we have to go back home." I like Erin's plan a lot more than Jerry's, but before Erin can say anything more, we hear the loud rumble of a growl come through the opening of the cave. It's so deep it sounds like distant thunder. I feel the hairs stand up on the back of my neck. A big tiger stands outside the mouth of the cave blocking our escape, and he's really pissed off that we have invaded his lair.

"Shit, we're trapped," Erin hisses. "We all have to rush him. And Jerry," she gives him a look that's filled with hope and fear, "you have to shoot that cat like you did the bear. Okay?"

"Don't worry. I'll hit him straight on as soon as I get a clear shot," he reassures us. We line up at the entrance and spot the tiger about twenty feet away. I notice how big that cat really is. We charge toward it and scream holy murder at the same time. It isn't coached; we yell because we're scared. It catches the tiger off-guard and backs him up a step. Jerry points the stun gun and blasts him just like he said he would. The charge knocks the beast over and we make for the rocks, but the tiger regains his feet in a split second and roars at us like he isn't hurt at all. Erin stops and turns around to snap some pictures. She clicks the camera a couple of times while the tiger paces back and forth, making up his mind whether to charge us.

"Okay, I got the photos. Give him another blast, Jerry!" Erin yells excitedly while she tosses her camera strap over her shoulder. Jerry aims the stun gun and fires. Nothing happens. He tries again. Still nothing.

"Shit!" he yells. "It's out of juice. I should have charged it up more!"

The three of us stand there, facing a tiger that's really got an attitude. He's staring straight at Erin, even though Jerry is the guy who shot him. It's like he knows that Erin's the one responsible for us being there. Erin figures out she's in trouble and turns to run like hell, but stumbles over her own feet and falls flat on her face. Jerry's so upset with his gun that he doesn't know what to do, so he throws it at the tiger and misses him completely. The tiger readies himself to pounce on Erin and leaps like he's coming off a springboard. The monster claws Erin's arm with his right paw making a nasty cut and drawing blood. I grab my pack and run at the tiger swinging it like a weapon. It smacks him on the side of his huge head. He backs up growling and turns his cold, angry eyes on me. He roars like he means it and crouches to leap at me. I realize that I'm as good as dead.

"Run, you guys!" I yell and get ready to swing my pack again. Suddenly a brilliant light explodes out of nowhere between the tiger and me, startling both of us. I have to shield my eyes it's so bright. Both Jerry and Erin must have to do the same. When I open them again, I am shocked to see Angus standing squarely between the ferocious beast and me. The big cat is now groveling on the ground, obviously terrified by what just happened.

"Be still," Angus commands in a voice so certain of itself that neither the tiger nor I are about to argue. In fact, the large predator relaxes like he's suddenly cool with the whole situation. He re-positions himself comfortably on the ground and licks his paw like nothing's the matter. He looks like a big old pussycat.

Angus turns to face the three of us. He appears a lot younger, like he's shed eighty years or more. His skin shines with health and his hair is now blond instead of white. He looks straight at Erin, who is holding her arm. It's bleeding pretty badly from the tiger's claw.

"You're lucky to be alive, young lady. Are 3D photos worth the price of your life and the lives of your two closest friends?"

"No sir," Erin answers with the meekest voice I'd ever heard her use.

"Well, lucky for you, destiny feels obliged to offer you three a little assistance. It seems your time is not yet up, despite your best efforts to toy with an animal who would heartily disagree."

"Destiny?" I ask.

"Source," my late history professor replies.

"We thought you were dead, Angus," Jerry says. "Weren't you burned up in the crematorium the other day?"

"My body was. I'm pure spirit now, Jerry. I put this body on to help you." He smiles, and it makes me feel like I haven't got a problem in the whole wide world. "I've gone home, children, and someday you will too."

"You mean when we die?" Erin asks.

"No, Erin. You must choose to live and not to die." He winks at us. "You'll have to figure out what the difference is. Meanwhile, you all go on back to the compound and get Erin to the healing center so they can take care of that wound. And fess up, too. No more lies and no more breaking the rules. There aren't that many, and what few there are are there for a reason."

"Yes sir," we answer.

"Good, now get going and I'll stay here and keep this tiger pacified until you're well on your way."

"Will we see you again, Angus?" I ask.

"Eventually we'll all be together, son. Now get."

I shed my shirt and wrap it around Erin's torn up arm while Jerry gathers up all our stuff. When he picks up the stun gun, the tiger growls softly, but doesn't move a muscle. Erin's eyes lock onto mine.

"Thanks for coming to my rescue. For a second there, I thought you might scare that tiger away."

"Yeah, well, if Angus hadn't shown up, I'd be torn to shreds," I answer. But inside, I'm experiencing something warm spreading through me that feels better than good.

Then I feel a hook in my chest, and I'm yanked into some kind of tornado, spinning around so fast I feel like puking. I hear a swooshing sound like a strong wind and feel it pushing against me from every direction. Even as I lose all sense of time and place, I am still aware. In the very next instant, I'm lying on my back, staring up at the water-stained ceiling of my bedroom in the Excelsior Hotel.

PART FIVE

I'm totally disorientated. Have I been lying here in bed this whole time? I glance at my watch. It's 7 a.m. Apparently, I've been asleep for hours, though my body feels like a bear waking up after months of hibernation. I sit up, rubbing my eyes, and try to get my bearings. I remember standing in front of the bathroom mirror... Then being yanked into some kind of time portal or spinning vortex! My jaw drops as it all comes back. I can recall everything that happened to me. Getting in over my head as a young and foolish priest in ancient Sumer and having my throat cut by an unforgiving general. I see my life in Rome as a well-heeled housewife with a major connection to the ruling family, and I can still feel the sharp disappointment when my affair with the young senator is stifled before it ever gets off the ground. I see my final adventure, chasing a tiger in the future with my two best buddies, and how Angus, our dead history teacher, saved us from being mauled at the last second.

I see everything as clearly as I did while living each of those lives... But was any of it real? I look back through the ages to the present and recall lying down on the bed and shutting my eyes before going into the bathroom and looking through the mirror. Maybe I never left the bed and just dreamed I did. Could this whole weird experience have been a dream? Even as I think it, I know it cannot be. I can recall every moment of joy, every face of a loved one, every sting of betrayal as clearly as the room around me. I know in both my heart and head that I cannot simply discount it as a dream. I have never recalled a dream with so much clarity before. It's like watching a movie.

As I look back at the different timelines, I sense there is something reminiscent about the three varied experiences, something very familiar about them and the people who were in them. Some thread connects me to all of the significant players in each story, a cycle of betrayal and trust, of wanting more than we had and paying for it either with our lives or with our own happiness. What is definite and undisputed is the fact that right now, in this life, I am the betrayed party. But in Rome, I betrayed my spouse, while in Sumer, I was the object of betrayal.

I take a deep breath and sense a major shift inside me. Whether it was all a dream or some kind of psychic adventure engineered by the Grim Reaper himself— something about that smile of his makes me wonder—I have a completely different regard for who I am. The thought of doing myself in no longer appeals to me at all. In fact, it seems like a laughable idea. What an inconceivable waste that would be. Yeah, I've been screwed by my wife and my best friend, but it no longer feels so devastating. I don't feel like the angry, self-pitying victim I was when I entered the Excelsior last night. In fact, the affair now has a ring of justice to it, like I'm paying off a debt. At any rate, the desperation I felt last night has dissipated.

Ted and Janice can have each other, and while I will miss them both, I no longer feel angry. It's as if re-living these three lives has put time between myself and this betrayal, letting it heal and be forgiven as time does to all wounds. In fact, my experience leads me to believe that time is more elastic than we think. Past, present, and future could all be happening at the same time. There is some aspect of ourselves that survives time and space. That lives forever.

I know now, as clear as this new day that calls to me, I will seek a fair and agreeable divorce from Janice so she and Ted can marry and build a life together. I still love her, and I love him too. They have made their choices, and I must make mine. While living the betrayals from different angles has given me the perspective to forgive, it is the recollection of Angus standing there in all that light that has awakened something new and exciting in me—a new purpose based on a much larger playing field and involving a deeper sense of belonging.

I raise myself off the bed and enter the sitting room. The Grim Reaper still hangs on the wall wearing his clever grin, and the knife still waits for me, glinting beneath the Reaper's scythe. I pick it up by the handle and carry it back to my bag, where I pack it away. The designated weapon for my personal destruction now looks like a harmless kitchen knife meant for chopping vegetables. Maybe I should return it to the draw it came from.

I feel something growing underneath my breastbone, and as my breath catches, I realize it is pure joy. I have a brand-new life to experience and explore! New journeys to make and people to meet and love. I also know I live in a world that may face a tough transition, and with this knowledge I can try to make some kind of difference out there. One thing is certain: I don't wish to work in the financial rackets anymore. I'll say my goodbye to Williams & Howe Capital Investments, cash in my options, and start all over again. What I end up doing is as big a mystery to me as last night's adventure, but what I have going for me is hope, a new and deep-seated hope that everything will be better than okay in the end. I know there's help out there somewhere, some older soul who's standing in the wings ready to guide me or encourage me, another Enheduanna or Caenis or even Angus. The world is not so lonely as it looks on the surface. There is guidance and support and direction coming from some creative Source that waits to be *revealed*. I only have to go out the door to discover who I am.

I collect my goods and go to check out of the Excelsior Hotel. I don't plan on ever coming back. There's a different clerk working the front desk. He's short and grimy looking. He takes my key and shoves it back into its cubbyhole. He barely cracks a smile and has nothing to say. Besides him, the lobby is empty. I look around one last time. The place looks even more tired and run down than it did last night. It's hard to believe that a dump like this could be the setting for such a profound transformation. I smile and head for the door.

There's a bounce in my step as I hit the sidewalk and feel the warmth of the morning sun on my face. I jingle my keys in my hand as I head to my car, and I can't help but wonder if there's a redder red in all the world than what glints before me, promising adventure. My stomach growls loudly, joining my heart and head in their eagerness for the next step. I decide to go someplace nice for breakfast. I feel like treating myself, and why not? Right now, I'm my own best friend, and together, we will begin anew. But first, I need to return that knife.

Several minutes later I pull in front of my house. Janice's car is in the driveway. Ted's car in nowhere in sight and I figure he went to work at the crack of dawn as all financial people must do to be in sync with the market. I approach the front door. I ring the doorbell. Moments later Janice opens it. She is obviously taken back by my sudden appearance.

"Hi," I say, "I need to pick up a few more things. I won't be long." She relaxes a little and steps back to let me enter the house I no longer live in.

"Are you okay," she asks nervously.

"Yeah, I'm fine, I reply. "I had a rough night, but I survived." I walk by her and enter the kitchen. I return the knife to its normal resting place. Then I walk to the bedroom, enter the closet and grab a suitcase that rests in the corner. I place it on the bed and open it. Janice is observing my movements from the bedroom door.

"I need a few more things to properly outfit my new life,' I say without any rancor at all. "I left in kind of a hurry last night. I won't be long."

"Jason, we need to talk."

"Yes, we do," I agree. "There's a lot to settle here. I suggest that we mediate. I won't be difficult, but I want a fair settlement for all of us. I plan to temporarily relocate somewhere in town, so I can be available for the negotiations. After that, it's a whole new ball game." I carefully pack the suitcase with a few sets of clothes to keep me in business for a while. I grab some personal items off the top of my dresser, add them to the mostly filled up suitcase and close and zip it up.

I turn and face my wife. "I'm okay Janice, seriously, I am. I accept the sudden change in circumstances and am ready to move on. I wish you and Ted well, I really do, and hope you two will enjoy your lives together. I'll contact you once I've relocated with the names of a few mediators. You can look into to if you want. We'll figure it all out."

I pick up the suitcase and move toward the door. She steps aside to let me pass by. I walk to the front door, open it, exit my house for what may be the last time, and head for my car. I open the trunk, drop my suitcase next to the other one, close it and get into the driver's seat. I start up my bright red Audi and drive away. It's breakfast time.